SOMETHING TO DYE FOR

Jay,
Thank you for all that you do.
XOXO
Aimee

AIMEE NICOLE WALKER

Something to Dye For
(Curl Up and DYE Mysteries, #2)
Copyright © 2016 Aimee Nicole Walker

ISBN: 978-0-9974225-5-9
aimeenicolewalker@blogspot.com

This is a work of fiction. Names, characters, places, and incidents either are the product of the author's imagination or are used fictitiously, and any resemblance to the actual person, living or dead, business establishments, events, or locales is entirely coincidental.

Cover photograph and interior photos © Wander Aguiar – www.wanderaguiar.com

Cover art © Jay Aheer of Simply Defined Art – www.jayscoversbydesign.com

Editing provided by Pam Ebeler of Undivided Editing – www.undividedediting.com

Proofreading provided by Judy Zweifel of Judy's Proofreading – www.judysproofreading.com

Interior Design and Formatting provided by Stacey Blake of Champagne Formats – www.champagneformats.com

All rights reserved. This book is licensed to the original publisher only.

This book contains sexually explicit material and is only intended for adult readers.

Copyrights and Trademarks:
Keurig
Andrew Christian
Michael Kors
Netflix
Phantom of the Opera
Dodge Charger
Miami Vice
Fiat
Three Stooges
The Ellen DeGeneres Show
Jell-O
Annalise Keating – How to Get Away With Murder
Red Lobster
Mr. Roger's Neighborhood
PBS
American Legion
Happy Days
Joanie loves Chachi
Mimi – The Drew Carey Show
Care Bear
Charlie's Angels
CSI
The Price is Right
Danger, Will Robinson – Lost in Space
March Madness – NCAA
Get out of Jail Free card – Monopoly
Superman – DC Comics
"Strip it Down" – Luke Bryan
"Like a Wrecking Ball" – Eric Church

Other Books by Aimee Nicole Walker

Only You

The Fated Hearts Series
Chasing Mr. Wright, Book 1
Rhythm of Us, Book 2
Surrender Your Heart, Book 3
Perfect Fit, Book 4
Return to Me, Book 5
Always You, Book 6
Any Means Necessary, Book 7

Curl Up and Dye Mysteries
Fatal Reaction (Series Prequel found on author's blog)
Dyeing to be Loved

Undisputed – coauthored with Nicholas Bella

DEDICATION

To Amy Keating Casey,

If I thought of you while writing certain parts of this book, then it stands to reason that you should get the book dedication. I crazy love your enthusiasm for your favorite teams.
#GoBucks #Who-Dey #Redlegs

ONE

Gabriel Wyatt

My ringing cellphone brought me out of a deep sleep. I had to untangle myself from Josh in order to roll over and pick it up from the night table. I squinted sleepily at the display, which said it was an unknown caller.

"Detective Wyatt," I said into the phone.

"Sorry to wake you, Detective," said a voice I vaguely recognized. "This is Sheriff Arless Tucker with the Carter County Sheriff's Department."

I sat up straight, going instantly on high alert. I knew that the sheriff of our county wasn't calling me in the middle of the night just to say howdy. "What can I do for you, Sheriff?"

"I'm at the scene of what appears to be a homicide on highway twenty-two and I was hoping to get your assistance," Sheriff Tucker said.

I was confused about why he'd be calling me because our jurisdiction didn't extend out to the county roads and highways. "Sure, Sheriff Tucker, but can I ask why you're calling me?"

"The man has been run off the road then shot in the head." Again, I wasn't sure where I came into play. "There was no driver's license on the victim, but we did find your business card in his wallet. Can you come down and ID the body?"

"Yes, sir. I'll be there in fifteen minutes." A sick feeling came over me as I realized who the victim most likely was. I disconnected the call and just sat there for a few minutes. If it was indeed Nate Turner, then what the hell was he doing in my county? I couldn't shake the feeling that he was coming to find me and had brought hell with him.

Josh let out a sweet sigh and the sound made me want to say fuck it and snuggle back down in the blankets with him. My conscience wouldn't let me ignore the request for help from Sheriff Tucker though. Besides, all he was asking me for was an identification, even though I found it odd that Nate didn't have his license in his wallet, but he had my business card.

I hated to wake Josh when he was sleeping so soundly in my bed, but I didn't want him to wake up and wonder where I had gone. I slid my hand beneath the cover and placed it at the small of his back while I leaned over and kissed his cheek.

"Hey," I said softly.

"Gabe," he said sleepily, "I adore your cock, but I'm too tired to ride your joystick." He never lost his snark, not even in his sleep.

"Oh, come on, baby," I whispered huskily in his ear.

Josh's hand snaked out from where it had been tucked beneath his chest and grabbed my dick then squeezed. "Just give me a few hours to rest my asshole and my mouth. Then I'll be all over this hunk of meat." His mouth opened wide for a yawn before he said, "Go do what you need to, but be careful. Wear extra layers so you don't become Detective Numb Nuts. I do have many plans for them."

I was quickly learning that Josh used humor and sarcasm to cover just about every emotion he had, especially when he wanted to mask affection and concern. My heart pinched tight in my chest and I wanted to tell him that I loved him, but he wasn't ready to hear it yet. He would only admit that he liked me. I was willing to accept that L word for the time being.

I pressed my lips to his ear and whispered, "I really like you." His only acknowledgment of my words was another sweet sigh as he returned to the land of dreams.

I threw back the covers and hustled my naked ass to my dresser to throw on clothes. I loved sleeping naked beside Josh whenever one of us slept over at the other's place, but the moments between leaving the bed and getting dressed felt like days in the drafty house I rented. Flannel and long johns were things I never expected to own when I lived in Florida, but I was a proud owner of several pair of long johns and a variety of flannel shirts. I could've moved back to Florida when the relationship that brought me to southern Ohio ended, but something kept me here. I glanced back over at the bed and saw the sleeping form of the man who touched me in ways I had never experienced or even expected. I altered my thinking from something kept me there to someone kept me there.

Josh Roman was worth freezing my nuts off.

Buddy moved from the foot of the bed to take my spot beside Josh, as if to tell me that he'd take watch over my guy. Whoever abandoned Buddy on a cold, rainy night in November did me a solid. I could've looked the world over and never found a dog as wonderful as him. "Atta boy," I said softly before I left my bedroom.

I remote started my car and made myself a cup of coffee while it warmed up. My chattering teeth was the only sound I heard in my silent neighborhood on the way to my car. I had learned not to let the sleepy town fool me; evil and depravity lived everywhere and Blissville was no exception.

I cranked up the heat and navigated my way through the streets of town then the dark county road, being extra careful to avoid patches of black ice. I saw the emergency lights flashing in the distance not long after I left town limits. I pulled over to the side of the road the best I could, without getting my car stuck in the freshly plowed snow from the recent storm that came through. I turned my emergency blinkers on and made my way over to the uniforms standing around the scene of what looked like a car accident.

"Hold up," one of the uniformed deputies said when I approached. "This is official sheriff's business." His tone of voice was grating and the arrogant look on his face had me instantly disliking him. There was a way of conducting yourself in a professional, authoritative way without sounding like a dick face, but apparently, the jackass missed that particular training session.

I pulled my badge off my belt and held it up. "I'm here on official business," I replied calmly, even though his attitude didn't deserve the respect I showed him. "Sheriff Tucker called me and asked me to come to the scene." His attitude didn't improve when I identified myself.

I heard the sheriff say, "Stand down and let the man through, Billy."

The brick wall had no intention of moving, which felt oddly personal to me for a man I'd never met before. As I shouldered past him, I heard the words "queer boy" being muttered beneath his breath. Ahh, that was the asshole's problem. I might not have known him but he'd apparently heard about me. If I hadn't been on official police business, I would've stopped and confronted him. I had a strong feeling that I'd get my chance in the near future; equally foreboding was the feeling that this thing with Nate Turner wasn't going away once I made an identification.

"Over here, Detective Wyatt." Sheriff Tucker walked toward the single-car accident and I followed behind him. The flashing red and blue lights from the deputies' cars mixed with the yellow lights of the tow truck waiting for the scene to be cleared so he could haul the car off. The only things that were missing from a typical accident were the EMTs and ambulance, but the presence of the county coroner van explained their absence.

"Holy shit," I said when I caught sight of the damage to the vehicle. It had hit a tree head-on and the impact to the car looked hard enough to kill a person without the extra bullet that the sheriff had told me about.

"Come over to this side," Tucker said, gesturing to the passenger side of the car. "Let me tell you, someone really wanted this guy dead." The sheriff shook his head slowly and stepped aside so I could get a view of the victim inside the car. "Ran the plates and the car came back as belonging to a Nate Turner from Cincinnati. That him?"

I leaned forward and looked inside the car. Nate's dead eyes stared at me from where his head rested on the deflated airbag. His skin was deathly white, his lips were blue, and dried blood splotched his face from where the bullet entered his forehead. The back of his head didn't fare as well when the bullet exited his skull, as blood and brain matter splattered the driver side door.

"That's him." I stood up and faced the sheriff. "What the hell happened here?"

"Looks like he lost control of his car over there," Tucker lit up tire tracks in snow with his flashlight, "came down the embankment and hit this tree head-on." Tucker walked around to the rear of the driver side of the luxury sedan and pointed to dents at the corner of the trunk and rear quarter panel. "He was obviously hit before he lost control." Sheriff Tucker turned off his flashlight and faced me. "The passenger window was broken–either from the impact or done purposely–and the killer leaned in and fired one bullet into Turner's skull. The bullet exited his skull and shattered the driver side window. We've been unable to find the spent bullet or the casing and any usable footprints in the snow were destroyed by the first officers on the scene." None of that was good news to hear when investigating a homicide.

Jesus, Nate! You should've called the damn cops like I told you. "Damn," I said to the sheriff. "Someone really wanted to make sure he was dead."

"How do you know him, Detective?" Sheriff Tucker asked.

"He owns a club in Cincinnati that I've been to a few times." My answer was met with a snicker from the dickhead deputy somewhere behind me. I thought our moment of reckoning might come sooner than I first predicted.

"Find something to do, Sampson," Sheriff Tucker bellowed loudly over my shoulder. Once my ear stopped ringing, I was grateful to have the full name of my new nemesis. Billy Sampson. "You were saying, Detective."

"I gave him my card when we met at his club a little over a year ago." I left out the part where Nate had gotten up close and personal with my ass. It wasn't relevant to the story. "He called me a little over a month ago and asked me to come see him. He said he needed my help."

"What kind of help?" the sheriff asked when I paused to breathe. *Damn, I was getting there.*

"Nate's car had been vandalized one night and then he started receiving threatening emails. He was visibly shaken by the tone of them and I thought he wanted advice on what to do."

"But he didn't?"

"He didn't say it out loud, but I'm pretty sure he didn't want the police department digging into his personal life or business dealings to find out who was threatening him," I told the sheriff.

"So why'd he call you then?" Tucker asked.

That question was trickier. There was nothing Nate had said during our meeting that indicated that he wanted me to do anything illegal. It was his body language, gestures, and the fact that he refused to involve the police. Someone killed Nate and I owed it to him to be as honest as I could be so that his killer was brought to justice. "I got the impression he wanted to hire me to find the person through non-legal channels. He didn't say as much, but it was the feeling I had. He wasn't happy about my refusal nor with me for repeating my recommendation to phone the police."

"Let's head to the station to talk," Tucker said. I couldn't tell from his tone if he believed me or not.

Regardless, I followed him to the Carter County Sheriff's Department. Once we arrived, he showed me to his office and asked if I wanted a cup of coffee. He had his own Keurig setup in his office so I figured why not. It wasn't like I was worried about them running my prints in connection to ones found on Nate's car. I had never touched that car, not even at the scene of the accident. I made myself a cup of coffee and relaxed into the chair across from his desk. I had done nothing wrong and had nothing to hide from Sheriff Tucker.

"Can you recall what the threatening emails said?" he asked.

"Vividly," I replied, setting my cup down on his desk. "The first one included a photo of Nate inspecting his damaged tires outside of his club. It told him how easy he could've been killed then, but where was the fun in that?" I looked at the sheriff and said, "I'm paraphrasing here. I can remember the content, but the exact wording might be off."

"Fair enough." He nodded for me to continue.

"The other email included photos of Nate inside his house. He was nude in them and doing various things like talking on the phone while holding a coffee cup or looking out the back door in the direction of the person taking the photo. The message said something about it was a shame to waste a cock like his then referenced cutting off his dick and making Nate choke on it."

"Ouch." Sheriff sat back in his chair and I could tell he was fighting the urge to cover his privates. It was a kneejerk reaction to hearing about someone losing their cock. "Was there anything else that you can remember?"

"Nate said he responded to one of the messages, I think it was the first one. He said that his email was returned with an error message that stated the email address he sent it to didn't exist. I also noted that the emails were sent at the exact same time of day each time they were sent."

"And that was?" he asked.

"Two in the afternoon."

"Do you mind if CSU looks at your car for evidence of damage and are you willing to have a gunshot residue test performed on your hands?" Tucker asked.

I had never been accused or questioned about an involvement in a crime. I had told Tucker everything that I knew. It galled me to be doubted, but I had nothing to hide from him. "I'll agree to both things."

"Good man," Tucker said, then rose to his feet. "I'll send a deputy in here to perform the GSR test."

A friendly deputy, who identified herself as Hannah Arnold, performed the test on my hands. I sat in Tucker's office and drank coffee while I waited for him to give me the all clear. It took him a lot longer than I appreciated, but he finally dragged his ass back into his office a little before six.

"You're free to go, Detective." No apologies for holding me longer than necessary or doubting me in the first place. "If you think of anything else…"

"…You'll be the first to know," I finished for him on my way out of his office.

I locked eyes with the homophobic deputy on my way out the

door. I wanted so badly to let Billy Sampson know what I thought about him, but I knew it wasn't the right time. I knew without a shadow of a doubt that our time to have words would come. Instead, I puckered up my lips into a kissy face at him and headed out into the cold.

A chill worked its way down my spine, that had nothing to do with the subzero temperature, as I made my way to my car. I was overwhelmed with a feeling that I was being watched, and not by some camera in the parking lot. This presence was dark and ominous. I looked around me to see if I could find the source, but I couldn't. Nor could I shake off the feeling that Nate Turner had practically brought his trouble to my front door.

TWO

Josh Roman

IT SHOCKED ME HOW ADDICTED I'D BECOME TO SLEEPING BESIDE Gabe, even though it was only a few nights a week. I hated waking up alone, especially in *his* bed, but I understood it would happen sometimes. I fell back to sleep easily enough after Gabe left because he had worn me out the night before. *I swear, the man fucked me like he'd never have another go at my ass.* I thought maybe it was the hard knock he took to the head in early December when he investigated the murder of our town's former first lady.

My heart still ached over Georgia's death and it seemed more tragic when the person who killed her was someone she trusted implicitly. The butler wasn't always the person who did it, sometimes it was the seventy-year-old housekeeper. I took every opportunity to harass Gabe and his partner, Adrian Goode, about being bested by an elderly woman. Adrian said he should've known better because his grandmother could still do a cartwheel at seventy-five years old.

I rose out of bed when my alarm went off on my cellphone. I liked to tease Gabe about being a wimp when it came to cold weather so I was glad he wasn't home to witness my sprint to his bathroom to start the shower. I grabbed my toothbrush and toothpaste then climbed beneath the spray of water as soon as it heated up to my preferred temperature–hot enough to please Satan. I tempered it with a tiny bit of cold water on the times that Gabe joined me, but he wasn't there so I could enjoy every second of depleting his hot water tank.

I had just stuck my toothbrush in my mouth and began to scrub my teeth when the shower curtain was yanked aside. I screamed in a horribly unmanly fashion and clutched my chest. I felt my face flush with embarrassed heat when Gabe started laughing at my reaction. I knew that dumbass wasn't laughing at *me* because I held the keys to his favorite kingdom; a portal of pleasure so thrilling I could put an amusement park out of business.

"Get in here, you're letting all the heat out." He wasn't wearing any clothes for me to grab so I snatched onto some chest hair and tugged. "You're lucky I didn't deep throat my toothbrush with your stupid stunt."

Gabe took my toothbrush out of my hand and set it on the shelf before he backed me up so that he too could stand beneath the scalding spray. For once he didn't complain about the burning water temperature so I knew the blood had already headed south toward his cock. "Mmmm. Deep throat." Gabe's moan sent thrills racing down my spine. He began kissing a path from my collarbone to my jaw.

"Oh no," I said firmly. "You nearly gave me a heart attack and my heart needs to rest now." I turned my back on him, as if I was angry, but all I really wanted to do was push my ass into his groin.

Gabe took the bait, grabbed my hips, and pressed his erection between the globes of my ass. "Forgive me," he whispered huskily in my ear.

I was ready to forgive him before the bulbous head of his dick rubbed against my greedy hole. My legs parted on their own accord to grant him more access. I couldn't imagine a time when I wouldn't want to take him inside my body. Gabe had done something I thought was impossible; he burrowed himself so deep inside my soul that I'd need divine intervention to extract him.

"You know what we both need to kick off our morning right." Gabe reached around and fisted my cock in his large hand. "It's adorable when you pretend not to want me."

It was hard to argue with him when I was grinding my ass on his dick like the cock addict I'd become. "Stop calling me adorable." I had to find something to fight him on or he'd think I was sick and take his hard-on away.

"Fucking adorable," he growled the same time he pushed a lubed finger inside my ass. I never asked, but I wondered if perhaps Gabe had been a Boy Scout when he was younger because he was always prepared. I somehow doubted that there was a badge for lube and condom preparedness, but if there was he surely had one. He never failed to whip out a stash from somewhere when the mood struck. In the shower, he kept them stashed on the shelf next to his shampoo.

After that, there was no more talking. Grunting, groaning, and moaning were the only things we could muster once he suited up and slid inside me. I braced my arms on the shower wall when Gabe started to move in earnest. He slid his hands up to pinch and roll my nipples, knowing it made me crazy. I laid my head back against his shoulder when it became too heavy for my neck to support. Gabe rubbed his morning scruff against my neck because he knew the response he'd get from me, just as I knew how he loved the feel of my beard against the skin on his inner thighs. He knew my body better than I did and after such a short period of time too.

He rode me fast until I sprayed my spunk all over the tile, then it was all I could do to hang on while he chased his own release. I could tell he was close by how tight he held my body and the animalistic growls that escaped his throat. He came hard and loud, driving me up on my toes as he spilled deep inside me. Gabe pressed his forehead to my shoulder and rested there until his breathing slowed down and his blood returned to his brain.

I could get used to this. It wasn't the first time I had the thought and I was certain it wouldn't be the last. I was more certain that I was nowhere close to being ready for cohabitating with him. The insane lust I felt for Gabe had turned into genuine affection, but we were still too new to be thinking of doing anything as crazy as move in together.

"Two more weeks until we go to Florida and you meet my parents." Gabe's words snapped me out of my post-coital fog.

I had always wanted to mean enough to a guy to be introduced to his parents. It had never happened, in fact, I seemed to have the opposite effect on men. They tended to want to hide me away in shame due to my sometimes–okay often–flamboyant nature. People often mistook flamboyancy for femininity and it couldn't be further than the truth in my case. I had always been the guy you fucked, not the one you took home to Sunday dinners. Until Gabe.

Gabe had thought of me as feminine at first, but he'd since seen the light. He also saw something in me that made him want to take me home to Florida to meet the parents. I still got a mushy feeling in the pit of my stomach every time I remembered opening the plane tickets on Christmas Eve. He figured the week of Valentine's Day would give me enough notice for my schedule. He learned in a very short time that my clients scheduled their appointments months in advance and there was no such thing as "off season" when it came to a woman's hair. Hair maintenance wasn't a sport; it was a lifestyle.

I finally had a man who wanted to show me off and all I could do was quake with fear. *What if they didn't like me? They probably loved his ex, Kyle, and we were nothing alike. Gabe could stand proud in front of his family with Kyle, the veterinarian. I am just a hair stylist...* That was when my panic came to a screeching halt. I had *never* been ashamed of what I did for a living. I wasn't just a hair stylist; I was a successful motherfucking business owner who made women, and a few men, feel good about themselves. I would not cower in shame in front of anyone for my career choice nor would I hide my success.

"Quit freaking out." Gabe's rough chuckle that followed his words had my spine snapping straight up.

"I was not." I sounded like I was five, at best.

"Babe, your body got tight enough with tension to snap off my dick when I mentioned meeting my parents." Gabe pulled his softening dick out of me just in case. "They're going to adore you."

"Will I adore them?" I thought it was a reasonable question, but Gabe's laughter said it was funny.

"You will. They're easygoing people who are fun to be around." Gabe kissed below my ear with a wet smack. "Just don't let my dad talk you into playing poker for money. You and your pets will be on the streets before you can blink an eye."

"You doubt my ability to play poker competently, huh?" I wasn't offended by his opinion because I knew it wasn't intended as an insult.

"Your face is so expressive, Josh. I can't imagine you being able to conceal the fact that you have a good or bad hand." See, he wasn't being derogatory so there was no need for my insecurities to flare up and cause an argument. *Look at me acting all adult-ish.* He had no way of knowing I was raised by the queen of card sharks since he'd never met my parents either. *Hmmm.*

"You know, you're not the only one whose parents live in Florida," I said. I bit back a laugh when I felt him tense against me. Seemed like I wasn't the only one who was nervous about meeting parents. "My folks can't be more than an hour north on I-95."

"It wouldn't be right going all the way to Florida and not spending time with your parents too," Gabe said. I could tell it was his good Southern manners behind the words more than anything. "We'll split our time between the parents."

"Um, Gabe." I turned within the circle of his arms to face him. "We don't have to spend every second of our time in Florida with either set of parents."

"True."

I felt a subtle drop in the water temperature and knew we wouldn't have long to wash before it dropped to frigid cold. That thought led me to Gabe's early morning adventure. "Where'd you get called out to this morning?" I handed him his shower gel then reached for my own.

"You won't believe it," was his answer. He shook his head as if he couldn't believe it either. He lathered up his hands and began washing his body. I loved the differences between our builds and coloring. Where I was slender, fair, and blond, Gabe was muscular, tanned, and dark. The sight was almost enough to make me lose my focus, but another subtle drop in temperature prompted me to get to washing.

"Try me," I replied drolly. I split my attention between washing and listening to Gabe tell me about Nate Turner's demise.

"I don't know what the fuck he was doing out here, but I guaran-fucking-tee it wasn't for good reasons."

"I don't believe it," I said in shock.

"I told you." Gabe's gloating remark and smirky smile earned a wet smack on his ass. "What was more shocking was the way the sheriff tested me for GSR and had my car checked over like I was the one who ran him off the road and killed him."

"GSR?" I asked.

"Gunshot residue." Gabe explained to me what happened when a person shoots a gun. "So the swabs came back negative and my car was cleared of any foul play." Gabe shook his head then his dark brown eyes widened. "I forgot to tell you the worst part."

I couldn't imagine what could be worse than getting called out of your warm bed to identify a douche bag club owner's brain-splattered corpse only to be treated like a suspect when all you did was tell the truth. But I was all ears. "What was the worst part?"

"Ugh, this awful homophobic deputy was on the scene and later at the station. I'm telling you, babe," Gabe said after releasing a frustrated breath, "Billy Sampson and I will go a round or two before long."

I could tell by the scowl on his face that he saw the way I stiffened when I heard Billy's name. Okay, meeting him was way worse than the cold, gruesome body, and the interrogation that followed. I hated the way my heart raced and my stomach churned from just hearing his name.

"I wasn't aware that he moved back." The words were barely a whisper when they crossed my lips. How had his return flown under my radar? My brain instantly returned to times so dark that I thought my life wasn't worth living, that no one would ever love me because I wasn't worthy. *Don't go there, Josh. You're much stronger now.* As if fate wanted to shock me back to the present, the water coming from the showerhead turned ice cold.

"Fuck!" Gabe reached around me and turned off the water. He reached outside the shower curtain and grabbed our towels off the hooks. He handed my towel to me before he began toweling his hair.

I stood their awestruck and watched the play of muscles in his chest and arms. I marveled for the hundredth time that Gabe wanted me the way I was. He thought I was worthy and I clung to those feelings instead of the sorrow that tried to move in and ruin my day at the mention of a demon from my misguided past. He looked up from what he was doing and caught me staring at him. The cocky grin he wore told me he mistook my interest as purely sexual. It often was sexual, but not right then.

"I really like you," I told him. "I just thought you should know." I looked away and began toweling myself off before I was blinded by his white smile. "You should've been in a toothpaste commercial," I groused.

"Aw, you say the sweetest things." He reached for me as I started to climb over the edge of the bathtub, but I eluded his grip. I'd be late for work if I gave in to the urge to play around with him.

Once we were dressed and in the kitchen, Gabe pulled me to him and asked, "Do you have time for breakfast?"

I did, but I was honestly still reeling from the bomb that Gabe inadvertently dropped on me in the shower. I needed to regroup and get myself together before my first client arrived. Besides, I wanted the opportunity to talk to my best friends about the latest development before the rest of the staff showed up for work.

"Raincheck?" I asked him.

"Anytime," was his swift reply.

The goodbye kiss he gave me at his back door was anything but swift and it was exactly what I needed to warm my heart during the walk home because two blocks felt like two miles in January. Gabe would've given me a ride home, but I found the brisk air to be exhilarating on most mornings. That morning all it did was wrap its icy fingers around my already stressed heart and squeeze.

Both Meredith and Chaz were running a little behind that morning so I didn't have a chance to speak to them about Billy's return to Carter County. I knew without a doubt that neither of them knew or they would've told me. I had practically befriended Chaz at birth and my beautiful queen came along in ninth grade. I knew without a doubt that I could count on them for anything, even if it meant they had to deliver unsettling news.

Not only were Chaz and Meredith late, my client was early, so there wasn't time to chat. I had to push aside all my conflicting thoughts and feelings so I could focus on making Mrs. Applegate feel like a million bucks. I closed my eyes briefly, found my center, and went on about my day as if nothing and no one could hurt me.

THREE

Gabe

"Captain, can I have a minute?"

Captain Shawn Reardon looked up from his desk and assessed me with keen eyes. I wasn't sure of his age, but I placed him in his late forties to early fifties. He struck me as one of the guys who went gray early but kept their youthful faces. His light blue eyes were a lot like lasers when they were locked on a person, as they were on me right then. I had worked for the man for three years and it was the first time I requested to speak to him privately instead of the other way around.

"Come on in, Gabe." Captain folded his hands on top of his large desk. "What's on your mind?" he asked briskly. Many people probably found his demeanor to be abrupt, but to me, he was a man whose every word and action had a purpose.

"I got a call in the middle of the night from Sheriff Tucker regarding a homicide on one of his county highways. The victim didn't have any ID on them, but he did have my business card in his wallet." The captain sat up straighter, if that was even possible, and listened as I told him everything that happened during my visit to Nate's office a few months prior and the early morning activities.

"Let me see if I understand you correctly. Sheriff Tucker called you out to ID a body and once you did, he treated you like a suspect. Did I hear you right?" Captain asked.

"Well, I wouldn't say…"

"Professional courtesy dictates that he should've at least called me, your superior, and informed me of what was going on. Did he ask you if you wanted a union rep present?" Captain's eyes turned an icy shade of blue and a vein popped out on his forehead as he became angrier with every word he spoke.

"No, but I…"

"It doesn't matter that you volunteered the information and agreed to the tests. There is protocol that he should've followed. I'll be calling that fat bastard's office later today." The level of animosity the captain felt for Sheriff Tucker was shocking. I was certain I resembled a cartoon character with bulging eyes and a gaping mouth after the captain's tirade. He rarely showed any emotion at all. I was beyond curious about the source of his dislike for the sheriff. He pinned me with narrowed eyes and said, "Never again, Detective Wyatt."

"Yes, sir."

My hearty agreement seemed to appease the captain and I could see his countenance returning to normal until once again his stoic façade was in place. "Do you have any idea what Nate Turner was into or why it seemed like he was coming to see you in the middle of the night?"

"I don't, sir," I answered honestly. "I just know he didn't want police involvement in identifying his harasser, well, not in the traditional sense any way. I have no idea why he was in this area at that time of night after a snow storm had moved through."

"It reeks of desperation. I have to ask you a tough question and I need your complete honesty, Gabe."

"You got it, sir," I replied.

"Did Nate Turner have reason to believe that you'd harbor or protect him from the person making threats?" Captain tipped his head slightly to the side like he was mulling over his next words. "Was there anything personal between you?"

"No, sir." Maybe our definitions of personal were different, but I didn't think the one time I got bent over Nate's desk in his office counted as personal. I had given the guy my card after I pulled up my pants. He tossed it in the trash then told me that he didn't do repeats. I considered the short time I was in his presence to be very impersonal, regardless of the fact that his dick had been in my ass. I was shocked when he called me out of the blue a year later and asked for help.

"I guess we'll never know what he was doing here then." The captain pointed his finger at me and said, "If Tucker calls you again…"

"I'll make you aware of the situation immediately." I rose from my chair and was prepared to leave when his next question caught me off guard.

"Do you think that you're in any danger?" I was used to an unreadable expression on his face, so the concern I saw in his furrowed brow and pinched lips gave me pause.

It was something that never occurred to me. I knew nothing about Nate's personal life or criminal activities so I couldn't possibly see how I would be in danger. "No, sir."

"Keep an eye out and report anything odd to me, Gabe." He nodded his head and returned his attention back to the paperwork on his desk. I had effectively been dismissed.

I found Adrian sitting at my desk with two cups of coffee. "You're looking rough, partner."

I gratefully accepted the coffee he made for me and tried not to wince over how sweet it was. Only Josh seemed to be able to make my coffee to my exact specifications. The baristas at The Brew came close, but I'd prefer Josh's coffee any day of the week. Of course, if I was getting Josh's coffee then that meant I was probably getting a piece of him too.

"Must be some good coffee," Adrian said. "You went from half dead to alert in just one sip."

"It's great, Adrian. Thank you." I let him believe his coffee, and not thoughts of Josh, breathed new life into me. "Hey, I need to tell you something that I should've told you sooner. I just never thought it would add up to anything."

Adrian listened raptly until I finished telling him about my early morning phone call and subsequent trip to the sheriff's office. "That's un-fucking-believable."

"It feels like a weird dream." But I knew the gruesome sight I saw earlier was real. I leaned toward Adrian and lowered my voice. "What does the captain have against Sheriff Tucker?" I told Adrian about how angry he became and even referred to Tucker as the "fat bastard."

Adrian threw his head back and laughed hard for several long moments. "Cap is married to the sheriff's only daughter."

"How'd I not know that?" I asked rhetorically. I wasn't one for gossip and the captain was a very private man, but I thought I would've at least known that much about him. "Damn, that must make for some interesting holidays."

"You know it." Adrian's desk phone rang and he answered it.

"Whoa," he said after listening for a few minutes. "We're on our way." Adrian nodded to my cup of coffee and said, "Bring it with you. The high school asked Officer Wen to bring Rocket for a random search and the dog alerted Wen to possible drugs in a locker. The principal opened the locker and found a huge cache of drugs."

"Pot?" I asked as I put my coat back on.

"He said it looked like a little bit of everything. Wen thinks the street value is around twenty thousand dollars."

I let out a low whistle. "Where does a high school kid get their hands on drugs like that?"

"I don't know, but you can bet your ass we're going to find out. There's no way we're going to let our town be destroyed by drugs," Adrian replied.

Blissville High School was a newly constructed two-story, brick building on the edge of town. Approximately six hundred kids in grades nine through twelve attended the school. The school district had a few controversial policies in place, but the biggest one was their search and seizure policy. The policy simply stated that the school had the right to bring in the K-9 unit to conduct random searches. If the dogs indicated to their handlers that contraband was found, the locker, or even a car in the parking lot, was opened and searched.

During my time in Blissville, the only thing confiscated had been small amounts of pot and sometimes alcohol. Nothing had prepared us for the number of drugs found in the locker that day. I had seen smaller busts in the homes of drug dealers in Miami.

"Holy shit," I said softly in the school hallway.

"Indeed," Principal Mary Rogers said. "I can't believe it." She closed her eyes then reopened them, as if she hoped to wake up from a bad dream.

"Still there," I told her.

"Indeed," she echoed her words from earlier.

"What can you tell me about the owner of the locker?" I asked her.

"Well, technically the school *owns* the locker, Detective, and the kids are permitted to use them." She tilted her head to the side and lightly tugged on her ear. "This particular locker hasn't been assigned this year. It's one of the few unassigned in this hallway."

"Someone knew the locker combination," Adrian said. "Do you have record of who was assigned to this locker last year?"

"He or she would've graduated," Principal Rogers said. "All these lockers in this hallway belong to the freshman class. They'll keep the same locker for their four years of high school. Before the seniors graduate, we check their lockers to make sure they're not damaged. Then we assign the lockers to the next group of incoming freshmen. We don't keep lists of previous assignments. We've never needed to do so."

"Someone knew this locker wasn't being used *and* they knew the combination." I looked back at the locker and watched as our team dusted for prints inside and out. "Anything we can use?" I asked.

"No, sir," Officer Kasey answered.

"Video footage?" I asked.

"The assistant principal is looking through it now with an officer, but we have no idea how long the drugs have been in the locker. We haven't had the K-9 unit in for several months so it's hard to say. The videos are only saved for thirty days before they're recorded over to save space in the mainframe." Principal Rogers ran her fingers over her pearl necklace nervously. "I don't like this, Detectives. This isn't a joint or two a kid has tried to sneak in. That," she pointed to the stash of drugs that officers were photographing and documenting before it was taken to the evidence room at the station, "was brought in with the intent to deal. I do not want dealers setting up shop inside my high school."

"Neither do we," I told her. "We need to interview any staff members that have access to the video equipment, the locker assignments, locker combinations, or have master keys to open any locker."

A small woman came running down the hallway toward us. "Mrs. Rogers, news vans from Cincinnati and Dayton just pulled into the school parking lot."

"I will make them available to you later today," the principal told us, "but right now I need to do damage control." She turned away and started walking back toward the school office. "Don't buzz them in," I heard her say. "They can stay outside until I've had a chance to speak to the superintendent." I couldn't help but smile when I thought about the vultures being locked out in the cold.

"Well, I guess there's nothing left for us to do now except to help them bag and tag the evidence. Then we can get some lunch," Adrian said.

"I hope you don't mind, but I have lunch plans with Josh," I told Adrian.

"Does he know this?" Adrian asked.

He had me there. Josh had no clue I was coming. He was regimented about his day and might not like me dropping in the salon during business hours, even with delicious food, but I felt like I needed to try. Something in the way he reacted to Billy Sampson's name struck me. It was almost like he folded in on himself rather than standing proud like I was used to seeing him. I didn't want to wait until after work to talk to him because it would allow him too much time to bury his emotions.

"It's a surprise," I told Adrian. "I'm hoping it's a good one."

I sat at the counter and drank a cup of coffee while I waited for

Emma to cook mine and Josh's food. I had no idea what Josh might be in the mood for so I just picked something and hoped he liked it. If not, I'd take it home and reheat it for dinner.

"Long time, no see," said a familiar voice on my right.

I turned and looked into the bright blue eyes of the man I used to share a home with. His eyes used to make my heart race when we first got together, but any romantic feelings I felt for him had been gone for more than a year–even longer if I thought hard enough about it. Instead, I saw a handsome guy with a great personality who passionately loved his job as the town veterinarian. I also saw a guy who deserved to find the man who was meant for him.

"Yeah, I haven't talked to you since before Christmas," I replied. I had run into Kyle at The Brew when I showed up hoping to run into a certain platinum blond with hazel eyes. Josh and I had been split up for over two weeks at the time, although I guess we weren't a couple at the time, and I was dying to see him again. Josh saw me having coffee with Kyle and got the wrong idea. I chased him out of the coffee shop and we took the first steps at amending our fragmented... *something*, as we both called it.

"I'm glad things worked out for you and Josh." His soft words reminded me that he had been nursing some frustrations that morning also.

"No luck with gamer dude?" I asked. I was shocked to hear that Kyle had started playing video games to pass the time once we broke up. Some guy he talked to online grabbed his attention and Kyle couldn't get him out of his system. Kyle wanted to meet the guy in person, but the guy disappeared before Kyle could mention it.

"Not yet, but I'm not giving up." Kyle smiled, but I noticed that his normal twinkle wasn't present in his eyes.

The waitress, Daniella, brought over the carryout bag with my order in it. After I paid her, I turned back to Kyle and patted him on the shoulder. "I hope everything works out for you." And I meant it. He was a good man who deserved to find happiness.

"See you around," Kyle told me before he placed his order with Daniella.

Josh was nowhere in sight when I walked into the salon. I noticed that his two partners in crime were also missing, so I suspected there was a pow wow of some sort going on. I didn't think they'd go upstairs in the middle of the day, which left the small kitchenette in the rear of the salon. As I approached the room, I picked up a piece of their conversation.

"Babe, we would've told you if we knew that asshole had returned to town. We'd never let you get caught off guard like that. How in the hell did we not know he was back?" Meredith asked. "Are you okay, Jazz?"

"I…"

"Fucknugget! Fucknugget! Fucknugget!" Josh's blue macaw squawked at the top of his lungs. I thought it was funny when I first taught him that word while I was recuperating at Josh's house from my concussion. Then Savage started to squawk it nearly every time he saw me and it wasn't so funny, especially when I was trying to spy. I decided to start working with him on new words.

Josh poked his head around the corner of the kitchen. "Surprise!" I held up the brown sack of food. "Hungry?"

Josh chewed on his bottom lip while his eyes raked up and down my body. "Starved." I wasn't sure if he was talking about the food or me.

FOUR

Josh

DAMN GABRIEL WYATT AND ALL HIS MANLY YUMMINESS. HE distracted me to the point of insanity. I was more addicted to him than Andrew Christian underwear and that was saying a lot. Hell, it had only been a few hours since his dick had been inside me and I was already jonesing for more.

"I'm out of here." Chaz grabbed Meredith's elbow and tugged her behind him.

"You never let me have any fun," I heard her tell Chaz, which was opposite of how it really was. Meredith was usually the one pulling Chaz out the door so that Gabe and I could have alone time.

"Mmmm, that smells good." I finally got a whiff of the food inside the carryout bag and my brain focused on something besides sex. "What did you get me?" I held up my hand to stop Gabe when he started to answer. "Let me guess." I sucked air into my nose dramatically and said, "I smell beef and mashed potatoes. That could be several items from the menu." I took another sniff and thought I caught a hint of honey glazed carrots. "Mmmm. You ordered me the pot roast dinner." I smiled at him triumphantly.

"You're good," Gabe said. He pulled me by the back of the neck and dropped a quick kiss on my lips. "So damn good."

I snatched the bag from him and set it on the table. "None of that or I'll lose my focus. Don't force me to ban you from the salon during business hours."

Gabe snorted as he took a seat. "Feed me and then I'll get out of your hair." Gabe smiled widely at his pun before continuing. "I won't even act like I want to take you up the stairs and peel off your clothes so I can kiss every inch of you. Nope, that's the furthest thing on my mind when you stare at my lips like that."

I was so close to saying "take me right now," but my growling stomach beat me to the punch. I unpacked and distributed our food then dug into the heaping pile of roast beef, gravy, and mashed potato heaven. "You didn't get country fried steak?" I asked.

"You've ruined me," he replied. His answer brought a smile to my face just like it did every time I asked the question and he answered in the same way. *My country fried steak is the bomb!* "Had an interesting morning, but I'm sure you've already heard all about it at the Come In and Gossip."

It was a good thing I hadn't taken a bite of food because it would've fallen out when my mouth gaped open. *Did he just mock my salon?* "Oh, no you didn't!" I clutched my chest with one hand and tried to look affronted.

"Oh, yes I did." Gabe didn't look a bit guilty for slandering my precious business. I would've been pissed if it hadn't been the God's honest truth.

"Yeah, I heard about the bust before you were even on the scene," I confessed.

"Jesus," Gabe mumbled around a bite of his buttery roll.

I pointed my fork at Gabe and said, "Leave him out of this." He smiled because it was the same exchange we had after sex the first time. "How big is big?" I asked. The leering smile on his face said his brain was still back in his bedroom on that cold, fall morning when I rode him like a bronco. "The drug bust," I prompted.

Gabe pinned me with a stern look. "What I tell you stays confidential."

"Goes without saying," I replied saucily. My clients might be full of gossip and chatter, but that didn't mean that I couldn't keep a secret. I was damn good at keeping secrets. Besides, Gabe wasn't telling me that Mrs. Jenkins switched laundry detergent or Mr. Hopkins stared a little too long at Mrs. Mayweather's ass in the Sac-N-Save parking lot. He was trusting me with something that could jeopardize his career. "Wait." I held up my finger when he started to talk. I got up and looked to see who might be lounging in the sitting room while waiting for their appointment. I had clients with hearing so acute they'd make the CIA envious. The sitting room was empty, but I shut the door in between the rooms for good measure.

"Huge!" Gabe said once I returned to my chair.

"Yes, babe, but what about the drugs?" I couldn't resist teasing him.

I thought Gabe was going to get up and strut like a peacock from my praise. "Almost as huge," he replied with a grin. Then he leaned forward and lowered his voice. "Seriously, we're talking a street value of a hundred thousand dollars or more. At first we thought maybe ten or twenty thousand, but it came back with a much higher value once we logged the evidence into the system."

"In a high school locker?" It was staggering to think that a kid in the school had the connections to gain access to a drug stash that size. "Whose locker was it?" I asked, even though I knew he wouldn't tell me.

"I don't know and I wouldn't tell you if I did." Gabe said exactly what I thought he would. "I'll let your three o'clock appointment tell you. I'm sure they'll know before I do." I was too hungry to comment on that snarkfabulous remark.

Who the hell was I trying to fool? "Just for that, I refuse to be your confidential informant." My response was met with a snort that I did choose to ignore.

I looked at my watch and saw that I didn't have much time before my next appointment arrived. I buckled down and ate the delicious lunch Gabe bought me. The small gestures of his affection meant more to me than if he bought me a fancy Michael Kors watch.

"That was so good, but now I need a nap." I rubbed my belly and said, "Carb City."

"I have an idea of how you can work some of it off later," Gabe said, reaching for me. "I still haven't seen your attic studio."

I wasn't sure why I hadn't shown him my pole dancing studio yet. I didn't think it was performance anxiety because I had competed in competitions, but then again, none of the spectators were Gabe. They were faceless people where he was my... *something*. What he thought mattered to me more than I ever thought I'd allow again.

"Soon."

Before he left, Gabe pulled me to him and pressed his forehead to mine. "You can trust me too, Josh." At first I wasn't sure what he was talking about then I realized that he probably caught part of what Meredith said to me. I figured he probably caught onto the shock I felt when I heard Billy's name in the shower. Hadn't he told me that my face gave away my thoughts?

"Soon," I repeated. I owed him the truth of my past, especially since it was still a minefield he tiptoed through. I worried that he would think less of me for allowing myself to be treated the way I had.

"Fair enough," he whispered before he dropped a sweet kiss on my lips. "Just so you know, nothing you say will make me *like* you any less."

"Thank you for lunch. It was very sweet of you," I told him when I walked with him back out to the salon.

"It's your late night and I don't want you hangry." Gabe stopped when he reached the door. "I thought Buddy and I might stop over around eight with pizza. I might even throw in a foot rub afterward."

I nearly moaned out loud because his foot rubs were fucking amazing. I sprung wood every time he dug his thumbs into my arches. Just thinking about it was enough to make me uncomfortable in a room full of clients. "Go, go now." There wasn't any venom in my words, only laughter.

I gave him a quick kiss on his cheek before I shooed him out the door. When I turned around to go to my station, I saw that every eye in the salon was focused on me. "Y'all go about your business before I add extra onto your bill today for the free show we just gave you."

Gabe and Buddy showed up promptly at eight like he said they would. He picked up two pizzas because our choices of pizza on some nights were on the opposite ends of the spectrum. I wanted the Hawaiian pizza with ham and pineapple and he wanted everything except mushrooms on his, including anchovies. Yeah, I totally made him brush his teeth afterwards; no way I was kissing his fishy lips.

I learned right away that *somethings* required a lot of work.

There was more manscaping to consider when I was showing off my dangly guy bits on a regular basis. Gabe liked my smooth balls, plus I didn't want him to get sac rash on his face from my scruffy nuts when he went down on me. We had schedules to juggle so that we got to see one another, and the debate about whose turn it was to sleep over at the other's house. I had to make sure that Gabe's favorite snacks were in my cabinets and he made sure to keep my shampoo and styling products on hand for me. Most importantly, and the only source for any serious debate, was the television shows we watched.

I was convinced there was a football game of some sort on every single night and, of course, that was what he picked to watch on his nights. I wanted to watch reality television where they fought and bitch-slapped one another. Neither of us like the other's choices, but we compromised. We were mature and shit. On that particular Thursday night, I lay on the couch with my feet in Gabe's lap and pouted a tiny amount because it was his night for television and of course there was a football game on, which meant I missed the new bitch-slapping premiere that was also on. At least I recorded the show and could watch it later.

Ugh, I would've been miserable if it hadn't been for the way those guys looked in their tight pants. I tried to find the positive in every situation, and those pants were it. After an hour or more of staring at asses, I finally noticed the shirt thingies they wore. "Oh, those shirts are hideous. Who picked out that shitty brown color?"

"They're called jerseys, babe," Gabe replied patiently. "The team owner picked them in honor of the team's name. They're called the Browns."

"Ugh, where is this team from? That color is just… I can't even."

Gabe rolled his eyes as if I was just too much for him sometimes. "Um, Cleveland."

"Oh." *Oops*. I had no idea about sports teams beyond Cincinnati or Dayton and my knowledge of those teams were sketchy at best.

I pulled my foot out of his hand and held up the other for him to work his magic on.

The game lasted way longer than I had energy for so I crashed hard somewhere around the third period, quarter, or whatever it was called. Gabe shook me lightly when the game was over and told me that he and Buddy were heading home.

"Stay," I said sleepily.

"Are you sure?" Two consecutive overnights in a row was something we hadn't done yet.

"Yep."

We stripped down and climbed beneath the sheets of my bed. Oddly, I couldn't go back to sleep once I cuddled up next to him. I blamed the brief chill I felt while stripping down, but I knew it was because I wanted to unburden my heart to him. There was something about the dark that made confessions easier.

"Billy Sampson was the first guy I gave my heart... and other parts to," I said softly. I felt Gabe tense beside me. I figured it had more to do with hearing that I had entrusted myself to someone so hateful than learning I hadn't been a virgin. "He was a bullying prick even back then, but I learned one day after school that the hatred he felt was more towards himself than me–or so I had convinced myself."

"I can't imagine it went well," Gabe said softly. He pulled me tighter against him as if he could protect me from the hateful memories of my misguided youth.

"He was like Jekyll and Hyde." I took a deep breath and exhaled it slowly. "When we were alone he was almost kind and caring, but when we were at school he still picked on me. In fact, he was worse after we had sex. I think it was easier for him to blame me than to accept that he liked boys. He made me promise not to tell anyone about us and I didn't. I think a part of me was actually afraid of him and what he'd do to me if I talked about us. I didn't even tell Chaz and Meredith about him until after he moved away."

"Did he hurt you?"

"Not with his hands," I answered. "He was just cruel and I put up with it for almost a year. I foolishly thought he was the best I could do. He started dating a popular cheerleader our senior year. I didn't know if it was to keep people off his back, or if he tried to convince himself he was straight, or was bisexual and didn't want to admit that either; I just knew I hated seeing them together. Billy told me that she meant nothing to him and that they weren't having sex. He promised that things would change for us once we graduated high school. I believed him right up until the girl got pregnant."

"Ouch," Gabe said.

"Yeah, and of course, in this town I'd heard it through the rumor mill before he had a chance to tell me himself. Hell," I laughed harshly, "I doubt he would've told me had I not confronted him about it."

"I'm almost afraid to find out." Gabe slid his hand into my hair and rubbed my scalp.

"He told me that I had never been important to him and he never had any intention of being with me beyond the fucking." The memory still hurt, but time and wisdom changed it from a sharp, stabbing pain to a dull one. "As bad as he sounds, he wasn't the worst of the losers I trusted. If you're a really good boy I'll tell you about my first year of college."

"College?" Gabe asked.

"Don't sound so damn surprised." I pinched his nipple. "It's downright insulting."

"Ouch!" I couldn't see him in the darkness, but I felt the sheets moving as he rubbed his aching nipple. "I wasn't trying to insult you. Damn!" He paused for a second and then asked, "What was your major?"

I prepared myself for his reaction. "Accounting."

The bed shook from him laughing so hard. "What? Why?"

"It's a story for another night," I told him. There was no damn way I was telling him anything else that night. My pride had taken enough blows.

"Oh, come on." The pout in Gabe's voice eased the tension in my body.

"Not tonight, darling. I have a headache," I said primly.

"Oh yeah?" Gabe took my words as a challenge.

I didn't even bother pretending that I didn't want to feel him inside of me. I opened my arms and my soul so that his goodness and light could fill me, banishing the remnants of my past until all I felt was him. It was quite some time later when Gabe collapsed beside me and pulled my sated body to him. I couldn't see his face, but I could feel the solid thumping of his heart beneath my hand. "You matter to me, Josh."

Had I not already loved him then, I would've fallen so hard.

FIVE

Gabe

"This is some crazy shit," Adrian said the next morning at the station. "I just can't get over the street value of those drugs." He rubbed his hand over his face and exhaled a heavy breath. "We've never had a bust that size in this town, or even in Carter County."

"I can't believe we have no clue who put them in the locker," I responded. "I find it awfully damn convenient the camera equipment isn't working. How long do they think it's been offline?"

"They're not sure," Adrian replied. "It's hard for me to imagine the drugs have been in that locker for long. If I'm a drug dealer and I hand off a stash like that to a pusher I'm expecting the money to come rolling in right away." Adrian shook his head in disgust. "You have a lot more experience with drug busts coming from a big city like Miami. What do you think?"

"It's hard for me to believe a dealer is going to trust a high school kid with that kind of volume. We could be looking at a mule, but the same doubts apply." In my experience, drug dealers only trusted teens to sell a little at a time. They had to turn in their cash before they could get more. Did that mean one of the adults in the school was involved? I had more questions than answer at that point.

Captain Reardon approached our desks with his long purposeful stride. "I hope you miraculously crack the case today. I have a family dinner tonight and I'll never hear the end of it," the captain said before he returned to his office. It was the first time he ever said anything about his personal life in front of me. It was a testament to how much the drug bust weighed on his mind.

Adrian and I grabbed another cup of coffee then headed to the school to conduct interviews with the staff and a few of the students who had lockers around the one where the drugs were found. I expected the morning to go by fast and to be rather dull; it turned out to be the exact opposite.

Our first stop was the principal's office. It was like any other principal's office I had visited during my misguided youth. Principal Rogers' office had the same boring tile floor and nondescript wall coloring as I expected to find, but the person sitting behind her desk was a surprise.

"My name is Delaney Sampson and I'm the superintendent for the Blissville School District." Her tone was very professional as was the handshake she offered before we settled down to business. Then shit got real. "I'll be overseeing the interviews today due to Principal Rogers' suspension."

"Suspension?" Adrian asked. His confused tone of voice

matched my thoughts.

Superintendent Sampson sat up taller, her posture looking so rigid she might break. "That's what I said." Her tone of voice was short, clipped, and as bitterly cold as the wind outside that day. I wondered if she was related to Deputy Dickhead when she first introduced herself. The arrogant look on her face that was identical to his negated my need to ask. Her demeanor told me that she didn't like to be questioned or asked to repeat herself. Too damn bad.

"I think we both know that Detective Goode heard what you said. He wasn't confused, he was questioning," I told her. Slipping into the role of bad cop was so damn easy for me. I had no use for misplaced arrogance and stupidity. "What we want to know, and have the right to ask," I added so that there wouldn't be any confusion, "is why she was suspended. Don't give me the standard lecture that investigations involving school district personnel are kept private either."

"It's to protect…"

"No, you're not protecting *her*," I said, interrupting the spiel she was about to give me. "What you've done is cast suspicion on her in the community and we'd," I gestured between Adrian and myself, "like to know why."

"It looks really bad for Mrs. Rogers," Adrian added. "The largest cache of drugs in our county's history is discovered and the principal is suspended the same day or the next." He shook his head.

"I'm not really concerned about your approval," she said icily. "The fact is that someone had access to our school building and tampered with our video equipment under her watch. I'm not saying she was involved, but she was careless."

I disliked the woman immensely. I promised myself that it wasn't personal and had nothing to do with Josh, but I wouldn't have placed my hand on a bible and swore that it was the truth. "Couldn't the same be said about you?"

"Well, I…" She stuttered and blustered like she'd never been challenged before meeting me.

"I think we're getting off on the wrong foot." Adrian held his hands up in the air, attempting to calm the situation. He was just as quick to fall into the role of good cop. "We asked, you answered. Let's move on." After receiving a barely perceptible nod from her, Adrian continued. "Let's start with the students and then interview the staff who had access to the video equipment and master key to the lockers."

The superintendent's reply was a brittle, "Fine." She looked at her list and rattled off the names of the two students on the list that Mrs. Rogers made. "Let's start with Regan."

Looking at a sullen, disinterested sixteen-year-old Regan Haines was like looking at myself twenty years ago. His insolence was plainly visible in his expression and by the way he slouched in his chair looking at his nails as if we weren't in the room with him. Others might've been put out by his behavior, but not me. At his age, I was angry at the world because my older brother, my hero, had been a victim of a convenience store robbery gone bad. I grew angrier and angrier with every day that his killer wasn't caught. I can honestly say that I don't know what would've happened to me had my football coach not given me a good shake when I needed it most. I transferred my emotion to the sport I loved most and then later into my education so I could be the best cop I could be. I didn't know Regan's reason for his attitude, but I was willing to bet it was from more than just boredom.

While his interview answers consisted of shrugs, the student who walked in after him was completely opposite. Lily Watson came into the office shaking like a Chihuahua. She took one look at Adrian and me then burst into tears.

"I did it!" She held out her hands in front of her like she expected us to cuff her.

Her confession took us off guard. She would've been the last person I suspected with her sweater set, pearls, and gray slacks. She looked like she was going to a church luncheon, not high school. I reminded myself that looks were often deceiving and my skills in that department were a bit rusty. I mean, a seventy-year-old woman got the drop on me and scrambled my brains. I once judged Josh as feminine because he had extra sway in his hips and wore vibrant clothes.

"*You're* confessing to putting the drugs in the locker next to yours, Lily?" Superintendent Sampson's voice was as doubtful as my initial reaction to her confession.

"Drugs? What?" Lily sounded as confused as the rest of us.

"What exactly are you confessing to?" Sampson spoke slowly, enunciating every word carefully.

"Well, not that," Lily answered. She began fiddling with her pearl necklace and chewing on her lower lip. "I don't even know what you're talking about." Had she been living under a rock? Josh heard about it before I arrived on the scene, yet a student didn't know it was going on in her own building.

Superintendent Sampson asked, "How could you not know?"

"Um… you see…"

"Lily!" The superintendent's loud, harsh voice was enough to scare me into a confession.

"I played hooky yesterday, ma'am. I stayed up too late watching Netflix the night before instead of studying for the biology exam. It counts for thirty percent of my grade and I just couldn't take the chance I'd fail it." Lily began to cry again. "My mom doesn't know I missed school yesterday. I called in and pretended to be her when I left a message on the student absentee voicemail box."

Superintendent Sampson let out a frustrated breath before she said, "We'll deal with that later. These detectives are here to ask you questions about the locker between you and Regan Haines."

"Oh."

"Lily, have you seen anyone accessing that locker? Students or faculty?" Adrian asked.

"No, sir."

"What about anyone selling drugs in the school?" I asked her.

"I'm not very social. I only care about getting good enough grades to get a scholarship so I can get the hell out of here." She raised her chin and looked at the superintendent. "I'll gladly take whatever punishment you deem necessary for my actions yesterday, but I'd appreciate it if you don't put that in my transcripts. I've had an exemplary record thus far."

"I'll consider it," Sampson said. Lily's plea must've struck a chord because she sounded less like a battle ax and more like a human.

The staff interviews were a lot less eventful and not nearly as entertaining. Each faculty member seemed to be shocked about the drugs, had no idea who was involved, and couldn't believe that any student had connections to someone who could move that volume of drugs around. I thought the morning was a complete bust until the final two minutes of the last interview with the geometry teacher.

"But you know," Doug Baxter said, almost as a second thought. "There was a band concert the night before the bust so the whole town had access to the building. And if the office was unlocked, then anyone who's gone to school here in the last twenty-five years knows where the school secretary keeps spare keys in her desk."

I looked over at Adrian who fell into that category. "Middle drawer on the right-hand side," he answered without being asked.

"Great! The whole damn town is a suspect," I told Adrian when we were on our way back to the police station.

"Including the secretary. She's about Wanda Honeycutt's age." Adrian didn't bother to hide the smile in his voice when he brought up the name of the woman who clobbered me.

"I don't know why you're so damn smug," I told him. "She hit you too."

"Yeah, but not as hard." Adrian laughed for a minute and then said, "Probably because you went all bad cop on her while I was nice."

"Fuck you, Adrian." My ire only made him laugh harder. I was glad I could give him something to laugh about after a morning of interviews that gave us more questions and suspects than what we started with. "Just for that, you get to tell Cap that we've got nothing to go on."

It was my turn to laugh at Adrian's misery, even more so when he returned from his solo trip to the captain's office with his tail between his legs. "I was going to name my firstborn child after you, but you can fucking forget it now. I thought Gabriel or Gabriella Goode sounded like sweet names for a baby, but not anymore."

I suspected that Adrian was just teasing me, but just the thought that I could possibly mean that much to him moved me more than I could say. Adrian had become more than just a partner to me, he was my best friend and my brother. "Nah, Sally Ann likes Josh better and we all know who the boss is in your home. You'll be having a Josh or a Josephine."

Adrian chuckled good-naturedly and I was glad to see the sting of the captain's bite didn't linger. "What do you have planned for tonight? Big date?"

"Not tonight," I replied. "Josh is taking Meredith to see Phantom of the Opera in Cincinnati for her birthday."

I didn't want to think about how much I was going to miss him or examine the reasons why too closely. Things had been going great with us, but there was still the lingering worry that Josh would slip away from me somehow. I had always known that someone had hurt him badly in his past and I was starting to get bits and pieces from him–both intentionally and by accident when he let little things slip. I had to remind myself daily that he was skittish and needed to take things slow.

I finished out my day at work and went home to Buddy. I fixed a big pot of spaghetti so that I'd have enough for leftovers that weekend. I kicked up my feet and watched college basketball until I couldn't keep my eyes open any longer. Of course, I was wide awake once I got in bed. At first I was irritated, but that disappeared the second I received a text from Josh asking if I was still awake.

Yep! I doubted he was coming over because that would be three overnight visits in a row.

Good. I'll meet you at the back door.

I moved faster than I thought I was still capable of in my haste to get to him. *Play it cool. Don't just rip his clothes off. Ask about his night.* I had good intentions, I really did. But he reached down and cupped my crotch and it was game on. I ripped the buttons off another dress shirt, probably the replacement one I bought him for Christmas, right there in my kitchen. It wasn't until the next morning that I even remembered to ask about his evening, but my dick was in his mouth and it was just rude to ask questions when someone had their mouth full.

Of course, I had to return the favor. I forgot about everything except making him curl his toes and yank my hair while I blew him. By the time I remembered *again* to have some fucking manners, Josh was already on his way home to get his day at the salon started. It might not have bothered a lot of guys, but it did me. From everything I had learned about his past so far, all he knew were men who wanted sex with him. I wasn't that guy. I wanted more from Josh, so much more. The only way he would believe it was if I started acting like it. I needed a plan.

SIX

Josh

SATURDAYS AT A SALON ARE BALLS OR TITS–WHATEVER YOU possess–to the wall. It's the only day a lot of clients can get in and I rarely have cancellations. Of course, there's always the one client you wish would cancel. It was just my luck that I had that particular client the morning after I stayed out late with my best girl then fooled around with my best guy for another hour or longer before I got to sleep. I might have been tired, but the gritty eyes and sore body were worth it.

Then she walked into my salon and I could feel all my happiness fading. Delaney "The Dragon" Sampson, as she was known to any kid who had her as a high school teacher, was a force to be reckoned with. She looked down her nose at my flamboyant style during my teenage years and I often got a homophobic vibe from her. Of course, she never said anything to me because my mother would have destroyed her, but that didn't mean she kept her opinions to herself at home in front of her family. I had often wondered if she was the reason why Billy hated himself and the attraction he felt for me. It took me a long time before I could look at her without seeing Billy, but I did it.

Over the years, Delaney moved up the ranks to principal and then later superintendent. She still had that watchful eye that didn't miss a single thing. Her disdain for me had faded, but I felt it was more because I held her hair in my hands rather than any enlightenment on her part. She reminded me of people who mistrusted, or just flat out didn't like, African Americans unless they played sports or sang songs that they liked. In the same vein, gay men were okay if they were helping decorate a house, baking goods, or styling hair, but open-mindedness often disappeared when the same gay men starting demanding things like equal rights. *Gasp!* It didn't make them any less racist or homophobic, but they convinced themselves otherwise. Maybe I was being too harsh, but I'd seen enough shit slung my way because of who I was attracted to and at Meredith for the color of her skin.

"Good morning, Mrs. Sampson," I said with a cheerfulness I didn't feel. She wasn't the only one who could fake it, unless we were talking about sex. I didn't have to waste energy on phony orgasms because my man knew what he was doing, but I'd bet the same couldn't be said about Mr. Sampson. He had Missionary Position Only and Two-Minute Man stamped all over his forehead. *Oops, look at me with all my judgment.*

"Joshua." She was the only person on the planet who called me that. It was only slightly better than the Joshy my mom still used sometimes. "I'm thinking about doing something different with my hair."

"Really?" I asked, playing along. We went through this routine every eight weeks. She'd look at shorter hairstyles in my magazines and books while I talked about subtle changes she could make with her hair color. Each time she'd leave my salon with the same blonde football-helmet style that she arrived with. You could lead a bad hair case to the chair but you couldn't make them change their hairstyle.

"What do you think about this one?" She held up the same picture she chose every visit.

As I always did, I said... Nope! I no longer feared veering away from my expected routine and responses. Instead, I was honest. "I don't like that cut for you. It does nothing to show off your heart-shaped face or the pretty shape of your eyes." Her gaze locked with mine in the mirror and I saw the surprise in her bright blue eyes. "I suspect you don't really like your current style either or you would not have talked about changing it every visit for the last five years. You're the kind of woman who knows what she wants and sets out to get it everywhere except when it comes to your hair. Can I show you which cut would look best with your features and shape of your face?"

She stared blankly at me in the mirror for a few minutes before she nodded imperceptibly. I turned the page and showed her a haircut that was similar to the one she chose, but the layers were longer and subtler. She flipped back and forth between the pages to carefully study the two different styles. I was prepared for her to tell me to just do the usual color and trim, but she shocked me when she said, "Let's do it." She pointed to the picture of the cut I suggested. "I also want to do that thing you suggested with the colors."

"Dimensional coloring?" I stood up straighter and felt a little perkier at the thought of doing something new for her. I loved clients who were all like "fuck it, let's try something new." I clapped my hands when she nodded. "Let me show you all the various colors I have so you can tell me what you're comfortable with." Interior designers had swatches of fabrics and carpets, I had hair samples for every dye color I offered.

"Is this too dark?" Delany asked. She ran her finger over a sample several shades darker than her current color.

"I will only be using it to make the blonde pop more." I found the exact colors the model used in the picture she liked then pointed out where the darker colors were used and how natural it looked.

"I love it, Joshua. You've been telling me this for years, but I'm not good with change anywhere but my career." It was the most human response and reaction I had ever seen from her.

"Most people aren't," I replied honestly.

Delaney settled herself in the chair while I went and mixed the dye for her hair. I was thankful that she wasn't one for a lot of small talk because I honestly didn't want to talk about her son. I could go the rest of my life without seeing or talking to him and be perfectly happy. When I returned to my station, I saw that Delaney was talking on her cellphone.

"I'm at the salon right now, but I'd love to watch the kids for you when I get home. I'm sure you and Laura could use a night out." My stomach sank because I knew who she was talking to. I just crossed my fingers that my name wouldn't be brought up. "Maybe you can drop them off to me when I'm done." Her eyes connected with mine in the mirror. "How long would you say before we're finished, Joshua?"

Damn it! "Two hours, give or take fifteen minutes or so."

Delaney broke eye contact with me as I started to work on her hair. "I should be done around four o'clock. Where are you two lovebirds heading?" I tried not to let her words make me sick. I wasn't sure who I felt worse for–Billy or his wife. It didn't take much thinking for me to choose Laura. "Yes, Joshua from high school. He has his own salon. It's lovely and he's wildly successful." There was a pause as she listened. "He's been doing my hair for years. In fact, he's finally convinced me to do something different with my hair. We're thinking red!" Delaney busted into laughter at whatever reaction Billy had. "Just kidding. We're just changing up the color a bit and I've chosen a new hairstyle." She paused again to listen. "I love you too, son. Yes, I'll tell Joshua hello from you."

I kept my eyes focused on her hair and avoided eye contact during the conversation beyond telling her how long I thought it would take to complete her hair makeover. I hoped that my mental cringing didn't show on my face, especially when she asked if I remembered her son from high school. I was so proud of myself when I was able to calmly say, "Sure do," without giving away any of the contempt I felt for the man. I couldn't stop myself from digging up one tidbit of information though. "I wasn't aware that he moved back."

"He's been back about six months. I'm so happy to be able to hug my grandbabies more than once or twice a year. Having kids is wonderful, but grandbabies are even better. My heart just fills to bursting when I look at them. You'll see someday when…" She broke off suddenly. I looked up and saw her eyes had widened and her cheeks had turned pink with embarrassment. "I'm sorry."

"Why are you sorry?" I asked her. "Same sex couples have children all the time. They either adopt or find a surrogate. I just might know what it feels like to be a grandfather someday." I had honestly never considered having kids of my own. I thought kids were adorable and precious, but being a father wasn't a role I thought about. I did plan on being the favorite uncle to Chaz's and Meredith's kids someday though.

Delaney looked relieved that I wasn't upset. "That's all very true," she said. "Times have really changed."

I couldn't get a read on how she felt about it, but I didn't linger there. I couldn't control her thoughts nor was I responsible for them. She sang my praises to her son in my presence, but who knew what she would say later behind my back. I was never one to back down from an argument or debate, but that didn't mean I went looking for them. My salon was a peaceful zone where serious topics like religion and politics were ignored in place of who was banging who–the truly important stuff in life.

"I heard Estelle Hayslip had her breasts done," I heard Meredith's client tell her.

"I got to touch them," Marci's client said. "They feel real and very perky."

Yes, all was right in my world again. Well, until ten minutes after four o'clock when *he* showed up with his kids to meet his mother. I had to admit, his spawns were adorable. I just hoped that they took after their mother in the personality department because Laura Sampson was one of the sweetest persons I had known in high school.

I was putting the finishing touches on Delaney's hair when Billy and his brood showed up. Even though I knew it was a possibility, I was still rattled to see him in my salon. Luckily, I had nerves of steel when wielding a straightening iron, or any other hot styling tool, and didn't singe Delaney's ears or neck. I felt Billy's eyes on me the entire time, but I completely ignored him.

"Asshole alert! Asshole alert!" Savage's word choices sometimes amazed me and made me want to kiss his feathered face. I mean, did that bird know his shit or what?

The clients in the salon burst into laughter and I refused to look over to gauge Billy's reaction.

Delaney surprised me by saying, "I love that crazy bird."

"Yes, well, I do apologize for the language your grandchildren just heard." I didn't mind Savage's potty mouth most of the time, but I didn't necessarily want kids leaving my salon repeating his filthy language. I tried leaving him upstairs during the day when I first brought him home, but he had separation anxiety so bad that he pecked raw spots beneath his wings. I hated seeing him so distressed and his beautiful feathers laying in the bottom of his cage. I carried him down to work with me every day since then and he'd become an instant sensation with my clients.

"I'll talk to them when we get in the car." She raised her brow skeptically and added, "But I'm sure they've heard far worse in movies or even songs these days." Lord only knew what they'd heard come from their own father's lips, but I bit my tongue to keep from saying that.

I put my straightener down and looked down at her. Delaney had her back to the mirror the entire time I dried then styled her hair. I loved the big reveal moment and hers was a big one. I should've been nervous, but I had a strong feeling she was going to love the new look. "Are you ready for the big reveal?"

"You look amazing, Mrs. Sampson," Meredith said.

"You really do, Mom." Billy's praise surprised me, but I didn't allow myself to even think about it.

"I'm so excited," she said. "Turn me around, Joshua." Delaney used her stern high school voice that always made me snap to attention when I was a teenager.

"Yes, ma'am." I turned her around without further delay and watched the wonder and surprise cross her face as she touched her hair.

"My God! I look ten years younger," she said in awe.

"At least," I replied smugly.

"You're amazing." Yeah, well, I'd heard her son say that to me a time or two, but for obviously different reasons. "Isn't he amazing, Billy?" I was so proud of myself for not allowing the groan to pass my lips or a grimace to form on my face. I decided I would develop a poker face if it was the last thing I did.

"He's something, all right." I wasn't exactly sure what the hell he meant, but like with his praise just before, I chose to ignore it.

"Well, I must get home and show this to Edward. He won't believe it's me." She rose from her chair once I removed her cape and continued to look at herself even longer. "Miracle worker." Her next action shocked the hell out of me. She snatched me to her and hugged me tight enough to cut off my airway and my circulation.

"Turn loose of him, Mom. He's starting to turn purple."

"Oh, you," she said, waving her hand dismissively at Billy. She turned back to me once more and said, "Thank you for your honesty, Joshua."

"You're very welcome, Mrs. Sampson. I'll see you in eight weeks, right?"

"You can bet on it."

I turned away and started to clean up the mess on the floor while she paid and greeted her grandchildren. I could feel Billy's focus on me at times, but I continued to ignore him. There was nothing I had to say to him and nothing I wanted to hear from his lips. Delaney called out a goodbye on her way out the door and I took my first relaxed breath since she arrived.

I went to the kitchen area and made myself a coffee then prepared to shut the salon for the day. I locked the front door after the last client left and asked everyone about their plans. Meredith had dinner and shopping plans with her mom and Chaz had mysterious plans he didn't talk much about. He seemed happy enough so I didn't press him for more details, but that didn't mean I wasn't curious. Marci had a dinner date with some guy she met online and we teased her the entire time we cleaned up the salon.

I had intended to lock the back door once everyone left for the night, but I got busy getting the deposit ready for Monday and forgot. I locked the deposit in the small safe I kept in the supply closet and returned my empty coffee cup to the kitchen. I heard the back door open when I was washing the dirty coffee cups, but thought nothing of it. Despite the rising body count in recent months, Blissville was a safe place to live. Unwanted people didn't just walk into homes or businesses. I turned, expecting to see Gabe's handsome, smiling face but found Billy Sampson standing in my kitchenette instead.

"Hello, Josh." His smile and tone of voice were friendly, but the predatory look in his eyes was that of a man who expected to pick up where we had left off ten years prior.

"What do you want?" I asked, but I already knew.

He laughed arrogantly then asked, "Is that any way to treat an old friend?" Billy swaggered a few steps toward where I stood frozen. "You can't think of a better way to say hello? Those plump lips were made for much better things than asking stupid questions."

His complete and utter arrogance snapped me to life. I couldn't believe the gall of that man. He actually thought I'd be so happy to see him that I'd drop to my knees and blow him. Fury flowed through my veins and I resolved to send that douche nozzle packing with no doubt about his place in my life. I was reminded of who I had become, despite the shit he kicked in my face when we were younger.

"I don't want you here, Billy, now or ever. You're not welcome." My voice was firm and there was no doubt that I meant it. Regardless of the scandal it would create, I decided that he would willingly leave on his own or I'd call the police and have him removed.

Billy wasn't the sharpest tool in the shed and he wasn't about to give up so easily. "Are you still jealous over Laura?" That was the only thing he ever took away from the argument we had when I walked away from him for good. His ego wouldn't allow him to contemplate that his actions were wrong; no, my jealousy was the issue.

"I envy her as much as I would a case of incurable herpes," I replied. "Get out of here and do not come back."

"I don't believe you." Billy reached for me, but paused when we heard a dog's vicious growl behind him.

"I'd believe him if I were you." Gabe sounded as angry and dangerous as the snarling dog on the end of the leash he held in his hands.

SEVEN

Gabe

"ARE YOU OKAY?" I ASKED WHEN JOSH'S EYES MET MINE.

Josh glanced at the vase of red roses I held in the bend of my arm then smiled at me. "I am now."

Buddy continued to growl menacingly and I held tight to his leash, just in case he wanted to take a chomp out of Sampson's sleazebag ass. If I hadn't already been crazy about the dog I would've been when he made his opinion of the man known. I'd always heard that animals were good judges of character and Buddy's reaction to the deputy proved it.

"Big Daddy's home!" Savage's words and timing were impeccable as always.

Josh's smile grew wider. "Did you teach him that too?"

"I know nothing of which you speak." I'd deny it until my dying breath. I shifted my focus back to Sampson who was looking between the two of us in confusion. "I believe Josh told you to leave." My voice was as menacing as Buddy's growl. A huge part of me really wanted to put the beat down on that mofo for hurting Josh the way he did, but I was an adult–one who swore to uphold the laws and not circumvent them when it was convenient for me.

Sampson ignored me and looked at Josh. "You can't be serious." He hooked his thumb in my direction and asked, "Are you for real with this guy?"

"Very real," Josh replied. "I want you to leave, Billy, and never come back. There's nothing for us to talk about and I don't want to be friends with you."

I could feel the hostility rolling off the dickbag when Josh reaffirmed my right to be there. The contemptuous look that Sampson gave me the morning I was called to the scene of Nate's homicide was child's play to the one he gave me in Josh's salon kitchenette. Instead of derision, I saw outright hatred in his blue eyes because I stood in the way of something he wanted. I wasn't fucking going anywhere so he'd just have to get the fuck over it.

Sampson shook his head like he couldn't believe what Josh told him. A lesser man might've gotten his feelings hurt, but I wasn't that man. I felt secure in my place in Josh's life. "Whatever." Sampson's words sounded like a teenager who didn't get his way. "I'll be seeing you around, Josh. This isn't over." Sampson bumped his shoulder against mine on his way to the door. I guess it was his way of trying to intimidate me, but it didn't work.

"Billy," Josh called out before he reached the door. He waited for Billy to turn then said, "It *is* over and has been for ten years.

Don't come back here."

Billy didn't say anything, but he didn't have to because the way he slammed the back door behind him spoke plenty. I unclipped Buddy's leash and went to Josh. I placed the vase and leash on the countertop beside him and studied him. I hated the tense lines on his face and the rigid way he stood. I pulled him into my arms and he resisted me. I worried that Sampson had undone some of the positive steps we'd taken forward, but then Josh held up his hands to show that they were wet.

He dried them on the towel beside him then turned to me. "Okay, now."

I pulled him against my chest and wrapped my arms tightly around him. My heart melted as I felt the tension drain from his body until he was the consistency of putty in my arms. Josh let out a soft sigh and I was glad that I took the initiative to come over to his house unannounced. I expected to find the door locked since the salon was closed, but instead I found an unwanted visitor inside.

"Do me a favor and keep the door locked, okay?" I asked. I knew he was used to growing up in a small, safe community where hardly anything bad happened, but like with most cities and towns across America, things were changing. In the span of just a few months, there were two murders, and two attempted murders, and the large drug bust. On top of that, there was Nate Turner's death not far from town. I still didn't know what the hell Nate was doing in my county the night he was killed, but I didn't think it was a coincidence.

Josh pulled back and looked up at me. I was happy to see that the lines of tension were gone from his beautiful face. "I learned my lesson." Josh looked over at the flowers and then back at me. "What's the occasion?"

"Do I need an occasion to do something nice for the guy I *like*?" I could see the battle brewing in his brain through his expressive eyes. Josh wanted to believe that I didn't have an ulterior motive in mind when I brought him flowers, but his experiences filled him with doubt.

"Are you even real?" Josh finally asked.

If we had been horsing around, I would've placed his hand over my crotch, but the seriousness I saw in his eyes told me a flippant or sexy gesture or response wasn't what he needed. Instead, I moved his hand from my waist and placed it over my heart. "Very real." I repeated the words he used earlier.

I felt a tenderness in his touch that wasn't usually present when Josh rose on his tiptoes and pressed his lips to mine. He was usually the one who turned things sexual between us because it was all he knew. I vowed to not let it happen that night. I wasn't saying no to getting him naked, but I wouldn't allow sex to be my primary focus that night. I controlled my dick, not the other way around.

"So, what did you have in mind tonight?" he asked when he pulled back from our kiss.

"I planned a special night in for us since you were out so late last night. I actually have quite a few things in my trunk, but I wanted to bring Buddy and the flowers in first."

I gave Josh credit for only looking wary for a few seconds. He was a guy who liked his routine and did not care for surprises, except on occasions like Christmas when they were somewhat expected. "That's very thoughtful of you and I must admit that I'm intrigued. Do you need any help carrying anything in?"

"Nope, got it all covered." I was sure to lock the damn back door when I returned from my car. "You're in for a real treat," I said when I unpacked the groceries from the bags. "I'm going to cook you a nice dinner, we're going to drink some wine, and then we're going to watch your favorite movies."

"This sounds great, but what are you getting out of all of this?" Josh asked.

It honestly broke my heart that not a single man had ever done something kind to make him feel special. I had turned away from him to look for a sauté pan, but I turned back around to face him so he could see the sincerity in my eyes. "Spending time with you and making you happy. That's what I'm 'getting out' of it."

I saw the moment he accepted my words as truth. "What are you making me for dinner?"

"Chicken Marsala and roasted vegetables." I turned back around and started the prep work for dinner, but not before I saw the stunned look on his face. He was probably expecting grilled cheese and tomato soup, which wasn't too far off from my normal cooking, but I was capable of more. It was important to me that he knew that and not just in regards to my kitchen skills.

"Can I help you?" he asked and I wondered if it was because I was touching his pots and pans. He was so damn particular about them that he rarely wanted anyone to wash them. Apparently, they were some high-dollar deal that he wanted to cherish.

"Nope."

"You want to listen to a football game or something while you work?" he asked.

"Nope." The night was about him and I wanted to prove that I didn't have to watch sports every single night. "You watch what you want." Television was a big deal because we were two men who were hardwired at birth to dominate the remote control.

"Okay." I heard the shrug in his voice. Soon his home was filled with the sounds of his favorite home improvement show while I cooked dinner for us.

My resolve to behave was pushed to the limits when Josh started showing his appreciation for my cooking skills by moaning after every bite. They were very similar to the sounds I made when I ate the food he cooked for me.

"So good." Oh man, Josh busted out the phrases he used when he was lost to the sensations we created together during sex. My dick started to wake from its slumber like a sleeping dragon, he was ready to come out and play. "Delicious." He licked a bit of sauce that dripped off his fork and onto his wrist. He wasn't helping me behave, but that wasn't his responsibility.

I refused his help to clean up after dinner and sent him back to the couch with his glass of wine. My body was so in tuned with him that I could feel when he chose to watch me instead of the television. His focus seemed to be more of the reflection type rather than making sure I didn't scrape the surface of the sauce pan with a sharp object. I realized that my actions surprised him and the skeptical side of him challenged my intentions, but he'd soon see. Hell, I was willing to go home instead of sleep over if that was what it took to make him see that my need for him went beyond sexual.

"Movie time," I said when I joined him on the couch. "What are you in the mood for?"

"I think I'd rather watch this show than a movie if that's okay with you." It happened to be one of his renovation shows that I happened to like also. It was a married couple who could find the beauty in just about any house. I was suspicious that he only chose it to make me happy, which must've showed on my face because he rolled his eyes. "There's a marathon on because the new season starts on Tuesday. I haven't seen some of these, and even if I did, I still love watching them."

"Okay," I said in surrender.

We watched a few hours of episodes and laughed several times at the husband's shenanigans and the wife's never-ending patience with him. They truly were a fun couple and very knowledgeable about what they were doing. My favorite thing about the show was how they tried to repurpose things when they could because shiny and new didn't fit everyone's personality.

"Relationship goals," Josh said sleepily from where he lay against my chest. His confession surprised me a bit, because the R word wasn't in his vocabulary. "*Something* goals," he amended, as if he read my mind.

I ran my hands through the silky strands of his platinum hair and could tell the moment he fell asleep. I didn't reach for the remote to change the show, I continued to watch the couple that Josh seemed to admire so much. It was true that they had a natural, genuine love for one another that came through loud and clear. They didn't smooch or hang all over each other, but you could see it in their expressions and the smiles they shared with one another.

I stayed in the same position so that I didn't wake him until the numbness turned into pain. "Wake up, sleepy head, so we can go to bed and be more comfortable." Josh just tried to burrow deeper into me rather than wake up. "If you cooperate then I'll take you to see Charlotte even though you haven't showed me your pole dancing studio." He'd been bugging me to show him my 1970 Dodge Charger that I kept in storage more than I bugged him about the studio.

"Just leave me here." Poor guy sounded exhausted and there was no way I was leaving him on the couch when there was a perfectly good bed waiting on him. I did the only thing I could; I carried him to bed. "What?" he asked when he realized he was being lifted in the air.

"I got you." They were the same words I said to him the night I shot and killed the man who broke into his home with the intention to kill him.

"Yes, you do." I tried not to take his words too seriously because he was half asleep, but they still made my heart speed up.

He woke up enough to help me remove his clothes and get in bed, but he was out like a light after that. I spooned up behind him so close that we shared a pillow because that was how he liked to be held. I discovered that I missed our closeness on the nights I slept away from him. The warmth of his skin against mine and his even breaths pulled me into a deep sleep.

The next thing I remembered, I opened my eyes to find Josh standing next to the bed fully dressed with a cup of coffee extended to me. It was a lot like the first time he stayed at my house, except I was happy to wake up there when he hadn't planned on staying at my house. I told him I'd wake him up and I did, but it was the next morning and not after a few hours like he'd been expecting.

"Breakfast in ten minutes." Josh set the coffee cup on the bedside table when I made no move to take it from him. "Hit the shower, *Big Daddy*, because you're taking me to see Charlotte before I have to do my tedious errands."

"You didn't cooperate," I hollered after his retreating back.

"Pick your battles, babe."

"Fine, but then I want a demonstration up in the studio."

Josh stopped and faced me. "Oh, honey, you're going to need a few days to rest up after the wicked things I want you to do to me on the hood of your car."

I whipped back the covers and flung my legs over the side of his bed. I tripped over my shoe and stubbed my big toe in my hurry to get to the shower, but my dick didn't care about anything as minor as that. "Fuck!" I heard Josh laughing over my discomfort and vowed I wouldn't be the only one limping that day.

EIGHT

Josh

IT HAD BECOME A COMPETITION BETWEEN US–CHARLOTTE VS THE pole dancing studio. As long as I live, I'll never forget the lust-crazed look in Gabe's eye the first time I mentioned my attic studio on our first dinner date. It was so fucking adorable how he tried to be a gentleman and wait for an invitation to a private showing the months that followed, rather than invite himself on up. It made me fall deeper in *like* with him. I'll also confess that I liked having the upper hand when it came to him, so it was quite a blow when I discovered that Gabe was keeping a secret also.

Sally Ann and Adrian had invited us over for Sunday football and chili once Gabe recuperated from his head injury. I can't even be sure who or why it was brought up, but Adrian said something about Charlotte or Gabe's obsession with Charlotte. At first, I was confused as fuck. *Who the hell was Charlotte and why would Gabe be obsessed with her?* I was overcome with an insane streak of jealousy and then I stamped that shit down quick. I never once got the impression from Gabe that he was also attracted to women and Lord knows there were enough sexually-engineered commercials on during football games to fire up any male remotely interested in lady bits.

Apparently long legs sold beer and models opening their mouths wide to eat a burger encouraged guys to want to eat at their restaurant. I didn't so much as see a reaction out of him. Then I realized it didn't matter who he was attracted to because I was the one he wanted. As insecure as I was at times, I was smart enough to know that attraction didn't equal unfaithfulness. Billy Sampson's behavior in high school colored my views for a long time, but I eventually figured things out. I also knew that Gabe wasn't the kind of guy to stray, which was a reassurance I never thought I would have in a rel… *something*.

Secure in my place in his life, I laid my head on his broad shoulder and asked, "Who's Charlotte?"

Gabe leaned away enough so he could look down at my upturned face. "I never told you about Charlotte?" I could hear the reverence in his voice when he mentioned her name and my earlier confidence started to fade.

"No, you certainly didn't."

"Oh. Hmmm." His nonchalant attitude caused me to narrow my eyes at him. He knew damn well he never told me about this Charlotte. The smirk he wore on his jutted chin made me want to twist his nipple clean off.

I was just about to blast him with standard Josh-like snark when Adrian spoke up. "What is Charlotte, not who."

Gabe sent Adrian a look that said he wasn't at all helpful, but I didn't agree. Charlotte wasn't a person; she was a thing. I began to think of all the things that men owned that they named, specifically a woman's name. I narrowed it down to two things: a boat or a car. Gabe didn't own a garage, but rental units were plentiful in Carter County and some were large enough to shelter either of those things.

"Boat or car?" *I asked him.*

"You show me yours and I'll show you mine," *was Gabe's husky whisper in my ear. He then turned and leveled Adrian with a fierce scowl.* "Not another word from you." *Adrian pretended to zip his lips then threw his hands up playfully in surrender.*

Gabe threw down the gauntlet that day and I was not about to give him a show on the pole–well, not the one in the attic, anyway–until he showed me Charlotte. I spent more time than I should've trying to figure out if she was a car or a boat. My first thought was that she was a classic car of some sort because his dad owned an auto body shop in Miami, but then again, being from Miami meant he probably liked the water. In the end, I decided she was a car because most boats that sailed in the ocean weren't the same ones that sailed on inland lakes in Ohio.

Even half dead, I would have heard his promise to take me to see her. It amused me when he tried to backpedal the next morning, but I wasn't letting up. He was going to show me his first and I was going to reward him handsomely later. I wasn't about to confess that I had a special song in mind for the first time I performed for him. I wanted to captivate him as surely as he had me and give him a night he would never forget.

It didn't take Gabe long to limp into the living room after his quick shower. It wasn't nice of me to laugh when he tripped over his shoe and cursed when he stubbed his toe. The wicked look in his eye promised that I'd be paying for my insensitivity. If he thought he scared me, he had another thing coming. I reached down and arranged my growing erection before I served up his scrambled eggs on a plate beside bacon and a blueberry muffin.

Gabe stepped behind me and pulled me tight against him. He rubbed his nose behind my ear and down my neck, knowing it drove me wild. "You spoil me."

I turned in the circle of his arms, looking into his eyes. "I wanted to give you a morning that was as special to you as last night was for me."

"I made you dinner and we watched television." I didn't like how he downplayed his kind gesture, but we both had our issues to work through.

"Well, I made you breakfast and then I'm going to bend over the hood of your precious car so you can fuck me."

Gabe groaned my name before he captured my lips in a kiss so devastating that I almost confessed that I more than liked him. I was on the verge of using the other L world when he broke our kiss, but then I noticed that the look on his face had turned from lust to suspicion.

"What makes you think Charlotte is a car?" he asked.

"You're not the only one with reasoning and deduction skills, Miami Vice." I pinched his nipple playfully before I turned back around to grab our plates. "Our lakes aren't deep enough for any boat you sailed in Miami and your father owns an auto body shop." I placed our plates on the table and then put my hands on my hips. I gave him my best smug smile before I said, "It stands to reason that you have a classic car stored somewhere in this county."

Gabe tipped his head to the side as if he was impressed then he shot my theory all to hell when he said, "Maybe it's a motorcycle."

My mouth dropped open as I pictured Gabe in a leather jacket and pants astride some manly looking machine. I imagined the vibration of the bike working its way through my body as I held tight to him with both my arms and thighs. "Well, I guess she better have one hell of a kickstand to support us when I straddle your legs and ride you."

"Jesus," Gabe groaned.

I may or may not have teased Gabe the entire thirty-minute ride to his storage unit with the things I wanted him to do to me. I was grateful that he was as worked up as I was by the time we stepped inside his unit because I couldn't handle being the only one to feel it. He was on me as soon as he shut the door. At first, I was too caught up in our heated kiss and the way his hands felt against my skin when they slid beneath my sweater. Eventually two thoughts penetrated my lust-dazed brain: it was dark as night inside but warm as could be.

"It's heated?" I asked after pulling back from his kiss.

"Nothing but the best for Charlotte." Gabe licked the seam of my lips before he bit down on my bottom lip. "Ready to meet her?"

I was more excited than I thought I would be. I mean, it was a hunk of metal either way, but she obviously meant a lot to Gabe and he meant a lot to me. I cringed internally after my hunk of metal thought, because I sure as hell didn't view my car that way. "Ready."

Gabe flipped on the light and I blinked against the sudden brightness in the unit. I could tell by the shape beneath the cloth cover that we were definitely talking about a classic car. Gabe walked over and slowly began to remove her cover, as if he was performing some automotive striptease. The gleaming black hood came into view and then the rest of the car inch by inch until just the rear of the car was covered. Gabe yanked the cover the rest of the way off and held up his hands like a dorky, but oh-so-sexy magician.

"She's a 1970 Dodge…"

"Charger," I completed for him. "My granddad had a red one named Dolly. She was his pride and joy too." I felt Gabe's eyes on me when I walked over to the gleaming machine. "She's beautiful." I reached for the handle and opened the door. I was pleased to see that her black leather interior was just as pristine as the exterior. "I can see why you like her so much." I heard and felt Gabe approaching me so I shut the door then turned to face him.

"Love, not like." The emotional crack in his voice told me that he might be talking about more than just his feelings for his car. I wasn't ready for that so I did the first thing that came to mind. I seduced him.

I reached between our bodies and stroked his erection through his jeans. I took to heart that I could get such an intense reaction out of an amazing man like Gabe. "It's been too long since I've felt you inside me." It had been twenty-four long hours too many and I was impatient to have him again.

I stepped away from him and walked around to the hood of the car. I unsnapped my pants and pushed them all the way down to my ankles so that I didn't risk scratching Charlotte's paint job with a snap or zipper. Gabe stood rooted to the spot until I began stroking my erection, then he stalked toward me with an intense look that said he was the predator and I was his prey.

Gabe stood behind me and removed my hand from my cock. He took my wrists in his hands and pushed his chest against by back until I was bent over with my hands braced on the hood. I was shocked that he wanted my handprints on his car, but then I lost track of all my thoughts when he said, "Don't move." His voice was a dark promise beneath the bright, sterile lights.

I expected to hear Gabe undressing in preparation to fuck me, but instead he dropped to his knees and parted my ass cheeks. My eyes rolled back in my head when I felt the tip of his wet tongue against the crinkled skin surrounding my hole. I expected him to dive right in, but I was wrong. Gabe took his time teasing my puckered entrance for several long moments before he pulled back to nibble on the taut globes of one ass cheek, then the other, while his large hands kneaded the muscles in my thighs. I needed more from him.

"Gabe," I moaned.

"Shhh, I got you," he replied.

I heard the sound of Gabe sucking on his finger before he pushed the tip inside my ass. Then I felt his tongue licking my sensitive pucker around his finger as he worked it in and out of my tight clench. Gabe growled as he lapped at my flesh like it was the best thing he had ever tasted. My head suddenly felt too heavy and I let it fall forward.

"More," I demanded.

Gabe obliged me by removing his finger so he could fuck my ass with his tongue. It was the most incredible thing I had ever felt and I hoped it wasn't something that I only received on special occasions like birthdays or Christmas in the future. Pre-cum leaked from my dick in a thin, clear line and landed on the hood of Charlotte.

"I'm getting cum on your car," I warned Gabe. His answer was to bury his tongue deeper inside me.

I wanted so badly to stroke my dick, but Gabe told me not to move and for once I listened to him without putting up a fight. I wanted to draw out my pleasure as long as I could and the combined sensation of his tongue in my ass and friction on my cock would have me coming too soon.

Gabe worked my hole until I was practically a pliant, limp noodle on the verge of collapsing onto the hood of his car. I promised him anything if he'd just take out his big cock and fuck me.

"Anything?" He rose up behind me and I heard the glorious sounds of him undoing his pants. "You'll give me anything I want? Like a private dance in your studio?"

"It was already a sure thing." I was embarrassed by the way I panted between words. "Fuck me already." Gabe made quick work of putting on a condom and lubing his cock. The slight burn of his penetration was so welcome I could've cried, but instead I shouted something that sounded entirely too much like hallelujah for the activities we were engaged in.

Gabe placed his hands on my hips and pulled back until only

the tip of his dick was inside me. I could tell he was going to torture me by teasing me and I wasn't about to take that. Instead, I pushed back until he was buried to the hilt inside me again.

"You little spitfire," Gabe growled. "You just have to be in control, don't you?" He leaned over me until his chest was pressed against my back. "One of these days..." He let his threat trail off, but he didn't worry me.

Gabe pumped his hips and gave me the fucking I demanded from him. I loved the sound of our flesh slapping together combined with his growls and my whimpered pleas of, "More." He wrapped one hand around my cock and the other around my chin so he could turn my head for his kiss.

God, I swore that every time we were together it was better than the time before. He made me feel things–want things–I never thought I'd experience. He wasn't the only one on the verge of throwing the real L word around, but the one functioning cell left in my brain refused to say something so special during sex. I wanted him to believe me when I finally fessed up to being in love with him and everyone knew that declarations made during sex couldn't be trusted.

Instead I went with, "I love... the way you fuck."

"I love... that I get to fuck you," was Gabe's reply.

We both meant more and we knew it. I figured we would turn our confession into a competition to see who caved first, kind of like when I squeezed my ass around his dick as hard as I could to make him come first. I wanted to bring him so much pleasure that he lost control and couldn't hold back.

"Damn it," Gabe said between gritted teeth. "I know what you're doing. It's not going to work. You're going to come first."

"I don't think so, baby." I reached between our legs and gripped his balls firmly in my hand and massaged them in a sure-fire way to make him... well, fire.

"Josh." I knew I would never tire of the way Gabe groaned my name when he came. His, "damn you," that followed was half-hearted to say the least. He never stopped pegging my prostate or jerking my dick when he filled the condom, but his rhythm did falter for a few seconds. "Come." Gabe sank his teeth in my neck where it curved into my shoulder and I couldn't stave off my orgasm any longer. Stars exploded behind my closed eyelids as my climax moved through my body.

Gabe was kind enough to catch me before I collapsed onto the cum-splattered hood of his car or maybe it was so I didn't scratch the paint with my coat zipper. Either way, I needed his strength as I came down off my high.

"Sexy," Gabe whispered huskily in my ear.

"Thanks," I said in between breaths.

"You too, but I meant that," he said. I opened my eyes and saw that he was pointing to the mess I made all over his car. "I love that I can make you come that hard." I could barely remember my name, yet, he could form complete sentences that made sense. I apparently wasn't doing a good enough job of rocking his world and planned to remedy that later the same week in my studio.

Gabe slowly pulled out of me and took care of the condom while I cleaned myself off with a shop towel he produced from somewhere. I couldn't keep the grin off my face when he lovingly cleaned Charlotte's hood with a microfiber towel before he recovered her.

"Thank you for introducing me to Charlotte," I told him once we were both tucked back into our pants and presentable to be seen in public.

"It's a big deal, you know. First Charlotte and then my parents." Gabe waggled his eyebrows then dropped a kiss on my lips and slid his fingers between mine before he tugged me toward the door.

"I can't wait to drive her once the weather turns nice," I said, knowing full well he wasn't going to allow that to happen.

"No one drives Charlotte but me," Gabe predictably said.

"Fine, Detective Butt Breath, but that means you can never ever take a spin on my pole." The thought of Gabe's much larger body spinning on my pole nearly had me laughing out loud. I adored him, but graceful and fluid weren't words I associated with Gabe, not even during sex.

Gabe stopped and turned to face me once we were outside his rental unit. "Which pole are you talking about?" His question caught me off guard. Did he mean that he wanted to bottom? For me? Gabe opened his mouth to answer me, but the loud, rumbling sound of a diesel pickup truck stopped him. We turned our heads sharply and watched as a dark truck with tinted windows drove between rows of units a few buildings down from his. I could tell his mind was in a place far away from sex.

"What's wrong?" I asked.

"I'm sure it's nothing," he replied.

I could tell by the grim line his lips formed on his face and the way that he gripped the steering wheel that his good humor and post-coital bliss seemed to have evaporated. He looked tense and coiled to react to something, but it didn't take me long to figure out why once we were on the road heading back toward Blissville.

The large black or dark gray truck came speeding up behind us and nearly hit us as it went around us, blowing black smoke all over the front of Gabe's car so that we choked on the fumes that came through the vents.

"I can't believe you had sex with that guy," Gabe said angrily.

"Who?"

"That's Sampson's truck," Gabe informed me. "I saw it parked outside your salon yesterday."

"Oh," I replied. "Hey, you can't blame me for who I slept with ten or eleven years ago. I was a dumb kid who wanted to be loved." In some ways, not a lot had changed. I was no longer dumb, or a kid, but I really wanted to be loved–especially by the man sitting to the left of me.

"I know, babe, and I'm sorry that I said that." Gabe blew out a frustrated breath. "I don't trust him or the fact that he happened to be at the same storage units as us at the exact same time."

"You think he followed us?" I asked. That seemed like way too much effort from the Billy I knew.

"I saw the look in his eye and heard the determination in his voice when he said it wasn't over," Gabe replied fiercely. He glanced over at me before returning his eyes to the road. "He can't have you because you're mine." I was about to preen in my seat until he said, "Even though you called me Detective Butt Breath after I made you come so hard you sang soprano."

"Well, you did just have your tongue in my ass," I told him.

"Which I later put in your mouth, so that makes you a Butt Breath too." He had a valid point and… eww. I hadn't thought about it until he said something. "So that means you kind of licked your own asshole."

"I hate you."

Gabe laughed because he knew it was the furthest thing from the truth.

NINE

Gabe

Josh made me feel a bevy of new emotions and most of them were amazing, but I really could do without the jealousy. How had I lived thirty-six years and not been jealous prior to meeting him? I never had a problem sharing my toys with my older brother when we were little. I never got jealous when one of my friends picked up a new buddy and started spending time with them. I never got jealous when a guy I was involved with noticed other men nor did I resent that they had a past prior to me coming into their lives. Why now? Why Josh?

Because you're crazy in love for the first time. I had only known Josh for such a short period of time, and most of that was spent hissing and spitting at one another or fucking, yet I had never been more certain of my feelings for anyone as I was with him. The thought of him with someone other than me made me ill and it didn't matter how unreasonable my feelings were. Hell, my ex lived in the same damn town as us and Josh wasn't insanely jealous–or at least not that he showed me. So why couldn't I get past a relationship that ended almost a decade before I met Josh?

Because there's something really off about Billy Sampson. I knew it the moment I met him that he was a jerk and it took me all of a minute or less to learn he was a homophobic jerk–or so I thought. It turned out that he really hated himself and the fact that he was attracted to other men. Those types of people were often more violent than a regular homophobe. I should've pitied him rather than been jealous of his existence, but I was angry that he got to see an innocent Josh that the world hadn't turned cynical and even angrier that he was part of the reason for Josh building walls around his heart.

I wanted that heart all to myself and I wanted it given to me freely. I needed Josh to be able to look into my eyes and tell me exactly how he felt about me without hiding his emotions behind snarky comments and sex. I craved the moment that Josh could be completely real with me and not worry that he would be let down and disappointed again. I also knew that I needed to earn that privilege with more than just words, which was why I pushed aside all of my irrational jealous feelings over his past with Billy Sampson so that I wouldn't ruin our day with a foul mood–especially after the sexy moment we shared in my storage unit.

I ended up taking Josh to run his errands rather than drop him off back at his house because I wanted to spend more time with him. I enjoyed our trip to Brook's Pets, but I could go the rest of my life without returning to the grocery story on a Sunday afternoon.

"What the hell is going on here?" I asked in disbelief. The parking lot was packed with cars and there were only two grocery carts left in the corral inside the store. "Is there a blizzard coming?" Every time the forecaster mentioned snow, regardless if it was a dusting or two feet, people ran to the store and bought out the bread and milk. Ohioans were strange individuals sometimes.

"It's Sunday at noon," Josh replied, as if that made any sense at all. He rolled his eyes when I just looked at him like he was from another planet. "All of the *good* people have just left church and they're grabbing their groceries before they go home. If I wasn't still blissed out from the O you gave me then I might be a little upset with you for making me arrive later than normal. I always get here and back home before the madness."

"You think we're bad because we don't attend church?" I asked him curiously.

"Not at all," he replied. "It was just something that was stressed by the older generation when I was younger. If you didn't go to church, then you were going to hell. Now, I get to go to hell for a much better reason." He rolled his eyes again at me and said, "No, I don't really believe that either. I'm just once again repeating the shit I've heard over the years, and not necessarily from people in my community." I wasn't overly religious, but I was glad to hear that Josh didn't think he was unworthy of His love like he had in the past with the men He created. "God loves everyone," he said confidently before he added, "especially those who make the world a more beautiful place." I knew when he pointed to himself he was referring to his career and not his looks, well, that was until he licked his finger and ran it over his eyebrow.

"You do make the world a more beautiful place." I leaned over and kissed his cheek and felt his skin flush beneath my lips. Sure enough, his face was a pretty shade of red when I pulled back. "I wonder what they'd call that shade in a lipstick," I pondered out loud.

Josh's response was to elbow me in the ribs before he walked ahead of me, pushing his cart with his head held high. I learned quickly that Josh didn't quite know how to handle it when someone served him up a bit of his own smart-ass medicine. I liked that I was unpredictable to him and kept him on his toes. I stood there longer than I should have, admiring his sassy, bubble butt as he walked away.

"I like you more and more each day."

I turned around and looked into Meredith's smiling eyes. I was curious what I did that made her so happy so I asked, "Why?"

"You're perfect for him," the woman dressed in her Sunday finest standing beside Meredith said. She had the same mocha-colored skin and keen brown eyes that sparkled with mirth as Josh's best friend. I didn't have to rely too heavily on my detecting skills to know I was standing in front of Meredith's mother. "You give that sass right back to him and keep him on his toes." I was glad to hear that my earlier speculation had been right. "Besides, I know love when I see it."

I leaned forward and said softly, "Don't tell him that or…"

"I'll scare him to death," she finished for me. "I know how my boy works, and yes, I claim him as my own. I promised Bertie that I would look after him when she moved to Florida and I take my promises seriously." She extended her hand to me and said, "I'm Wilhelmina Richmond, by the way. My friends call me Willa." I shook her hand and after a long awkward pause she added, "That includes you too."

"It's wonderful to meet you, Willa." The earlier mention of Josh's mom reminded me that I would be meeting her in a few weeks. I wanted to do something nice when I met Bertie, perhaps gift her a bottle of her favorite perfume or something, and asked Willa for suggestions.

"Do you really want to make a good impression on Bertie?" she asked me.

"Yes, ma'am."

"Respect," she said then looked at Meredith. "Take note of how a man should talk to your mother." I raised my brow, wondering what she was referring to but decided to ask Meredith later because I knew Josh would double back and look for me before too much longer. Willa locked her eyes on mine and said, "Treat her son the way he deserves to be treated and I promise you that she's gonna love you." It sounded too simple to be true, but that's exactly how I would feel if I had a son or daughter.

As I predicted, Josh returned to my side mere seconds after Willa finished her sentence. "Mama Richmond," he said before he was wrapped tight in a hug. "I miss your face."

"Boy, I've lived in the same house for nearly fifteen years. Do I need to print off a map for you or are you just playing hard to get?" Then she looked at me and amended, "Or, perhaps you've been very busy." Josh wasn't the only one who blushed after Willa's comment. "I remember what it was like when things were new."

"Mama," Meredith said, but her admonishment was ruined by her snort.

"I'll stop over tomorrow," Josh promised, tugging on my arm to get me to follow. "This guy made me late and I have to get a move on if I'm going to make dinner an amazing event."

"Dinner is always an amazing event," Meredith countered.

"Thanks, love," Josh told her as he walked backwards. I took the cart from him in fear that he'd run someone over. "I'll see you tonight." He then blew air kisses at Willa and said, "And you tomorrow."

"What's for dinner?" I asked Josh once he turned back around. I hadn't missed a Sunday dinner since he first invited me after we kissed and made up after he returned from Thanksgiving with his family in Florida. I was the first guy Josh ever invited over to the precious night he only shared with the two people closest to him in the world–Chaz and Meredith.

"You're in for a real treat," he said proudly. "I'm making you beef stew and cornbread." I didn't miss how he said he was making it for me.

My mouth watered at the thought and I groaned so loud that people turned to look. "He's making cornbread," I said, as if that explained everything.

"*Homemade* cornbread," Josh amended. "Not some crappy box mix." Some lady, who'd just tossed a name brand box of cornbread mix in her cart, gave him the side-eye and sped away.

The rest of the trip through the store was less eventful and Josh refrained from insulting anyone else with talk about his superior cooking skills. He did take his sweet old-fashioned time squeezing the produce in a way that made me think of the way he milked my balls right before we arrived. I couldn't tell if he was dilly dallying to annoy and tease me or if he was that particular about his fruit. I patiently pushed the cart without saying a single word and exchanged sympathetic looks with other men who were in the same boat as me. I couldn't wait to get back ho… to his house and smell the amazingness that I knew his beef stew would be.

It seemed like days before we were once again back in my car heading to Josh's house to put away his groceries and pet supplies. A light snow had begun to fall while we were inside the store so I was paying more attention to the roads than whatever Josh was saying at the time. I had seen just how quickly the roads got slick when the temperature hovered around or was below freezing and wrecking was the last thing I wanted to do that day.

"Are you paying attention?" he asked primly.

"Not really." Hey, I wanted points for honesty, but it didn't look like I was going to get them.

"That just added an extra day on before you get to see my studio and the special routine I have planned for you."

I sat up straighter in my seat and glanced over at him quickly to see if he was joking. He was not. It was the first time he ever mentioned a special routine and I was damn determined to knock that day off my sentence. "I'm sorry, dear." The snort Josh gave told me that my voice was anything but the contrite one I had planned.

"I was *saying*," Josh said exaggeratingly, "that I read an article online yesterday that said a lot of gay couples start looking alike after they've dated for a while. I'm just stating for the record that we," I saw him gesture his finger between us out of the corner of my eye, "will never be that couple."

I gasped as if I was truly affronted when I was actually excited that he thought of us as a couple, even though the R word had yet to be used by either of us. "Are you saying that you think I'm ugly?"

"Don't play dumb with me, Detective…" He skipped whatever insult he was about to use when I pinned him with the same scowl I gave perps when I played bad cop. "I simply meant that I like how different we are as individuals. I think we complement each other."

His words made my heart dance in my chest. "I agree," I told him. I turned to face him once I was stopped at a four-way stop. I hooked my finger in his jacket and pulled him to me for a quick kiss. "Besides, there's no way my boys want to be trapped in skinny jeans after all these years wearing Levi's."

Josh laughed hard, but I wasn't sure if it was due to my words or the idea of me crammed into skinny jeans. I loved how they looked on him, but there was no amount of money in the world that would entice me to wear them.

"I like the way you look in my t-shirts though," I told him once I resumed driving back toward his house. If I was keeping score of the number of times I rendered Josh speechless it would probably be a total of two times after he heard my t-shirt comment.

I wouldn't say he stiffened exactly, but there was a sudden stillness to him. Josh was never still. I worried that I went too far or pushed too fast until he placed his hand on my leg and patted it. "I like wearing your shirts because they smell like you." I had to swallow hard twice to dislodge the lump of emotion stuck in my throat.

I knew there was so much more to his words than him admitting that he liked my body wash.

I pulled into his driveway at the rear of his house and parked next to his teal green Mini Cooper convertible. I wanted so badly to expand on the emotional exchange that we both had, but I didn't want to push my luck. Instead, I posed to him the question that just popped into my head. "What's the name of your car?" I knew that there was no way in hell that Josh didn't have a name for her. He loved that car as much as I loved Charlotte. His pink-tinged cheeks told me that he was embarrassed about the name he chose for his car. He mumbled something beneath his breath, but it was too soft for me to hear. "What was that?"

"Princess!"

"It's cute," I replied, "like the car and like…"

"Do not say like her owner." Josh's shrewd eyes locked on my twitching lips as I fought back the urge to laugh.

"I would never."

Josh's response was to get out of my car and walk around to the trunk so he could start unloading groceries. I was feeling a tad sassy myself and didn't push the button to open it for him. Instead I sat in my car and watched him through my rearview mirror until he lowered his head and looked at me through the rear windshield and mouthed the words "two days."

I popped the trunk almost as fast as I could spring an erection. The smug smile on his face told me that he had me right where he wanted me–by the balls. Yeah, well, I had my own little victory with him admitting he liked to smell like me. In my book, it made us both winners. If I had my way, we both would be celebrating our victories together after his friends went home.

TEN

Josh

I WASN'T ADDICTED TO GABE. I WASN'T ADDICTED TO GABE. I wasn't... oh, damn it. I was fucking addicted to Gabe. I had spent a few consecutive nights sleeping beside him and then found that I couldn't sleep once we went back to separate beds. I was surprised I wasn't shaking from withdrawal and scheming to find a way to get my next Gabe fix. My brain cautioned me to slow things down and that I was allowing him to get too close too fast, but my heart and body told my brain to take a damn vacation from overthinking for a damn change.

I reached for my phone on the bedside table to text him but stopped myself. It was well past midnight on a work night for him. He needed his sleep to concentrate on solving his drug case and Lord knows I didn't let him rest much over the past weekend. I also knew he wouldn't be sleeping much on Wednesday when I did my big studio reveal and routine for him.

Instead of pestering Gabe, I got out of bed and fixed a mug of chamomile tea to try and help soothe me to sleep. I curled up with Diva on the sofa and turned on a rerun of my favorite cooking show. "Who's the best kitty in the world?" I cooed while I scratched her ears. Diva purred loudly and bumped her head against my cup of tea so that I had to put it down and use both hands to please her.

Diva curled up on my chest and tucked her head beneath my chin. The warmth of her fur and gentle vibration of her purring worked better than any tea and I found myself nodding off right when the judges were about to test the food that the reality show contestants prepared. The show invaded my dreams and the panel of celebrity chefs was replaced by Chaz, Meredith, and Gabe. The wide-eyed, hopeful culinary students morphed into different versions of me. There were three Joshes, all in different outfits and obviously, none that I would've picked. That flannel shirt lumberjack look didn't work for me at all.

Sunday dinners morphed into a judging contest and instead of normal brilliant dishes, I served up octopus tentacle stew and ox tail carbonara. What. The. Ever. Loving. Fuck!

"This tentacle stew is a tad bit under seasoned," Chef Gabe said with a scowl on his face. "It's not your best dish in this competition, Josh."

Lumberjack Josh looked crestfallen but what the hell did he expect serving up nasty shit like that? Next up was Emo Josh dressed all in black and who clearly had a heavy hand when applying eye liner. I worried that the black skinny jeans he wore were so tight they would cut the circulation off to his cock.

Chef Chaz took a bite of ox tail carbonara and spit it back out. "I can't even…" He waved his hand dramatically and a member of the crew came and took the offensive plate away.

Last up to be judged was Preppy Josh, who I admit was my favorite. That light blue Oxford button-up shirt and pink sweater tied around his neck was a little much for me, but of the three Joshes he appeared to be taking the competition most serious.

"This is an unusual spin on country fried crow," Chef Meredith said after taking a bite. She tilted her head to the side as if she couldn't decide if that was a good or a bad thing. She took another small bite and then smiled broadly. "I like it, Josh. There's this little burst of heat at the back of my throat that gives it an extra something. Well done."

"Yasssss, bitch." Preppy Josh twirled in celebration.

"*Excuse* me," Chef Meredith said. I could tell by the look on her face that she'd be serving up some crow for Preppy Josh to eat. Dumb fool. Meredith opened her mouth to blast him, but I was ripped out of my sleep by the sound of a car alarm going off.

I had always heard that moms could always tell their crying baby apart from others in a room and I believed it because I could clearly tell my baby's cry of distress from my neighbor's Fiat 500. "Damn cat," I muttered as I set Diva on the sofa and rose to my feet. Diva was insulted by my comment and snagged my pajama bottoms with her claw before I could walk away. "Aww, not you, baby girl. I was talking about that unfortunate cat who lives next door who sets off a different alarm almost nightly. Scruffy or some stupid shit name," I told Diva.

She retracted her claw and permitted me to leave. I put on my robe and slid my feet in my slippers before I grabbed my car keys. My Princess sometimes played hard to get and required me to stick my key in the door rather than push a button on the fob before she would stop her crying.

I flipped on the outside light next to the back door and made my way carefully down the icy steps to the driveway. If I ever cleaned out all the crap in my garage, I could store Princess inside and not worry about her alarm being set off by a dumb cat. I slipped and slid my way over to the car and couldn't believe what I saw when I got there. All four of my tires had been slashed. I unlocked Princess to turn off the alarm then stood there staring at my baby and wondering who would violate her in such a hateful way.

An eerie feeling came over me, as if I was being watched. I looked up and down the alley, but didn't see anything out of the norm other than the street light closest to my driveway was out. It had been working when I walked Gabe to his car earlier that night because I remembered remarking about how pretty the snowflakes looked in the beam of light. The light could've gone out on its own, but I had a sneaky suspicion that wasn't the case. I was too freaked out to investigate so I returned inside the house and called the police.

Somewhere in the back of my mind it should've occurred to me to call my hunky detective of a boyfriend first, but it didn't. Unfortunately for me, one of the officers who arrived on the scene called him instead of me. In my opinion, four uniformed officers to answer a vandalism call seemed to be a tad bit excessive. Hell, I didn't even know we had four cops on duty at one time. Regardless, one of the three extra cops had nothing better to do than call Gabe while the first officer took my statement and completed a report. The thunderous look on Gabe's face when he arrived made me want to hide in my closet, but those days were long past.

I also noticed that the Three Stooges suddenly got busier once he arrived. One of them even found a clue, admittedly one that validated the uneasy feeling I had when I first discovered that my tires had been slashed. "Detective Wyatt, it appears that the street light in the alley was purposely busted. I found shards of glass below on the ground beneath the light," he said, interrupting the stare down

Gabe was giving me.

"Stay inside where it's warm and don't bother trying to lock me out. We are going to have a conversation when I return." Gabe's tone of voice and high-handed behavior should've pissed me off, but the shaking I felt in my body had nothing to do with fear or anger. Damn him.

My tea from earlier was ice cold and disgusting so I made a fresh cup, made myself comfy on the sofa, and flipped on a new show I hadn't seen before called Who's Your Fryin' Daddy? The host went to carnivals and county fairs from coast to coast and featured deep fried favorites. I got so caught up in the weird shit that some people liked to fry that I was able to temporarily forget the damage to my poor, pitiful Princess until Gabe returned upstairs by himself.

"Where's the other officers?" I asked. I tilted my head to look around him, hoping that one or more would be following behind him, but no such luck.

"I sent them all on their way," Gabe replied sternly. Instead of sitting on the couch next to me or the club chair beside the couch, Gabe squatted down in front of me. "Are you okay?" I was glad to see that concern had replaced the majority of the anger he felt earlier, although I could still see it simmering around the edges of worry in his eyes. I wasn't out of the woods yet.

"I'm fine, Gabe, but Princess…"

"Forget the car for a moment, Josh. Your insurance company will replace the tires. Princess will be fixed. It's you that I'm worried about." He released a shaky breath and I realized that his concern went deeper than I had first realized. I knew that Gabe had a protective streak, but I thought his reaction to a little bit of vandalism was disproportionate.

"What am I not understanding here?" I asked him.

"Tell me exactly what happened?" Gabe avoided my question, which irritated me. It was the middle of the night and I'd had very little beauty sleep so I wasn't surprised when I felt the ugly coming to the surface.

"Why don't you read the report?" I fired back.

"Now is not the time for your attitude, Josh. I'll overlook that you called the police department instead of me... for now, but I need you to answer my question. What exactly happened?"

I wasn't one to give in easy. "Well, I couldn't fall asleep so I fixed myself a cup of warm tea and curled up with the cat on the couch. I was watching some food reality show and next thing I knew I was having a dream. You were there, Meredith was there, Chaz was there, and..."

"Josh!" Gabe rose to his feet and paced angrily away from me while sliding his hands through his hair. He turned to face me and gave his hair a theatrical yank to let me know how mad I drove him. "Damn it! You could be in serious danger and..."

"Wait a damn minute! How do you jump from four flat tires to serious danger, Gabe?" I was too shocked to come up with a cutesy name for him just then.

"Remember when I told you about the threats made to Nate Turner?" Gabe asked. I nodded my head but failed to see what I had in common with a sleazebag night club owner who might've been involved in illegal activities. I didn't so much as cheat on my taxes. "His tires were slashed just like yours."

"Coincidence," I said to Gabe, but I couldn't shake the feeling that he might be right. I did feel an ominous presence when I stood outside.

"If Nate hadn't turned up dead in our county then I would agree with you, but he did," Gabe said. He took his coat off and tossed it over the arm of the couch. "Josh, I have no clue what Nate was into or why he appeared to be bringing it to me, but it can't be a coincidence. I'd love to pin this on Deputy Small Dick, but in all fairness, this doesn't seem to have his name on it."

Gabe was making serious accusations and basically telling me that my life could be in great peril, but all I could think about was how much I had rubbed off on him already. His Deputy Small Dick talk made me smile and brought happy tears to my eyes.

A look of panic crossed Gabe's face then he said, "Josh, don't cry. I won't let anything bad happen to you." He pulled me into his arms and said such sweet things to me that only made me shake harder, and at some point, Gabe realized I was trembling from laughter and not fear. "What can you possibly find funny about this situation?"

"Deputy… Small… Dick…" I laughed so hard that I gasped for air between each word. "You might not look like me yet, but you're starting to sound like me."

Gabe closed his eyes as he struggled to find patience with me. If he planned on sticking around long, and I hoped that he did, then he would need to discover a huge well of it inside him. "It's late and nothing is going to get resolved by us not sleeping."

"You're staying?" There was no disguising the hopefulness in my voice.

"I'm staying."

Once we were tucked beneath the covers, I nestled up close to him and placed my head on his shoulder. He ran his hand up and down my back, but I wasn't sure if he was trying to comfort me or himself. "Much better," I said sleepily. The excitement was wearing off and I could feel sleep coming for me.

"Why weren't you able to sleep?" Gabe asked. There should've been a rule about asking questions when someone was tired and their guard was down.

"You know," I replied.

"Maybe I want to hear the words," Gabe said.

I remembered the scared look in his eyes when he returned upstairs by himself and I wanted to do something that would ease his worry, even if it was just for the night. "Because you weren't here," I admitted.

"I wasn't sleeping either," Gabe told me. He pressed a kiss against my forehead. "Just say the word when you're ready to change our sleeping arrangements."

I knew he was talking about more than the frequency of sleepovers. I also knew I wasn't ready for it yet. "You'll be the first to know," I simply said.

"Probably not," Gabe said. "I predict that I'll be the..." he paused to count in his head, "third or fourth person to know."

"Fourth?" I knew that Meredith and Chaz were probably one and two in his mind. A while ago, he would've been right, but I discovered that I didn't want to talk too much about my relationship with Gabe. For one thing, I didn't think I'd be able to find the right words. Second, what we had felt too special to dissect over coffee with friends–not that I wouldn't hesitate to turn to my friends if I needed help.

"Yeah, you're right," he said. "The entire town will probably know about it before I do. You'll do something cutesy like drop a change of address card for me at the post office early one morning and word will spread through town like wildfire before lunch."

"That sounds about right," I said after mulling it over. "Wait, you're the one moving?"

Gabe snorted. "There's no room for a pole dancing studio at my house."

"It always comes back to the damn pole dancing," I said, but I couldn't keep the smile out of my sleepy voice.

"Go to sleep, babe," Gabe whispered into the darkness. "You'll have a busy day tomorrow reporting your claim to your insurance company and then making arrangements to have Princess towed to have new tires put on. Unless..."

"I'll take care of it." I appreciated that he was going to offer, but I had the day off and was quite capable of doing the tasks he mentioned.

"I'll leave my Charger for you in case you need to drive someplace. I'll have Adrian pick me up here in the morning." Gabe loved that car with the remote start, heated seats and steering wheel. I couldn't believe he'd let me drive it, but then I realized that I probably ranked higher in his life than even I knew. The scale was leaning majorly toward the thrill side, but there was still an edge of terror remaining when I thought about how close we'd come in so little of a time. *Breathe, Josh. Don't fight it.*

ELEVEN

Gabe

"You want to tell me why you didn't call me last night?" I asked as I toweled dried my hair after a shared shower with Josh. I tried not to be insulted and offended or take it the wrong way, but it was hard to do. He needed help, I wasn't the first person he turned to, and it didn't sit well with me. At all.

"It was a kneejerk reaction," he said with a casual shrug. Truthfully, I felt he was way too nonchalant about the entire vandalism ordeal.

"Kneejerk reaction." I rolled his words in my mind while I repeated them out loud.

"Yes, when there's trouble you call 911." He looked at me like I lost my mind.

"But you didn't the night that Oscar Davidson broke into your home to kill you. You called me," I reminded him, as if he could ever forget. I sure as hell wouldn't forget sprinting through dark back yards in my attempt to save him from a fucking mad man.

"I did."

I hung up my towel and placed my hands on my hips. "Why?"

"I can't take you seriously with you standing there all naked and sexy looking," Josh said. He was clearly stalling because he could barely stand up after the orgasm I had just given him, so there was no way he was ready for more. I crossed my arms over my chest and gave him my best menacing scowl. I was freezing my naked ass off, but I wasn't budging from the topic. "That's not helping because I can still see your dick."

"Josh." My tone said I was done playing.

"Fine!" He snatched his towel off the rack and began rubbing himself furiously. "I wanted to hear your voice one more damn time." I couldn't see his expression because Josh kept his eyes focused on what his hands were doing, but the flush on his body told me he was embarrassed. "Even then I knew there was *something* more between us, even if I didn't want there to be. If those were going to be my last moments…"

I closed the gap between us and tugged on his towel until he looked up at me then tugged until he was as close as I could get him considering the side of the bathtub was between us. "They were never going to be your last moments."

"How do you know that?" he asked skeptically.

The answer to his question was simple: he was meant to be mine. At the time of his attack, I knew only two things about him: he drove me crazy and I couldn't get enough. We hadn't known each other long then and we weren't sure we liked each other. I suspected that my move to Blissville was fated, but to be with him instead of Kyle. I wouldn't tell him any of that right then because he wasn't ready to hear it. *Soon*, I told myself. To him, I said, "I know these things."

"Yeah? But you didn't see…"

"… Blah blah blah," I finished for him. The Wanda Honeycutt jokes were getting old. I wasn't the only one fooled by her sweet church lady routine and at least I could say I'd only known her for a few months. The rest of the knuckleheads knew her their entire lives and never saw her devious nature.

"Josh," I said seriously. "Call me first next time."

Josh scrunched up his nose and frowned. "Damn, I hope there isn't a next time," he replied.

"Me too, but if there is…"

"… You'll be the first to know," he said obligingly. Josh lowered his voice and whispered, "We're starting to finish each other's sentences. Next thing you know, you'll be wearing…"

"I'm not wearing skinny jeans," I said cutting him off. I lightly bit his bottom lip then stepped back so he could get out of the tub and get warmed up. I couldn't help but notice Josh's nips were hard enough to cut glass. I noticed his hot, naked body even though he had milked every last drop of spunk from my balls in the shower. I figured only death would keep my eyes from feasting on his beauty, but I doubted even that would stop me.

Josh pulled out one of my suits and ties from the depths of his giant closet once we returned to his bedroom. I watched as he opened his underwear and sock drawer and removed a pair of my boxers and dress socks that were mixed in with his stuff. My heart would've smiled if it could over the sweet, domestic moment.

"I ironed this shirt after I laundered it, but it could probably use another pass," Josh said, inspecting the pale blue shirt he held up in front of him.

"It's fine the way it is." I hooked my finger in the knotted towel at his waist. "Thank you." I kept the kiss chaste because I knew Adrian would be on his way and I didn't want to keep him waiting. The only thing I paused to do was watch Josh pull on a pair of neon green bikini briefs. Again, there was no way I wouldn't notice the way the fabric clung to the taut globes of his ass.

"Keep looking at me like that and you're going to be late."

I snapped my head up and caught Josh watching me in the mirror. "As if you don't know how fond I am of your ass." I resumed getting dressed before I pulled him to me for one last kiss.

"Be easy on the gas pedal if you drive my car. It's rear wheel drive so the power comes from the ass end. If you stomp the gas pedal you'll spin the tires; it's especially bad on wet or slick roads," I told Josh.

"I won't hurt your precious car." He rolled his eyes. I was surprised he didn't make a crack about the power coming from his ass end too.

"I wasn't worried about the car getting hurt." He could pretend that we didn't have a similar conversation the night before all he wanted, but I could tell by the soft look in his hazel eyes that he remembered just fine. "See you tonight." It wasn't a question; it was a promise. He wasn't the only one who had a hard time sleeping alone after spending so many nights together.

"Big Daddy! Big Daddy!" Savage never failed to bring a smile to my face.

"Dirty Bird," I teased as I walked by.

"Dirty Bird," he repeated.

I waited downstairs, and away from the temptation of Josh, for Adrian to pick me up. When he arrived, his smile was so big that I needed sunglasses to shield my eyes from the sun glaring off his white teeth. "Shut up," I warned as I got into his car.

"I didn't say a damn thing," he replied. "But if I was going to say something, it would be that you look remarkably chipper for a man whose boyfriend called the police instead of him."

"Good thing you're not saying anything," I said wryly.

"Crazy week for you, partner. First your former fuck buddy gets killed in our county, then the drug bust, and now your boyfriend is getting harassed. What's the likelihood that it's all coincidental?"

"Well, I think two of the three are related," I told Adrian, but then I stopped to think it over. "Do you think Turner's appearance in our county had something to do with the drugs?"

"I think it's something we really need to consider," he replied.

Captain Reardon was waiting for us when we arrived at the station. "Gabe, I need to see you in my office."

I exchanged a brief look with Adrian before I followed the captain to his office. "Yes, sir?" I asked once I was sitting across from him.

"Are you aware that all incoming and outgoing email is monitored?"

"Yes, sir," I replied, but I wasn't sure where he was going with his question. I knew that I hadn't broken any police department policies regarding email conduct-well, not that I was aware of anyway.

"What you might not know is that during the monitoring process emails containing certain words or phrases are flagged and directed to our IT department for further scrutiny," Captain Reardon said. I raised my brows, still unsure of what was going on. "Apparently, an incoming email to you was flagged and forwarded for review." He picked up a piece of paper and slid it to me. "Congratulations on having the first flagged email since the process was implemented a decade ago, Detective Wyatt."

"Um, thank you," I replied hesitantly. I looked down at the printed email and couldn't believe what I read.

Gabe,

I know you didn't want to get involved in my situation, but I wasn't sure who I could trust anymore. I did take your advice and contacted the Cincinnati Police Department about the threats against me and things went from bad to worse.

Please call me. 555.0045

Nate

I looked at the date on the email and saw that it was dated a few days before he was killed. He *was* coming to look for me. "Fuck," I said in disbelief. "Why are we just now getting it? What phrase in that email slowed things down rather than sped them up?"

"As I said before, this was the first time an email showed up in the review inbox and it was overlooked. There's been illnesses and… you know, it doesn't matter. I'm not making any excuses because it's entirely possible that Mr. Turner's death could've been prevented. Internal Affairs will be launching an investigation into the situation, which will include you since you were the intended recipient."

"I understand, sir. I have nothing to hide," I told him.

"I believe you, Gabe. Regardless, you will have union representation during any interview," he firmly said. Then he did something so uncharacteristic of him. He broke eye contact and fidgeted with the buttons on his sleeves while mumbling something beneath his breath that sounded a lot like, "pompous old goat," but I couldn't be sure.

"Sir?"

Captain cleared his throat. "Internal Affairs will also be keeping a close eye on the detectives with the sheriff's department too since they're investigating Nate's homicide." Ahhh, the "pompous old goat" comment was directed at his father-in-law.

"Fair enough," I replied. I tried to modulate my voice so the dread I felt over potentially dealing with Billy Sampson again didn't show. "I assume they'll be looking in to CPD as well." It wasn't that Nate said the police department was corrupt, but the vague comment could be construed that way, so an investigation was the only thing to do.

"Oh, you can bet on it." Captain retrieved Nate's email and slid it back into the file. "I'm waiting for a call from your union rep,

Jillian Rosewood, to see when she's available for your interview. I'll let you know when everything is set up." I could tell by his brisk tone that our conversation was finished and he was ready to move on to other tasks.

"Yes, sir." I rose from my seat and exited his office.

Adrian nodded his head toward the coffee station that was set up in the rear of the room. "What's going on?" he asked when we were out of ear shot from everyone else. Adrian listened intently as I told him about the email and the pending interview with IA. "That's some serious shit." Adrian rubbed the back of his head in shock. "Someone has to be held accountable for overlooking that email."

"Agreed." There wasn't anything I could do to help Nate Turner any more, unless I somehow was called upon to investigate his homicide, but that was highly unlikely. I could, however, make sure that Josh stayed safe, and by doing so, potentially solve Nate's case.

I tried to convince myself again that morning that it was a fluke, a coincidence. I wanted to think it was Sampson's jealous tantrum, but my gut was telling me it wasn't him. My fears were confirmed when the desk sergeant stopped at my desk with an envelope for me.

"This was dropped through our mail slot and is addressed to you," O'Malley said. He set it on the corner of my desk and walked away. All I could do was stare at it while a strong sense of foreboding snaked its way up my spine and burrowed inside my brain.

"Partner, you look like you're about to get sick," Adrian said when he returned from the bathroom. "What's this?" He reached down to pick up the envelope, but I stopped him.

"Gloves," I told him. I opened the bottom drawer of my desk and pulled out two pairs of black latex gloves. My heart was in my throat when I picked up the envelope with gloved hands. My name was written crudely in blood red marker on the outside.

"I don't like this, Gabe," Adrian said.

"That makes two of us." I released a deep breath and opened the envelope. Inside were several photos of Josh. "These were taken this week."

"How do you know?" Adrian asked.

"These running tights are brand new," I replied. Josh loved the bright aqua blue stripe down the side of the gray pants and I loved the Andrew Christian jock in the same shade of blue he wore beneath them that day. "Oh, God," I said when I came to the last picture. "This was last night." It was a photo of Josh standing in his driveway with a shell-shocked expression on his face. "He flattened his tires and then purposely set off the car alarm so Josh would come out."

Confirming my worst fears that the person who stalked, threatened and killed Nate had moved onto Josh didn't make me feel better. There were times in life that a person wanted to be wrong, but Josh was in danger and the pictures proved it.

"Whoever killed Nate thinks you know more than you do," Adrian said, confirming my thoughts. Fear gripped my heart and made it nearly impossible for me to think. "We need to bring Captain up to speed."

I knew Adrian was right, but all I wanted to do was find Josh and hold him tight before I put him on a plane to a destination far from here so I would know that he was safe.

TWELVE

Josh

As much as I hated how quickly word got around a small town, it sometimes had its perks; such as my insurance agent calling me before I had a chance to call her. "I heard you had a bit of trouble last night," Holly Givens said over the phone not five minutes after Gabe left for work with Adrian.

"Just a little," I told her.

"Well, is it as bad as the rumors at the diner this morning?" she asked.

"Ohhh, how bad did they say it was?" In the grand scheme of things, four flat tires weren't that big of a deal. I was glad it seemed as if my reality was better than the rumors, which wasn't always my experience.

"Four flat tires, hate messages scratched into the paint, and a busted windshield," she responded.

"Wow! The town really thinks someone has it in for me." I paused for a minute to think it over. Did they think I deserved that kind of reaction from someone or were they just having fun with the speculation? "What did the hate messages say?"

"Funny," Holly said with a laugh, "no one seemed to know that. It was just 'downright hateful.'" I could tell she was quoting exactly what she'd overheard because she changed her tone of voice to a shocked whisper. We had two murders in our town and one right outside of town in less than six months and two attempted murders–counting mine–yet, my vandalism garnered as much attention.

"Huh," I said, not sure what else to say. "Well, you'll be glad to know it's just the tires."

Holly went on to explain how coverage for replacing tires worked. Apparently, the insurance company depreciates for the wear and tear on the tires. "It's not a replacement cost policy like you have on your home and business," she told me, "so you will have more out of pocket expense than just your deductible. I just wanted to give you a heads up so that you're not surprised when your adjuster talks to you later today." I heard her fingers typing busily in the background. "You have rental car coverage if Earl can't get you in at the Tire Store today. Just give me a call and let me know if you need it."

"I sure will, Holly. Thank you for your help." She'd been the agent for my family almost all my life having taken over the agency when her father retired. I never even thought about shopping around for insurance because the service I got from her was impeccable.

It turned out that Earl was booked up for the entire week so I called Holly back and arranged for a rental car to be delivered later that day. Holly told me that my adjuster would be out to look at the damage and measure the amount of tread that was left on each tire. "He'll cut you a check on the spot."

I hung up from her and decided to check my inventory. There wasn't anything else I could do about the situation and dwelling on the fact that someone might want to hurt me *again* wasn't productive or healthy. I fell into my old habits of seeking comfort from routine.

That lasted for all about fifteen minutes before Chaz and Meredith came rushing into the salon.

"Baby, are you okay?" Meredith asked.

"Oh my God, dude! What the hell is going on?" Chaz asked. "Who'd you piss off?"

"I bet it was that fucking Sampson," Meredith said.

"Fucking loser," Chaz added.

I wasn't sure what I could tell them, so I went with the safest response. "We're not sure who's responsible."

Meredith snorted. "I pity the dumbass when Gabe gets ahold of him."

"It could be a female, Meredith," I admonished. "Remember Mrs. Honeycutt."

"Yeah, don't be sexist, Meredith," Chaz piped in. "Women can be and do anything, which doesn't exclude being a psychopathic killer."

Meredith wasn't amused by either one of us, but chose to ignore us rather than give us a lecture. "Is Gabe still sleeping or something?"

"No, he went to work," I replied before resuming my count of shampoos and conditioners in stock. I had software that automatically deducted the merchandise from stock when a purchase was made, but I double-checked each and every Monday. Perhaps one day I'd just rely on the figures the program gave me, but I doubted it.

"His car is here," Chaz said, stating the obvious.

"Seven, eight, nine…" I began counting bottles out loud so they'd take the hint.

"Holy shit!" Meredith's loud exclamation caught me off guard and I lost track of how many anti-frizz shampoos I had. "He left his car for *you* to drive," Meredith added. I didn't like her emphasis, as if I was a bad driver or some shit.

"No way!" Chaz at least had the decency to downplay his reaction when he said, "Not that you're a bad driver…" I was sure he and Meredith were exchanging looks behind my back during his pause, "maybe just a tad fast."

"There's a lot of horsepower beneath that hood," Meredith told me. "Are you sure you can handle it?"

I rose from where I was bent over then turned to face her with a smirk on my face. "I'm absolutely certain I can handle a hard, fast ride."

Meredith rolled her eyes. "Well, I guess you can test it out when you drive over to visit my mama today."

I had promised to visit with Willa and I would keep my word. I also decided I'd take Gabe's car to the store and buy some apples. I was going to bake him a pie that was so good he'd probably come in his pants. Of course, I kept that part to myself.

I updated Chaz and Meredith about what Holly said about the coverage and rental car. Once they were sure I was okay, they left me to finish my inventory so I could move on to the rest of my day. I decided to review the schedule for the upcoming week later because I wanted to get my errands over and get back in time for the adjuster to arrive, and later, my rental car.

I confess that I was a little bit apprehensive about driving Gabe's muscle car, but that vanished the moment I hit the button twice to remote start his growly beast. Princess was equipped with heated seats, but not a heated steering wheel or remote start. I looked down at my wardrobe and realized that driving Gabe's car would require an outfit change. The t-shirt and jeans I had put on that morning wasn't bad ass enough to wear when driving… Wait a minute. Gabe never told me what he named his new Charger, just his classic. No way a guy who loved cars as much as him drove an unnamed car. I made a note to ask him about it.

I put on a pair of dark denim jeans, a light gray V-neck cashmere sweater, and swapped my wool coat for my leather jacket. I added a handsome scarf and my aviators for a nice finish before I ventured outside. I quieted the voice in my head that wanted to remind me about the potential danger I was in and tried not to look at my beautiful, damaged Princess. Then I noticed that Gabe's Charger wasn't running and I worried that I had broken it somehow. *Or someone had tampered with it.* I waved off that notion and called Gabe.

"Is everything okay?" Gabe asked instead of greeting me. He sounded even more worried than the night before and I rolled my eyes.

"I didn't hurt your car," I replied sarcastically. "Well, at least I don't think so."

"What's wrong?" His tone became less worried and more amused. Gabe laughed when I told him about starting the car then deciding to change clothes into something nice to drive her. "The remote start only lasts for ten minutes," he explained. "So, you must've taken longer than that to get dressed and get down to her. Josh?"

"Hmmm." I was distracted by the affectionate way he said my name.

"You could wear a burlap bag and look good." I heard the smile in his voice.

"Aw, you're so sweet," I replied, "but I'm not shaving days off of your pole dancing sentence." I had special plans for him that night and needed time to put them in place.

"One of these days you're going to take my compliment for how it's intended and not suspect an ulterior motive," Gabe told me. He sounded like he was making it one of his life's missions.

"Maybe," I said without commitment. "Anything I need to do special since I let the remote start run too long?" I asked, getting him back on subject.

"Nope. Just press and hold your foot down on the brake then hit the start button," Gabe said. "Josh, be safe. I don't want anything to happen to *you*."

"I'll be careful." I knew he was talking about more than my driving. Even if Gabe was overreacting, it always paid to be careful.

I chose to buy my apples before heading to Willa's because I knew she'd need plenty of time to fuss. While I was at the store, I looked into some bath oils and scented candles. Blissville was at least a good thirty minutes away from a decent mall, but we had some local ladies who made bath salts and oils, candles, and soaps. I loved to support my small community and buy local when I could. A thought came to me just then and I made a mental note to call Marabeth Adams to see if perhaps she wanted to sell her items in my salon. Better yet, maybe we could develop an exclusive fragrance for my clients.

The thought had me practically dancing through the aisles until I came face to face with a person I had never wanted to see again, let alone twice within a few days. What the hell was he doing at the grocery store in the middle of the fucking day wearing that smug grin? Billy Sampson was about to find out just how much I had changed from the naïve boy he once knew.

"Are you the rotten bastard who slashed my tires?" I demanded hotly.

Billy threw his head back and laughed loudly. "As if I care enough about you to put forth the effort," he said once he was done mocking me.

"You know; I find it odd that you happen to turn up everywhere I go lately." I was not convinced by his performance.

"I don't know what you're talking about," Billy replied.

"You let yourself into my home uninvited and got belligerent when I asked you to leave. You just so happen to turn up at the same storage facility that Gabe uses, and now here you are in the grocery store the same time as me." I shook my head sadly, as if he was the most pitiful creature on earth. "Lord help you if you were the one who slashed my tires."

Billy wore a cold sneer on his face by the time I was finished. I knew he was prepared to blast me with something cruel, but I was equally prepared to deflect it so that it didn't penetrate my soul. That loser wasn't penetrating anything on me ever again.

He looked around and lowered his voice so that no one would hear what he said to me. "You think pretty highly of that tight little ass, don't you? I have to say that I've had much better than yours and by guys who appreciated my attention more than you ever did. I have zero interest in resuming anything with your whiny ass. Our house here is quite a bit smaller than the one in Texas so we have a lot of items in storage until we can find a bigger place. My wife needed something from our unit and that's why I was there yesterday. I'm here now to pick up diapers for my baby. It's pure coincidence that we're here at the same time. As for last night, I was on duty because I work nights. It was the only shift available in the department when we moved back." He stepped closer and his voice took on a menacing tone when he said, "I came to your house on Saturday because I wanted to tell you to keep your mouth shut about what happened between us in high school. If you so much as breathe a word…"

"You'll what? Flatten my tires like a punk teenager?" I rolled my eyes and added, "As if I would want anyone to know I had your pencil dick in my ass. People think I have standards in this town and I don't want to disappoint them."

Billy's face turned as red as a fire engine and I worried that I'd gone too far. "Look at you all smug about your happy little relationship. How long do you think a guy like him is going to want you, Josh?"

They're just words, not truth. "I'd put my relationship with Gabe against yours with your wife. At least Gabe and I are completely honest with each other. Can you say that?"

"You little shit, I should…" he paused then smiled over my shoulder. "Hi, Mrs. Burkett. How are you today?"

I looked over my shoulder and saw my favorite neighbor pushing her cart in our direction. "Hello, Billy," she said happily. "I'm doing wonderful. How are you doing?"

Billy moved off to talk to her and I continued on my way. I just needed vanilla ice cream to complete Gabe's dessert for the evening. I chose the gourmet vanilla bean because nothing was too good for him.

I sighed a breath of relief when I saw Billy leave the store when I approached the self-scan checkout. Everything he said to me could've been the truth, but I didn't believe him. The fact that he'd been living in Carter County for six months without approaching me gave validity to what he said, but it didn't help his case when I saw that he didn't have anything in his hands when he left the store. Maybe they were out of diapers or perhaps he could get them cheaper elsewhere, but I somehow doubted that either of those reasons were true. My gut told me he was there to intimidate me, although I wasn't sure why.

I shook off all thoughts about him as I scanned and paid for my groceries because none of them were pleasant or productive for a happy life. I refused to let his scorn and hatefulness ruin my good mood or cast doubt on my relationship with Gabe. He knew next to nothing about me and absolutely nothing about Gabe. I didn't have a motherfucking crystal ball to know that everything would work out perfectly between me and Gabe; I was fine with that. The beauty was in the journey as we grew as individuals and as a couple; I wouldn't trade that for all the certainty in the world.

It wasn't until I arrived back home after my visit with Willa, who let me store my ice cream in her freezer while we visited, dealt with the adjuster, and signed paperwork for my rental car that a huge realization dawned on me. I had spoken the word "relationship" out loud and the world didn't come to an end. It was just unfortunate that I used it when speaking about Gabe to Billy Sampson and not said directly to Gabe. I couldn't take back what I said to Billy, nor did I regret it, but I did wish I had used the word while talking to Gabe first. I decided I would pull up my big boy jock strap and make Gabe aware that I had upgraded our status from a *something* to a relationship.

THIRTEEN

Gabe

CAPTAIN REARDON HAD LEARNED THAT THE IA INTERVIEWS wouldn't be happening until the next day, but that didn't stop him from seeking out some information for himself. He was shocked and very worried about Josh when he found out about the tire slashing and subsequent photos being dropped off at the station. None of us were surprised when the envelope didn't turn up any fingerprints other than O'Malley's and the photos were free from any prints. The only differences between Josh and Nate's initial photos were in the method of delivery, lack of message in Josh's situation, and Nate only received one picture of him checking out his tires on the first contact where Josh, through me, received several. I wasn't sure what that meant beyond the person responsible had to be found and fast.

"The threat has come to us so we can't just sit back and wait for IA to do their thing," Captain Reardon had said, echoing my thoughts. "I'm going to reach out to someone I know and trust in the CPD and hopefully get some answers for us. I want to know about the detectives that were assigned to Nate's case and I want to know what he told them. I'd rather not try to protect Josh blind."

By the end of the work day, I hadn't learned anything new. I wasn't operating on the theory that no news was good news. I needed cold hard facts so I could make sure that not a single precious platinum blond hair on Josh's head was harmed. The stress of the situation wore me down quicker than any physical excursion I had ever experienced.

I stopped at my house long enough to grab a few more suits and Buddy's things. I wasn't asking Josh for permission, nor was I waiting to be invited. He wanted me there, I wanted to be there, and I hoped he would cooperate when he heard about the photos. I didn't want to ride roughshod over him anywhere except the bedroom. I wanted him to drop the change of address slip at the post office on his own, not feel pressured to do so by circumstance.

I unhooked Buddy's leash and let him run up the stairs while I followed behind at a more leisurely pace while trying not to get angry at finding the back door unlocked again. The truth was, I was nervous about seeing Josh. I was worried that I would do something or react in a way that would scare him on multiple levels for a few reasons. I didn't want him terrorized over the photos or my feelings for him.

"You're such a good boy," I heard Josh say to Buddy followed by, "you're such a slut for a belly rub."

I'm not sure what prompted my next move; perhaps it was to

lighten my own mood or make Josh smile. I ran the rest of the way up the steps, tossed my stuff on the couch, and threw myself down next to Buddy on the floor to present my belly to Josh too. Buddy looked completely confused, but Josh threw his head back and howled with laughter over my theatrics. Then he dropped down to his knees and began rubbing my belly. As if someone flipped a switch, my thoughts went from lightening the mood to sexy time as soon as I felt the heat of Josh's hand through my dress shirt.

"You're such a good boy," Josh said to me as he straddled my hips and pressed his ass against my crotch. The voice he used wasn't high pitched like he used on Buddy; it was low and sexy. He rocked against me and said, "You're kind of slutty for an entirely different kind of rub." Josh lowered his upper body over me until his lips were just a hairsbreadth away from mine. "I like it."

I grabbed his hips and rocked his ass against my growing erection until my engine was at full throttle and ready to ride. "I could get used to this kind of greeting," I told him honestly as I pulled his sweater over his head.

"I could get used to giving it," Josh said as he made quick work with my tie.

We only separated long enough to get undressed and for Josh to retrieve a condom and lube from his bedroom. His modern glass coffee table didn't have any nifty little drawers in it like my old one did. I learned to keep those hidey holes stocked for when Josh came over because he liked being my halftime show. I lost track of how many third quarters I missed on football games because I honestly couldn't have cared less.

Josh suited me up and lubed my cock before he reached around and stretched his own ass for me and fuck if that wasn't a sexy sight to behold. Just when I worried he was enjoying it too much and didn't need me, he removed his fingers and lined the broad head of my dick to his hole. He sank down on my rod until his ass rested on my pelvis.

I dug my fingers in his hips in my attempt to get him to move, but I could tell he was in the mood to draw out my pleasure. It was a wonderful problem to have and I lay there and watched the beautiful, graceful way his hips moved as he rocked back and forth slowly. His movements were fluid and effortless; I knew that I'd lose my mind once I finally saw him on his pole.

No matter how many times I was inside him, it still felt new and amazing to me. I mentally promised to make sure I paid him back with sexy surprises of my own rather than let him be the one to always surprise me. I let Josh have his fun teasing me until I couldn't take it anymore then I rolled him onto his back and fucked him hard enough to scoot us both across the floor. I could feel the burn of the hardwood rubbing raw spots on my knees but didn't care about anything but making him come so I could empty myself inside him.

I made sure to peg his prostate in a way that guaranteed he'd happily blast his spunk all over his stomach and give up his little challenge to see who came first. There would be nights when he won, but that wasn't one of them. My restraint wasn't much to brag about because I unloaded inside the condom as soon as his greedy ass clamped down on my cock during his orgasm.

I carefully pulled out of his ass and rolled over onto my back so I didn't squish him on the hard floors with my weight. The floor was a lot less forgiving than a bed, as my knees could attest. I doubted the tender skin on his ass fared any better. I was just about to say something about the unlocked door when I became aware of a delicious smell wafting in from the kitchen. It short-circuited my brain and I could only think about one thing.

"I smell baking apples," I said.

"Uh huh," he replied.

I looked over and smiled at the blissed-out expression on his face. "Are you baking a pie?"

"Uh huh."

"It's my favorite," I told him.

"Uh huh."

I reached over and lightly pinched his nipple to snap him out of his orgasmic coma. He opened his eyes and turned his head to look at me. "I never told you that apple pie was my favorite dessert."

"Not with words," Josh replied softly. He chuckled at the confused look on my face. "The first time I ever laid eyes on you was at Edson and Emma's diner. I had stopped in to pick up my carryout order and you and Kyle were there eating. You bit into a piece of apple pie and this orgasmic look spread across your face." He got quiet for a second and I thought he was finished with his story, but then he spoke again. "I had never been as envious as I was of that stupid piece of pie. I figured I would live my entire life and never incite that kind of passion from another person." Josh reached over and laid his hand over my heart. "I was wrong."

I captured his hand and brought it to my lips for a kiss. "You were." I don't know what my pie-eating face looked like, but I was certain it paled in comparison to the one I made when I was with him–whether it involved sex or not. There was never going to be a piece of pie I enjoyed more than him.

"Oh my God. I think I just came in my pants," I said after I had my first bite of pie an hour later. "I might be a fool for telling you this because your arrogance when it comes to cooking is already off the charts, but this… It's the best thing I've ever had." I poked the crust with my fork and saw it flake up. "The crust is perfection and the pie has the right amount of sweetness without being too much. This ice cream is just ridiculous."

"Arrogance?" Josh asked. "It's not arrogance when it's the truth, babe."

I wasn't about to get into a debate with him and risk my ice cream melting and making my pie soggy. I hated soggy pie crust. I'd take his word for it and save any argument I might have for a day that I didn't have pie in front of me, or after I got to see his studio.

"That's what I thought," he said when no argument was forthcoming from me.

I listened to Josh tell me about the conversation with his insurance agent, Chaz and Meredith, Mama Richmond, and someone named Marabeth who makes soaps, oils, and bath stuff. As talkative as he was, I could tell there was something he wasn't telling me.

"Spill it," I told him.

"I ran into Deputy Small Dick at the grocery store." He bit his lip and I couldn't tell if he was worried that I would be upset that he ran into him or what was said. Turned out it was both.

"He's a dumb bastard who doesn't know a damn thing about us," I told Josh.

"I know."

"Then why are you upset?" I asked. Then I realized he had used the R word when he rebutted what Deputy Small Dick said. "You said the R word."

"To him and not you," Josh said quietly.

My heart about melted when I realized what had him upset. It wasn't that he saw Billy or the things he said, it was that Billy was the first to hear that Josh and I had a relationship and not just a *something*. "Josh, I've known for quite some time that what we have is way more than just *something*, it's *the thing*." I tugged his hand and pulled him closer. "Although it's nice to hear that you know it too."

This kiss we shared was long and sweet. I was sure it was going to lead to something even longer and sweeter, but his cellphone rang and interrupted us. Josh looked down at his phone and groaned. "Someone must've called her."

"Who?" I asked.

"My mother." He let out a long sigh and said, "You might as well get settled in for football. This won't be a brief conversation."

He wasn't kidding either. It took him until halftime to calm his mother down, but I couldn't blame her. Listening to him reassure his mom made me feel guilty because I hadn't told him about the photos yet and because I let me dick's demands sidetrack me from the conversation we needed to have about leaving his door unlocked.

"What's with the scowl?" Josh asked when he got off the phone with his mom.

I reached up and snagged his hand as he approached the couch and tugged him down to sit in my lap. "There's been a recent development that I probably should've told you about the minute I came home."

"But I went and distracted you with my hot body, my amazing dinner, and then pie," he said, running his hand through my hair.

I hoped he was as forgiving when I told him what happened. "An envelope was dropped through our mail slot for me at the police station today. Inside were pictures of you that were taken this past week and early this morning when you discovered your tires had been slashed."

Josh's skin paled and he blinked rapidly. "Like Nate," he said.

"Yes and no," I replied, then told him about the differences.

"So, it could be a copycat," Josh said, narrowing his eyes.

It wasn't a working theory in my mind, but I would've been foolish not to consider everything. "It could be, but who here knows about Nate and his connection to me?" I asked.

"Billy knows," Josh said.

"True." I couldn't dispute what he said.

"I didn't believe him when he said he just happened to be at the same places as me these past few days, nor do I believe his excuse for wanting to talk to me. Plus, he left the store without buying the diapers he said he was there to pick up."

I wished it could be as simple as Billy being a complete dickhead and taking advantage of circumstance to cause trouble for us, but I suspected it was a lot more complicated than what Josh said. Instead of voicing my fears, I said, "Maybe."

I kept going back to the email that Nate sent me, specifically the possible implication that the CPD could be involved. There was nothing worse in my book than a dirty cop. I wished that I could believe that they didn't exist, but I had seen the truth with my own eyes in Miami.

"Miami Vice," Josh said, snapping his fingers to get my attention. My scowl hardly fazed him. "I need to know something very important from you and I need you to be completely honest with me."

"Okay."

"How'd I look in the pictures?"

"Josh," I replied with extreme exasperation.

"I'm serious, babe. Those pictures are going to end up in the hands of a jury of my peers and I need to be prepared to defend myself if necessary."

I thought I was fluent in Josh speak, but he stumped me. *Jury? Defend himself?* "What?"

"The jury will consist of people in my community and they'll all be judging me and my abilities as a stylist if I look unfortunate in the pictures they show in the courtroom." He talked very slow, like he was talking to someone with an addled brain. "So, tell me. Was my hair a mess? Did my skin look blotchy?"

I thought back to the photos I held in my hands earlier that morning. They represented my worst nightmare, which was the thought of losing him to the same person who killed Nate Turner. To him, they were equally as devastating, but for a completely different reason. He was serious as a heart attack about what he said. I didn't have the heart to tell him that the picture from last night, while not flattering to him, was completely adorable to me. His hair was standing up all over the place as if he'd ran his fingers all through it and his pink cheeks made it obvious he'd just been woken from sleep. None of those things would make him a bit happy, so I did what I had to do. "You looked amazing." I hoped the pictures never made it into his hands because he'd surely call me a liar, but it was my truth.

"Now, let's talk about how I found your back door unlocked again."

Josh grimaced then said, "I'm sorry. I'll do better."

"Promise me, Josh, because I can't stand the thought of someone hurting you."

"I promise."

"That's good because there are better ways to spend our time than arguing," I told him.

"Yeah?"

I playfully pushed him off my lap and onto the couch cushion beside me before I jumped to my feet. "Yes, like eat more apple pie!"

"I don't know where you put it?" Josh remarked.

"Yes, you do," I said, waggling my brows obnoxiously.

"Ew, Gabe. No." Josh shook his head sadly. "We can snark all we want but we don't do cheesy."

"Mmmm, cheddar cheese is great on pie."

"You're hopeless," Josh said.

I was hopelessly in love with him and the beautiful smile that he gave only to me.

FOURTEEN

Josh

"That's your rental car?" Chaz asked the next morning when he arrived to work.

"More like rental tank," Meredith amended. "I bet Gabe approves of you being surrounded by all of that metal. Does it have airbags to cover every part of your body?"

We were all staring at the gleaming red monstrosity in my driveway through the window in the kitchenette. I had been shocked the day before when the rental car agency pulled up. I saw the Big

Red pull in followed by a sleek sedan. I perked up thinking I'd look mighty fine driving that sleek number so you can imagine my shock when they handed me the keys to the giant SUV that looked big enough to transport Blissville High's soccer team. They informed me it was the only rental left when they presented the rental agreement to me.

"Why can't I drive that?" I asked, pointing to the sedan.

"That's my personal car, sir," Car Guy 1 said. "I followed behind Jerry so I could give him a ride back to the office." I referred to Jerry as Car Guy 2.

"Hmmm," I said looking down at the daily rate for rental. "You're going to make sure you don't charge my insurance company for the higher rental price or try to get me to pay the difference between a car and SUV rate though, right? It's not our fault you had insufficient inventory to meet our needs."

"We wouldn't dream of doing so, sir," Car Guy 2 responded, but I noted he sounded more surprised I would know the difference than insulted I would suspect something like that.

I was used to people thinking I was a "dumb blond" and it didn't help them take me seriously when they found out that I worked at a salon. I more than worked there, I owned it. You can't be a successful business owner and be gullible at the same time. "Then let's mark out these rates and write in the correct ones, fellas." I slashed through the figures like I meant serious business, and I did.

"Of course," Car Guy 1 said, but he was looking a bit nervous.

I knew damn well that big giant monster wasn't the only vehicle left to rent off their lot and I had half a mind to drive over there after we were done and prove it. Still, I had better things to do, like bake Gabe's pie, and it turned out to be one of my favorite memories in our young *relationship*. So, I let them off the hook with a simple rate change and their initials on the form. Well, I did give a copy of the revised rates to my adjuster so he would know how much to pay them when they sent the bill. My days of playing the fool were over!

"I didn't read the owner's manual," I told Meredith. "I'm hoping like hell not to drive that big bastard."

"You and everyone else who lives in this town," Chaz muttered.

"Again with the damn driving remarks." I threw my hands up in the air and walked away. "It was one parked car," I said referencing the only accident I had, "and there was an inch of ice on the streets."

"Which is why you shouldn't have been out," Meredith said.

I was saved by my first client of the day who just happened to be Gabe's ex. "Good morning," I said cheerily to Kyle. I got immense pleasure by overhearing Chaz choking on his own fucking saliva when Doctor Feel Me Good walked in the door.

"Well, it is for some," Kyle replied with a smirk. He walked over to my chair and had a seat. "Not all of us started off our morning the way you probably did."

I know it wasn't deliberately said to remind me that not that long ago he was the one waking up beside Gabe and getting morning… I killed the thought before it went there. Regardless, that's exactly where my brain went.

"I didn't mean that the way you're taking it." Kyle sounded extremely contrite and uncomfortable, which I felt was only fair since I was also ill at ease right then.

I met his eyes in the mirror and I saw how sorry he really was by the grimace he wore on his face and the way he bit his lip. It was actually a great look on him; it made him appear more human. Kyle was the type who always came across as confident, as if nothing or no one bothered him. Having known Gabe, I could see where that would irritate him. Gabe wanted real and honest responses from me at all times, whether it be anger and annoyance or joy and happiness. Kyle was a person who was sometimes hard to read. His smiles and responses came across as generic, or at least in public they did. I had no way of knowing what he was like privately.

"I know you didn't," I replied honestly. Kyle had told me on more than one occasion that I was good for Gabe. I wasn't sure what he'd said to Gabe about me and I honestly didn't care. What mattered was what Gabe thought about me and he really, really liked me. A lot. I could've teased Kyle about how silly that would've been since I was about to hold his hair in my hands, but I let it go. Instead, I wrapped the cape around his shoulders and asked, "Just a trim today?"

"Yep." Kyle entertained me with stories from veterinary school like he always did since he started coming to my salon when he moved back with Gabe. He'd never talk about his clients in Blissville because that would've been unprofessional and unethical and he was an upstanding guy–one Chaz would give his left testicle to be pinned beneath on the closest firm surface. I tried my best not to let my overactive mind wander there. That didn't stop me from smirking when Kyle greeted Chaz when he walked by on his way to his post at the front door. "How's Harry doing?" Kyle was referring to the hairless cat that Chaz owned.

Chaz's eye bugged out of his head and he choked on his own saliva again, as if Kyle was talking about his cock and not his cat. "Um, he's doing good," Chaz finally squeaked out.

"You feeling okay?" Kyle asked, completely unaware of the effect he had on my best friend. I had never seen two more clueless people than them. If Chaz had been paying any bit of attention, he would've noticed how Kyle sat a little straighter in his chair–as if he needed any more height–and how his eyes brightened.

"You need to sit still," I admonished Kyle with a light whack of my comb on his beefy shoulder. "You'll end up with a crooked cut or much shorter hair than you'd prefer. People will either think I've lost my touch or that you started going back to Burt's Butcher, um… *Barber* Shop."

"Neither of those things will do," Kyle replied good-naturedly. "Speaking of Burt's, when do you suppose Gabe will trust you to cut his hair?"

"That's a good question," I replied. "He's due for one." I decided

I would suggest a trim that night and see where it got me. The worst he could say was no and it would only hurt my feelings, but no big deal. I could take it. Maybe.

I was glad my day started with an easy client like Kyle because it allowed me to ease into my day rather than be thrust into chaos right out of the chute. It turned out that Kyle was definitely the calm before the storm.

Hair emergency–a catastrophic event at levels so high they could permanently scar a person for life if not immediately remedied. The occurrences could be self-induced or the result of a freak accident. Also referred to as "you ain't getting lunch today" among hair professionals.

There were weeks I went without a single hair emergency walking into my salon and then there were days when several of them came rushing inside almost at once. I promised myself I would write a book after I retired because I was certain it would be a best seller and land me on Ellen's show. Chaz pointed out that Ellen would be retired long before me when I mentioned my book idea to him. I told him to shut the fuck up because I couldn't imagine a world without Ellen smiling, dancing, and doing amazing things every weekday.

That day, I had three hair emergencies run through my doors with their eyes bugging out of their heads and a forlorn expression on their faces. They looked at me with so much hope in their eyes, as if I was the Jesus of hair disaster fixes, that I couldn't turn them away. It would mean working through lunch, but I didn't have the heart to say no.

I was used to seeing kids cut their own hair and Mom or Dad rushing them in to see me, but the opposite happened to my first client–well, except the kid didn't drive them to my salon. She looked to be around four years old and much too short to see over the steering wheel.

Wow, little Tabitha did a number on her mommy's hair too.

There was no fucking way we were avoiding short-as-fuck bangs. "I can't believe I fell asleep," Victoria said. Tears flowed down her face and little Tabitha, unaware of how much trauma she caused, sat in her mommy's lap and lovingly caressed her mother's face.

I worked Victoria in between routine maintenance appointments. By the time I was finished, those tears of horror were tears of happiness. "I look like that one actress in that one movie." I had no fucking idea what she was talking about, but she totally rocked those motherfucking bangs.

"Um, might I make a tiny suggestion?" I asked. I hated to ruin the good mood she was in, but with the shorter bangs it was obvious as hell the woman had zero maintenance program for her brows. They looked like two sasquatches stretched across her forehead that were nearly holding hands above her nose to form one long brow.

"Okay," she replied timidly when I suggested a brow wax. "Will it hurt?"

"Stings a little, but it's totally worth it," I replied.

She loved her new brows so much, Tabitha got a mani/pedi in the little kids' chair, I got a huge tip, and Victoria bought several new products for her hair and skin. "Let's go get a brownie and hot chocolate from The Brew," I heard Victoria tell Tabitha as they left. I knew next to nothing about raising kids, but I thought it was completely possible that Victoria was giving Tabitha the wrong impression about actions and consequences.

Next through my door was a complete surprise. Nadine Beaumont, wife to the sleazy town mayor, entered my salon looking like a Hollywood A-lister trying to go incognito while drawing attention to themselves at the same time. I could see the floral print of the scarf she wore around her head beneath the hood of her red wool peacoat and her oversized sunglasses, on a cloudy day, was a nice finishing touch.

I'd banned Nadine from my salon when she broke the heart of my dear friend who happened to be her former boss and wife of the man she screwed behind her back. They had a soap opera style throw down in my salon that caused damage to my property and face. Nadine had tried to apologize to me since then and she looked truly sincere when she said that she wished she could take it all back and make things right with Georgia. Unfortunately for her, she came to that realization *after* Georgia was murdered by her housekeeper.

I realized two things since I refused my services to her. Nadine's marriage to that son of a bitch was a bigger punishment than anything I, or anyone else, could dole out to her and sometimes people truly were sorry about their misdeeds and perhaps deserved second chances. I might've been willing to extend the olive branch to Nadine but it would be a cold day in hell before I did the same thing for her loser husband. I had thought about calling Nadine and trying to make amends with her, but I wasn't really sure how to approach the subject without looking desperate for business, which I definitely was not.

"Josh," she said breathlessly. "Please take me back." Again with her daytime soap opera theatrics. "I just can't go on like this."

She had the eye of everyone in the room. Her attempt to hide the disastrous effects of whatever was beneath the scarf told me she was tired of being the talk of the town. I led her into the kitchenette and closed the door so we could have some privacy.

"What have you done, Nadine?"

She burst into tears and I'm not talking about a few tears here. I mean full on body shaking sobs. "There's so many things," she managed to say in between sobs.

"Honey, I meant your hair. I'm just the *Hair* Jesus, not the *real* Jesus."

"I know," she said pitifully. Then she lowered her hood and slowly unwound the long scarf from her head.

"Holy fuck!" I knew my exclamation was loud enough to be heard in the next county just as certain as I knew it didn't help to dispel the curiosity of the clients in my salon. "Who did this to you, Nadine? There has to be laws against this type of treatment to your formerly beautiful hair."

"It… was… the… new… salon…" She got her words out in between sobbing hiccups.

"What new salon?" Just how busy had I been with Gabe's dick up my ass that I didn't know a competitor had moved into *my* territory.

"Bargain Beauty Salon," she whimpered. "I didn't know what else to do since you kicked me out."

Now look, I was all sympathetic about her hair up until that point. *She* was the one who said such horrible things to Georgia in *my* salon. For all I knew, *she* was the one who gave me a shiner. My mind reeled with what to do. I could send her on her un-merry way, and force her to deal with the disaster she presented me on her own, or I could be kind and help her out. If I decided to be kind, I then had to choose whether to take her out into the middle of the salon so she could be an example to anyone who thought about leaving me for a "bargain," or I could be a kind human being and keep her away from prying eyes.

I really must've wanted to get on the *real* Jesus' good side because I said, "Stay here, Nadine. Let me go whip something up to try and remove that lemony-yellow-Jell-O look you've got going on there." *Hey, I at least got my digs in.*

I didn't think anyone could outdo Nadine in the hair disaster department, but I was so, so wrong. Laura Sampson won the title hands down. She stood timidly in my salon with her hair looking like it got caught in a motherfucking electric mixer, like cake mixing gone wild. There was even some kind of brown substance in her long locks.

"Girl, what the ever-loving-fuck happened to you?" I asked.

"Kids! Kids happened to me, Josh!"

"Honey, come sit down," I said, gesturing to my chair.

I know that people who knew my story would think I had something against Laura, but the truth was I didn't. Laura had always been kind to me in school and, as far as I was concerned, she was another one of Billy's victims. Laura plopped down in my chair and I gingerly stuck my hands in the tangled mess to figure out what the hell she'd gotten into because she was crying too hard to help me.

"Aha," I said when I located the huge wad of gum in her hair. The gooey brown substance was peanut butter. She had hoped the oil in the peanuts would break down the gum and help ease it out of her hair.

"I tried ice too," she said. "Nothing worked. I had to wait until my mother-in-law finished work before I could come in. Billy's been gone for a few days and…"

I filed away her statement about Billy to be dissected later. The only thing that mattered was finding a way to remove the gum and make her feel beautiful again. It didn't take me long to figure out what had to happen. "Honey, I'm afraid I'm going to need to cut your hair."

"Billy is going to be so mad at me," she said tearfully.

I hated men who thought they had the right to tell their wives how to wear their hair. Were those assholes up and styling their women's hair for them every day? It was the same story all the time. "My husband doesn't like short hair." "My husband only likes straight hair." Well, the world never had and never would operate that way.

I kept my opinion about her asshole for a husband to myself and said, "I'm sorry, honey. If I could find another way…"

"Just do it," she said. "It'll grow back and if he had been home like he should've been then maybe it wouldn't have happened. I never let the kids sleep with me when he's home. I didn't even know one of the little buggers had gum in their mouths. I'm just lucky and grateful that they didn't choke on it."

By the time I was finished, Laura loved her hair. She gave me a tight squeeze and a nice tip before she left my salon looking much happier than when she arrived. I just hoped her happiness stayed with her once Billy decided to drag his ass home from God knew where.

"It's not my problem," I told myself when I finally trudged upstairs at the end of the day. "Hey, babe," I said when my eyes landed on Detective I Can Fuck Like a Machine.

Gabe looked up at me from where he sat on the couch watching his sports talk program. "Hey, yourself." I noticed he was staring at me longer than normal, as if he was assessing me.

"What?" I asked.

"I kind of miss the streak of color you used to wear in your hair," he replied.

I narrowed my eyes at him before I stomped to my bedroom to put on more comfortable clothes.

"What did I say?" I heard him ask in confusion.

"Men," I said to Diva who was curled up on my bed.

FIFTEEN

Gabe

"What about men?" I asked Josh. He was so worked up about something he didn't even hear me follow him. I leaned in the doorway and waited for the show to start. Little did he know, I wasn't in the mood to participate in whatever little tantrum he wanted to throw.

"You're always telling people how to wear their hair and shit," he snarled over his shoulder.

"*I'm* not always telling people how to wear their hair," I told him. "I simply just made a comment that I missed the color streak in the front of your hair. You're the guy telling people how to wear their hair."

"I make suggestions, but I always leave it up to them." He narrowed his eyes when he realized what he said wasn't much different than what I said. "I see what you did there."

"What's really got you upset, babe?" I went to him and tugged him into my arms, earning a glare from Diva who was enjoying the loving she was getting from her human. I listened to him talk about his crazy day and how it ended with Laura Sampson's visit.

"Where's he been?" I asked when he got to the part where she said Billy had been gone for a few days. We knew damn well that he'd been in town because both of us saw him multiple times the previous days.

"I didn't ask because it's not my business." Josh stepped away and began to take off his clothes. "These damn hair disasters make a man hangry."

As hard as it was for me to do when his clothes started coming off, I took a step back. "I'll make dinner. How's spaghetti and garlic bread sound?"

He pursed his lips and tipped his head. "I have stuff to make spaghetti and garlic bread?"

"You do now because I stopped on the way home. It sounded really good to me, but if you'd rather…"

Josh held his hand up to stop me. "No. Spaghetti sounds great. Just let me finish getting my pjs on and I'll help you."

"I can handle spaghetti," I tossed over my shoulder on my way to the kitchen.

I felt his presence in the kitchen before I heard him because my guy was like a ninja. Josh poured himself a glass of wine and leaned against the counter instead of going into the living room to watch TV. "Okay, you heard all about my day so let's hear about yours. How'd it go with IA?"

I started to tell him about the interview, but didn't get past their names before he interrupted.

"Wait! Their names are Officers Ronnie Cobb and Lonnie Popp?" he asked, as if I was joking. "What did Ronnie and Lonnie look like?"

"Really?" I asked him.

"Yeah, you're right. Besides, I bet they're much more interesting in my mind than in real life." I had no doubt that he was correct. Other than their names, nothing about them stuck out in my mind.

"They were really serious as all Internal Affairs officers are," I told him.

"You've dealt with them before?" Josh wanted to know.

"Yep," I replied.

"Is that common? I'd think a guy could go his entire career in law enforcement and not have a run-in with IA, but you've done it twice in how many years?" It was actually three times so I held up three fingers. He cocked his head to the side then looked me up and down. He was probably right about it being unusual for me having a run-in with IA that many times, but I had nothing to compare it to. "What happened the first time?" he asked.

As much as I wanted to tell Josh what happened, I couldn't. "I can't talk about it, babe. It's an ongoing case from about four years ago."

"Wow, it must've happened right before you moved here," he said, but not in a fishing sort of way. Josh knew how seriously I took my job and never pried for information out of me that I shouldn't share.

"The second time?" Josh asked.

"Oscar."

"Oh." Josh blinked a few times then his expression morphed into concern. "I'm sorry, Gabe."

"You have nothing to apologize for, babe. You did nothing wrong," I assured him. "I will never be sorry that you survived that night and ended up in my life. Never."

My words sounded awfully close to a declaration that he wasn't prepared to hear. He cleared his throat and said, "Anyway, back to your current interrogation."

"Ouch." I dropped my hand between my legs and rubbed my balls as if he'd just kicked them. My theatrics garnered an eye roll but little else. "Jillian Rosewood, my union rep, was awesome. Picture Annalise Keating," I said to give him a visual, "and…"

"Which wig?"

"Josh," I said in a warning tone, "do you want to hear this story tonight or are we going to drag this out all week long?"

"Detective Butt Munch," he grumbled before he took another sip of wine. "You know how much I love Annalise."

"Why yes, Josh, I do like to munch on your butt and yes I know how much you love Annalise," I replied before I moved on again. "Jillian kept Ronnie and Lonnie," Josh chuckled when I said their names again, "on the straight and narrow."

"Did you learn anything about the photos of me or who sent them? Did you get the impression that Ronnie and Lonnie thought there was someone in the CPD involved in this case or just you?"

"Me?"

"Oh come on, you know they're looking hard at you, especially since you've already tangled with IA twice before." Josh let out a sad sigh and shook his head. "They think you killed Nate then vandalized Princess and dropped off the subsequent photos of me to divert attention."

"You're pretty damn good at this," I told him. "What happened after that?"

"Annalise, I mean, Jillian reminded them that you had an alibi for the night Nate was killed," he pointed to himself, "so you couldn't possibly have been the one to run Nate off the road and shoot him in the head. Frick and Frack–because I can't say their real names without laughing–are now willing to concede that you didn't kill Nate yourself, but they suspect you know who did. By now they might've even talked to a few patrons of Vibe, or even their bartenders," he added excitedly, "and know about your personal visit with Nate not long before he died. Add in the email…" Josh let his words trail off.

I shut off the burners beneath the meat sauce and noodles. "You're really good at this," I told him. To the best of my knowledge, they didn't know about my hookup with Nate. If they did, it wasn't mentioned to me. I wouldn't have denied it, but I wasn't volunteering information either.

"I'm good at a lot of things," he boasted. Was it a boast if it was true?

"Yes, you are." I drained the pasta and returned it to the pot then poured the pasta sauce over top of it. Josh handed me the slotted spaghetti spoon. I mixed the sauce and noodles while the bread baked for the final minute. "I'm going to go in there tomorrow and thank her for her time, but I have my own representation."

Josh pinched my ass hard before he opened the cabinet to get the plates out. "Don't be snarky," he told me. "There's only room for one snarkicist in this relationship." Josh turned and swayed his perky ass over to the table.

"Hey, you said 'relationship' without stuttering or breaking into hives," I replied.

"You want to make it three days?" he asked. Little did he know, I wasn't waiting another damn day before I saw his studio. I knew him better than he realized. He was wanting to make it perfect for me and the only thing I needed for that to happen was him. He was my perfection. "Snarkicist?"

"Snarkicist. S-n-a-r-k-i-c-i-s-t. It's someone who uses snark as a main form of communication, often in a passive-aggressive way."

"You learn that talk in Psychology one-oh-one when you went to school to become an accountant?" I asked, knowing it would get a rise out of him. He stood silently with his back to me for so long that I thought I'd gone too far. "Josh…"

He turned around suddenly when he heard the apologetic tone in my voice. "I take it back, Detective Snarky Pants. There *is* enough room in this relationship for two snarkicists."

"Good thing," I told him. "I'm not going anywhere."

"On a serious note," Josh said once we sat down and started to eat, "you're not really under a lot of scrutiny, are you?"

"Some," I said with a shrug. "I can't blame them and I'm not worried about my job because I haven't done anything wrong. The only thing that concerns me is that while they're focusing on me they're letting a killer get closer to you."

"I think it's smoke and mirrors," Josh said. "I think the vandalism was done to get to you, as were the pictures, so you'd stop investigating something bigger."

"Adrian and I have batted that around a bit, but neither of us are willing to stake your life on it."

Josh insisted on washing the dishes and I let him because I did the same thing for him when he cooked. That's the way it worked in my house growing up and I was glad to see it was working for Josh and me. I was on him the minute the last dish was dried and put away. I gently threw him over my shoulder–he did just eat after all–and carried him to the door that led to the attic. He fussed and put up a little fight, but settled down when I swatted him on his plump ass cheek.

I flipped on the light switch at the top of the stairs and stood in awe of his studio. One wall was nothing but mirrors and the rest were painted in a medium shade of gray. Huge, vibrant watercolor paintings of male ballet dancers were hung on the walls. It appeared that ballet was another one of Josh's loves and I wondered if he ever took lessons or just loved it from afar. Regardless, it was another nuance of his personality that I stored in my heart.

Then my eyes feasted on the pole in the center of the room. I had never in my life seen one of them before, except in movies. I had never seen a man pole dancing anywhere except in my imagination after Josh told me about his hobby.

"Will you put me down now?" he asked.

"Will you promise not to run?" I put him down without waiting for his answer because I knew in my heart he was done running from me. I also knew that Josh liked to do things on his terms and timeline. He wasn't just Josh anymore; he was part of an *us*.

"I wanted to wear something sexier or…"

"I don't need sexy outfits, scented air, candles, or anything else except you. Hell, I don't even need the pole, but I'd sure like to see what you can do."

He studied me closely for several long moments while he chewed on his bottom lip. I hated the insecurity I saw in his eyes and was about to call the whole thing off when he stood taller and straightened his shoulders. "Prepare to be wowed." Josh set about lighting candles and adjusting the lights in his studio anyway. He pulled a chair over for me to sit at directly in front of the pole, but far enough away that I couldn't touch him.

Josh took a deep breath and then stripped down to his underwear, which happened to be the aqua jock strap that I loved. You can bet both my dick and I perked right up when I feasted my eyes on his firm bubble butt. Josh pushed play on a remote then slit it across the floor so it was out of his way. My mouth fell open when the sexy, bluesy music from Eric Church's "Like a Wrecking Ball" began playing. If I was going to create a soundtrack to make love to, that song would be my first pick.

I watched as Josh mounted the pole and began to perform a routine of spins and moves that were both beautiful in their execution and perfectly timed to the sultry beat of the music. I watched in complete awe as he appeared to be walking on air at times or supporting the entire weight of his body with one hand. Every move he made was flawless and appeared to be effortless, but I saw the way his abdominal muscles flexed beneath the skin.

My need for him grew with every sexy beat of the music until I couldn't take it anymore. Josh ended his routine when I rose from my chair. He stood with his back pressed to the pole and watched as I stalked the rest of the way to him.

"You're so beautiful and sexy," I said, "and all mine."

I didn't give him a chance to respond, but I didn't need his words to know that he was as turned on as I was. He shook in my arms, his lips trembled beneath mine, and he dug his fingers in my ass to pull me closer. I knew the way he panted into my mouth had nothing to do with physical exertion and everything to do with his hunger to have me inside of him.

It wasn't arrogance on my part for saying that because he pulled his mouth away from mine and directed me to where he hid condoms and lube for my big night. I retrieved the items like he asked me to, but I didn't just lube up and fuck him like he expected. I turned him around to face the pole then dropped down behind him to get at his sexy ass.

I took my time teasing the crinkled flesh that Josh had teasingly called my pleasure portal more than once. At the time, I had snorted because it sounded so corny but hell if it wasn't true. I teased his ass with my tongue and took my time stretching him open with my tongue and two fingers until he begged me to fill him. His body shook with anticipation when I rolled the condom on and added more lube.

I rose to my feet then turned Josh to face me. I lifted him up and he wrapped his legs around my waist then I pressed his back against the pole. Josh hooked his arms around my neck and pulled my face to his for a hot, searing kiss. I captured his gasp in my mouth when I entered him. The music he danced to was on repeat and I showed him that he wasn't the only one who could perform to music. Yep, it was the perfect song for making love.

Josh dug his nails in my scalp to get me to fuck him harder, but the tempo I set felt so fucking good that I never wanted to stop.

I ignored his attempts and pinned him tighter against the pole to prevent him from fucking himself on my dick and continued with the pace that, although he fought, made him moan and whimper in pleasure.

"I've got you, Josh." I needed him to know, that no matter what, I had him covered regardless of the pace life set or the obstacles it threw at us.

"I need…" His words came out in pants.

He wanted to take control because the things I made him feel scared him. If he could just take control, then he'd feel grounded. Well, his feet weren't on the ground, they were wrapped around my waist and I wanted to show him that he could trust me–then and always.

It would've been easy to sit in the chair and let him ride me, but easy wasn't the answer. I kissed him through his panic until he relaxed completely in my arms. Josh's body gave off the signs that he was close to coming and I kept making love to him until I felt the hot splash of his cum on my stomach. Once I got what I needed from him, I relaxed my grip and let him take over.

Josh reached behind him and gripped the pole above his head with both hands and pushed against me until I stepped back enough so that his body was at an angle. I placed my hands on his hips when he began to move, riding my cock by undulating his hips in a hypnotic way that had me on the edge too fast.

"It's my turn," he said, when I moved to take control back.

Josh rode my cock until my legs shook and threatened to give out. He smiled wickedly and his hazel eyes gleamed a darker hue as he worked me until I thought I would die if I didn't come. The smooth way his body moved had to be illegal, because I was surely addicted to him as others were to narcotics.

"Josh," I said between gritted teeth. I needed more friction and for him to move faster. I. Was. Right. There. Josh laughed wickedly the moment I came inside him. My orgasm was a slow roll through my body until I shattered into a million pieces.

I don't remember falling to my knees with Josh wrapped around me, but that was how we ended up. He cooed and kissed my face as I returned to the land of the living. "Look who's back," he said lovingly.

"I think you nearly killed me," I told him.

"No, that'll be my reverse cowboy. I'm only going to bring that bad boy out on special occasions like birthdays and anniversaries."

My heart rate tripled when Josh mentioned anniversaries, as in he planned on having them with me. "Who are you and what have you done with *my* Josh?"

"I'm still *your* Josh," he said. It was one of the sweetest exchanges we'd ever had. I was impressed on how far we'd come in a relatively short time. Then he said, "So try to avoid getting framed and sent to prison for this Nate Turner case. It would be *murder* on our sex life."

"There's *my* Josh."

SIXTEEN

Josh

BEFORE I KNEW IT, GABE AND I WERE BOARDING A PLANE TO MIAMI for Meet the Parents Week. An itty-bitty part of me expected Internal Affairs to ban Gabe from traveling due to his shady past in Miami. Okay, that was a huge exaggeration on my part because I had no clue what the deal was in Miami. A few months ago, I would've taken it personally that Gabe didn't trust me with the story. I knew him enough to know that he did trust me and would tell me if he could. Gabe was a man with a lot of integrity; if he was told not to discuss the case then he wouldn't discuss the case.

I wasn't thrilled with the early departure time because the guy beside me in seat 11A kept me up half the night before our trip. Apparently, vacations, or the fact that I was meeting his folks, made Detective Sex on a Stick very horny. Limping up to meet his parents after a night of Gabe liberally using my ass wasn't my idea of a fun time. Luckily for him, and my sore ass too, he splurged and bought first class seats for us so I could stretch out and be as comfortable as one could be on a plane.

I enjoyed the convenience of flying, I loved taxiing down the runway and lifting off, but I didn't like air turbulence or landing. The flight was quick and devoid of much air turbulence, which made me happy because I was already anxious about meeting Gabe's mom and dad. I didn't want anything to amplify my tension and turn me into some spastic version of me for when the big moment came.

My spirits soared the minute we grabbed our luggage from the little spinning thing–I could never remember the correct name–and headed toward the airport exit because I could see through the windows that the weather was glorious. Gabe promised me that both the air and water temperatures in Miami in February would be in the '70s. I expected Gabe to veer over to the rental car agencies, but he kept walking toward the exit.

"There they are!" His exuberant announcement had me looking around for a celebrity or something. Who was it? Britney? Cher? Beyoncé? My heart rate was already accelerated from anxiety and I worried that I'd have a heart attack or stroke out before I got to meet Mom and Pop Wyatt. Next thing I knew, Gabe powerwalked his sexy ass over to an African American man and a Hispanic woman with their arms open wide to embrace him.

"My baby," the woman said when she wrapped her arms about Gabe.

"Welcome home, son." The declaration was followed up with a hearty back slap.

I had followed behind Gabe at a more leisurely pace wondering once again if I looked presentable enough to meet Al and Martina Wyatt. To Gabe this might've been a simple introduction, but to me it was *everything*. Gabe had gone from being my *something* to my *everything*. The swift changes to my life were both terrifying and exhilarating, and depending on the day, I either embraced or denied it. That day I chose to embrace it because his parents looked at me with huge, welcoming smiles on their faces when I approached the trio and I forgot to be afraid.

"Mom and Dad," Gabe said reverently, "this is Josh."

The Wyatts didn't bother with formal things like handshakes, they were huggers. Martina snatched me up first and smelled like cinnamon, sugar, and love; her hug was as equally as warm. Al smelled like sunshine and strength when he pulled me in against him; his hug was equally as firm. I was happy that the slap on my back wasn't as sharp as the one Gabe received.

"We are so excited to meet you," Martina said. Her smiling lips trembled for a second before she bit them.

"He looks surprised to meet us," Al said. "I bet Gabe neglected to mention he was adopted again."

"It shouldn't matter what race my parents are," Gabe told his father.

"It's his way of testing people." Martina looped her arm through mine and the four of us made our way to the exit. "Let me tell you that plenty of people have failed him."

"We don't give a lot of thought to our family dynamics," Al said. "Miami is such a melting pot of diversity and our situation isn't unique, but we've learned that others aren't quite as open-minded."

"Their loss is my gain," I said, earning a huge smile from Martina.

I learned fast where Gabe got his love of classic cars from when Martina and I followed Al and Gabe to a gleaming, cherry red Cadillac convertible that had to be from the '60s. The white top was down and the white leather seats were as clean as if the car had just rolled off the assembly line in Michigan. I worried that I had packed too much for a week–okay, Gabe said I did– but I got over it the minute Al opened the trunk of that monster. Hell, I could've fit Princess inside the trunk.

"Sweet ride, Mr. Wyatt," I said.

"None of that mister stuff. Just call me Al," he said. "Nice to see that you found one that can appreciate classic cars when he sees one." My appreciation of classic cars came more from envisioning my sexy boyfriend driving them, or better yet rimming and fucking me over the hood, but I didn't think that Al wanted to hear that.

"He *loves* Charlotte," Gabe said. At least I was the only one who picked up on the slight fluctuation in his tone or saw his wicked smile in the wide back seat of the car.

"I bet," Al said. The humor in his voice said I wasn't the only one to pick up on that after all.

"You must be hungry," Martina said once Al had maneuvered out of the parking lot and onto a street. "I thought we'd go back to our house for a while and visit before we drop you off at the rental car agency."

Their home was an upscale, two-story Spanish style home in a subdivision built around a golf course. As beautiful as it was, I couldn't help but remember a conversation that Gabe and I once had.

"I'm not so scary, you know," Gabe had said.

"Said the alligator to the little yappy dog that was standing along the side of the lake before he ate him."

"There aren't gators in those ponds, are there?" I whispered to Gabe as we walked to the front of his parents' home.

"This is Florida and they can be found everywhere, babe." I could tell by the look on his face that he was remembering the conversation too. Then he leaned over and loudly nibbled my neck, making me laugh and twist to get away from him.

His parents went inside rather than wait on us to stop fooling around. Gabe pulled me to him for a long, lingering kiss before he linked our fingers and led me inside. The ambience of Al and Martina's home was the exact opposite of Gabe's in Ohio. His parents' home was filled with warm colors, inviting furniture, and family pictures were on every surface. Gabe's home was sterile in comparison and didn't have a single family photo sitting around.

"You didn't get any of your mother's decorating skills, did you?"

"Nope, not even one. I admire a home that's put together well, but don't have the first clue how to make it happen. You remind me a lot of my mom," Gabe said.

I could tell by the reverent tone of voice that he meant that as a compliment, but comparing anyone to your mother is a recipe for disaster. "Babe, that's just wrong on so many levels."

"I wasn't saying that because…"

"I know," I said, cutting him off. I knew he wasn't saying that I was feminine in any way. "I meant that our relationship shouldn't resemble anything you have with a parent. That's just gross."

"I was only referring to your effortless cooking and decorating. You make having a warm and inviting home seem so easy."

"You're forgiven." I stood up on my tiptoes and gave him a kiss before we continued to the kitchen.

"Jesus, you two," Gabe said when we found his mom and dad kissing in the kitchen. "See, what did I tell you?" he asked me.

On our very first date, although I didn't call it that at the time, Gabe told me that his parents still acted like newlyweds between bites of country fried steak–that I later put to shame. His revelation was the first thing, other than sex, that we had in common. What he thought was gross about his parents, I found completely charming. Of course, I suspected we'd have the exact reverse situation when he met my parents in the middle of the week.

"It's our house," Al told him, "and we'll neck if we want to." Al gave Martina one last peck on the lips and then waved for his son to follow him out to the garage. "I want to show you the next purchase I'm planning on making."

I learned from Gabe that Al not only had a successful auto repair shop, he restored and rebuilt classic cars that had been abandoned. Some he kept for himself and others he sold for a considerable profit. I too was curious about the next project, but I could see that Martina wanted some alone time to talk to me one-on-one.

"Do you want to help me fix brunch?" she asked. "Gabe told me what a marvelous cook you are so try not to show me up in my own kitchen." She winked playfully at me then walked to her refrigerator.

It would give me something to do with my nervous hands, besides look like I had a medical condition, so I jumped on it. Martina pulled a casserole dish out of the refrigerator and set it on the counter. It appeared to be some type of French toast that you make the day before and let sit overnight. It looked scrumptious and I made a mental note to get the recipe from her later, especially if Gabe liked it, because I suspected that swapping recipes wasn't on her mind right then.

"Do you have any food allergies?" she asked as she pulled fresh produce from her crisper drawer of her refrigerator. "I put a lot of veggies in Gabe's scrambled eggs and I don't want to add an ingredient that offends or attempts to kill you."

"I don't have any allergies and I like just about everything except liver and onions." I began washing the vegetables in the sink as she pulled them out. I chuckled as I washed the button mushrooms because I thought of the faces Gabe made every time someone tried to slip one into a recipe. He thought cream of mushroom soup was the most disgusting thing he'd ever seen.

"What's got you so tickled?" Martina asked.

"Oh, I was just laughing about Gabe's hatred of mushrooms." I was still recalling funny memories so it took me longer than normal to realize that Martina was standing as still as a statue. I turned and found her studying me with her head tilted to the side.

"Gabe doesn't hate mushrooms," she replied softly.

I realized that I was standing on very shaky ground and worried that my next words could make or break my relationship with her. "Oh, of course he doesn't. I was confusing him with my best friend Chaz." I giggled a little bit. "I blame it on my lack of sleep from...um..." I turned back and picked up the paring knife to either cut the veggies, slit my own throat, or defend myself from a marauding mama bear.

Martina didn't move so I began slicing and dicing peppers and onions. I felt her eyes on me the entire time and I was afraid to blink. "Don't slice those," she said softly when I reached for the mushrooms. "Gabe doesn't like them." Her voice had a sadness to it that made me look up at her. I felt so bad that I upset her, even if it was accidentally. "I can't believe I didn't know that all these years." Martina shook her head.

"He probably didn't want to upset you," I replied. "He made me chicken Marsala for dinner once and put all of the mushrooms on my plate. He picks them off his pizza rather than complain about them if they end up on there by accident."

"There's more to it than him just being thoughtful," Martina said, "but thank you for trying to make me feel better." The oven beeped to let her know that it was preheated so she slid the French toast casserole into the oven then set about cooking various types of meats. "You care a great deal for my son, Josh. I can tell that so I'm going to let you in on a little secret the way that you did for me just now."

"Okay," I said, almost hesitantly.

"Gabe isn't just a pleaser by nature; a lot of it's from circumstance or his misguided notion that he needs to be a certain way to be loved. I think that possibly comes from being adopted. He's told you about his older brother, Dylan, right?" I nodded my head. "Well, Dylan was mine and Al's biological child. We tried for years to conceive again, but it just wasn't in the cards. The daughter of a long-time family friend became pregnant when she was a senior in high school and decided to give her baby up for adoption. As difficult as that time was for her, it was the answer to our prayers. We brought little Gabe home from the hospital and our family was finally complete." Martina smiled sweetly as she recalled the memory.

"Gabe has known since he was old enough to understand that he was adopted. It seemed like there was a part of him that felt he needed to work harder to earn or keep our love. He adored his older brother so he wasn't really competing with Dylan, but there was definitely a force pushing him to be perfect. It got worse when Dylan was killed. Someone actually had the gall to say that we had lost our only son, as if Gabe didn't count because he wasn't ours biologically. Al and I never felt that way so we don't know where the idiot got the notion, but it didn't matter because Gabe heard what the fool said and took it to heart. It seemed like it validated feelings and fears he'd harbored for years."

"Wow, some people don't know when to shut the hell up," I told Martina. It broke my heart to think of Gabe feeling unloved and unwanted.

Martina chuckled then said, "They sure don't. Losing Dylan was a terrible heartbreak and I was so far gone in my own grief that I didn't see how close I came to losing Gabe too." She brought her hand up and rubbed her throat as she blinked away tears. "He became unruly and stopped caring about life. I don't know what would've happened to him had his football coach not stepped in and helped us. Gabe channeled his emotions into the sport he loved so much and I swear to you it saved his life."

I decided I'd never complain about watching games with him again. I knew he loved the sport, but I never realized the emotional importance it had in his life.

"Anyway," Martina waved her hand as if she was pushing the sad memories aside, "his refusal to tell me he doesn't like mushrooms is an example of Gabe being worried more about pleasing me than himself. I'm glad you told me." She stood on her tiptoes and kissed me on the cheek.

It wasn't long before Gabe and Al returned from the garage chatting about cars. Martina and I finished getting brunch put together then we gathered around the table to enjoy the feast. I bit my lip to keep from laughing when Gabe took his fork and tried to secretly poke through his scrambled eggs looking for the offensive mushrooms. Even more funny was the look on Martina's face as she watched her son.

"Gabriel Allen Wyatt," Martina said loud enough to make us all jump. "I cannot believe you've been picking out the mushrooms all these years. Where the hell did you put them?"

"You told her?" Gabe asked me accusingly, like I told her that he liked to eat ass.

"Don't you even think about blaming this on Josh," she said, pointing her fork at him. "Where did you put the mushrooms all these years? They were never on the plate when you were finished."

"He fed them to the dog when he thought we weren't looking or hid them in his napkin," Al said. "What?" he asked when his wife stared at him in shock.

"You knew?" Martina asked Al, who just shrugged.

While his parents exchanged looks, I received one of my own from Gabe. In the grand scheme of things, Gabe not liking mushrooms wasn't a big deal. His willingness to keep it from his mom for thirty-six years because he wanted to please her *was* a big deal. I couldn't allow Gabe to sacrifice his own happiness just to please me. There would always be a mutually pleasing compromise, such as getting mushrooms on only half of a pizza or getting separate pizzas like we often did. We could use the same logic for whatever difference we had. It wasn't my way or his way; it was our way. I just needed to make sure he knew it too.

SEVENTEEN

Gabe

OTHER THAN THE MUSHROOM CONFESSION FROM JOSH, OUR VISIT with my parents went even better than I expected. While Josh was giving away my secrets, I spent time with my dad in his garage. He showed me the car he was hoping to buy and the plans he had to restore it if everything fell into place.

"Josh is really different than the other guys you brought home," Dad said once we finished with the car talk. Two things happened: I felt myself getting defensive over Josh and I regretted that I had ever brought anyone else home to meet them. Josh wasn't just another guy; he was *the guy*. Dad must've sensed that what he said upset me because he was quick to set me straight. "I meant that in a very good way, son."

My ire turned to curiosity in a flash. "Why?"

"Well, he's mature in a way the others weren't, even though I'm guessing he's younger than you," Dad said.

"By six-and-a-half years," I told him.

"He's one of those who are wise beyond their years, an old soul. I don't know if it's his personality or a side effect of life, but it's there nonetheless."

"I think it's a little bit of both," I told him honestly.

Heart-to-heart talks weren't something we normally did, but I knew my dad was always there for me if I needed him. I was surprised when my dad said, "He's comfortable in his own skin and his place in your life. I like that about him the most."

"Me too," I agreed. When I first saw Josh, I got the same impression about him being comfortable in his own skin. I realized later, that while it was mostly true, he used that as a shield to hide his deepest, darkest vulnerabilities. I wasn't arrogant enough to believe that my love for him was enough to excise those hurts completely, but I did see him blossom and grow more confident in other ways once he realized that I wanted him just the way he was.

Josh's confidence could never be confused with arrogance. He had no idea how much he lit a room up when he entered it, the insane way people were drawn to him, or the tight hold he had on my heart. I wanted him to know that I was his, and his alone. I needed him to know that his happiness enhanced my own. I wanted him to know that I pinned my hopes and dreams on a smart-mouthed, sexy salon owner. I just needed to wait for the right moment to present itself.

"I sense that you're holding something back," Dad said. "You and I both know that we don't always get another chance to tell people the way we feel about them. Sometimes," my dad's voice broke, "they walk out that door to get their dad a carton of his favorite ice cream because his throat was hurting and they don't come back. Gabe, if you love that man half as much as I think you do then you tell him."

My dad's words brought back all the grief we felt when Dylan was killed and reminded me that someone made threats against Josh, maybe not so much with words, but the pictures said a lot. I knew that my dad was right and that I had to create the moment and not wait for it to happen on its own because I may never get the chance. I had already planned a nice dinner at the steak and seafood restaurant in the hotel where we were staying so I mentally added a romantic stroll on the beach. What was more perfect than that?

Things were going according to plan too. We got to our hotel room, put up our clothes, and went down to the restaurant where I'd made a reservation. Josh chose the wine, I chose the appetizer, and the evening was off to a great start. Then I looked over Josh's shoulder and locked eyes with a man I had never hoped to see again.

Jimmy De Soto had been my partner when I made detective. Jimmy D, as he was called, accepted me instantly without a care that I was gay. He took me under his wing and showed me how to be a good detective. Jimmy was someone I had deeply respected and admired during the two years that I worked with him. I had noticed slight changes in his personality after he and his wife of fifteen years divorced, but I thought they were temporary and wouldn't impact his job. Turned out I was dead wrong.

Jimmy and I worked vice, which I'd never tell Josh or he'd never shut the hell up with the jokes, and the last case we worked together ended in the worst possible way. We arrested a guy during a drug bust who we thought we could flip. Ace was a young, brash, and proud gang member who refused to cooperate. The decision was made to hold him for the forty-eight hours permitted by law in hopes that he'd give us some names for a lighter sentence. Ace was busted with a large cache of drugs on him plus a wad of cash, so he was facing some hard time for dealing. Jimmy was convinced that he could get names if he sweated him out long enough.

Midway through that fateful day, my dad called to let me know that my grandfather suffered a massive heart attack and it didn't look good for him. Jimmy encouraged me to leave to be with my family and promised that he and another detective from vice would take over the interrogation. Granddad lingered for a few days before he passed away. My mom, dad, and I took turns staying with him around the clock so he wouldn't be alone.

When I returned to work after the funeral, Jimmy wasn't the same guy who had patted me on the back and told me he'd be praying for my family. I learned that he and another detective from vice got angry when they couldn't get the kid to flip so they took him and dropped Ace, who had just turned eighteen years old, off in the middle of a rival gang's territory. Ace was killed and a gang war ensued.

The two detectives involved said that they didn't do anything wrong and they dropped Ace off where he told them to, but there were two things wrong with that story. One, they had no business dropping him off anywhere. We didn't operate a transportation service out of MPD. Second, I heard Jimmy callously say, "He would've died anyway." I hated that kind of ignorance and I was honest when interviewed by IA afterwards. Jimmy was put on paid administrative leave while the case was investigated.

The days after I gave my statement to IA was wrought with tension and discord. Many of my fellow officers felt I should've just kept my mouth shut and that my loyalty should've been given to Jimmy over the investigation. It was that line of thinking that I didn't agree with and I never backed down or apologized for telling the truth. My refusal to conform to their ways made my life a living hell at work, but I had no regrets.

Not long after everything went down, Kyle announced that he was moving back to Ohio. I jumped on the chance for a new start for my career and my relationship with him because I thought that my job stress played a big role in the decline in our relationship. Kyle was willing to give it a try too, but we learned that a relationship between us just wasn't meant to be. I got my fresh start with my career and found the love I had been searching for. I had put my time with the MPD behind me and focused on my new life. The look on Jimmy's face said that he hadn't put my involvement behind him.

As best as I understood it, Jimmy was forced into an early retirement. They couldn't prove that he deliberately set Ace up to get killed and Jimmy sure as hell didn't confess, but his behavior, if not criminal, was unethical. A person I had once admired was someone I came to resent. He represented a level of evil and corruption that I'd never understand. I'd heard through the rumor mill that Jimmy blamed me and my testimony for the reason he was forced out of the department, although he never once said anything to me about it.

"Should I be concerned that you're looking that intently at another man?" Josh asked, bringing me back to the present.

I hadn't been lying when I told Josh I couldn't talk about it. Criminal charges were never filed against Jimmy and I figured it was part of his retirement deal. Ace's family sued the city of Miami and won a settlement. I had to fly back to Miami and give a deposition, but I wasn't called to give testimony during the trial. My union rep had advised me not to discuss the case with anyone because criminal charges could be filed if new evidence was introduced, say someone's guilty conscience got the better of them.

I tore my eyes from Jimmy's sneering face and focused back on Josh. "A ghost from the past," I told him, "and absolutely nothing for you to worry about."

"Do you want to leave?" Josh asked worriedly.

I shoved all thoughts of Jimmy aside and reached for Josh's hand. "No way. I can't wait until you try their seafood. There's nothing like it in Ohio." I knew what he was going to say so I cut him off. "Red Lobster doesn't count. You'll see."

I was so busy enjoying Josh's seafood porn faces that I didn't even know when Jimmy left the restaurant. I laughed at the crestfallen expression on Josh's face when he looked down and saw that his plate was empty.

"I don't know why," he said after I commented on his cute little pout. "I couldn't eat another bite if I tried."

"How about we work some of it off with a nice stroll on the beach?" I asked.

The breeze coming off the ocean rustled through Josh's fair strands of hair as he titled his head back and breathed in the air. He closed his eyes and inhaled deeply before he released the breath slowly. "It's beautiful here," he said.

"This part is," I agreed. "There are parts that are going downhill; the neighborhood I grew up in is one of them. I can't speak for everywhere, but the middle class is getting smaller and smaller here. I wish I could say it was because they were moving up, but that's not the truth. I hate seeing empty buildings where thriving businesses used to be and neighborhoods where kids can no longer safely play in their yards."

"I think that's happening everywhere," Josh said. "Politicians are too busy fighting each other instead of fighting hunger and poverty."

"True," I said. "How the hell did we get onto such morose subjects on a beautiful night like this?" I asked.

"You started it," Josh said petulantly, making me laugh.

"You're right, I did."

"So, can I assume that the 'old ghost' in the restaurant has something to do with the things you can't talk about because I don't see that guy being an old boyfriend."

"You assumed correctly, even though I'm not sure how you did it," I replied.

"He's not your type," Josh said with an arrogant lift of his chin.

"Look who's stereotyping now," I admonished, then playfully nudged him with my shoulder. "I thought you weren't my type once upon a time."

"You were dumb then," Josh quipped. "Besides, I don't care what you say, Mr. Rogers was never going to be your type, regardless of his neighborhood."

I laughed when I realized that Jimmy did somewhat look like the guy from the kid's show that ran for decades on PBS. "You got me," I confessed.

"But will I keep you?" Josh asked playfully.

"I guess time will tell."

Josh pulled his hand from mine, rolled up the legs of his jeans to mid-calf, and removed his shoes. "I've been here for an entire day and haven't gotten my toes wet yet."

I waited until he was ankle deep in the water before I hollered, "Look out for the alligators."

"What?" he shrieked. "Jackass," he yelled when I threw my head back and laughed at him.

I removed my shoes and rolled up my jeans too, then followed him into the water. It was a beautiful time of the night with the sun going down and most of the beach goers looking for something to eat after being in the sun all day. It seemed like I didn't have to force "the moment" because it was upon me.

Josh jumped in my arms, wrapped his legs around my waist, and his arms around my neck. I didn't even care that my clothes were getting soaked from his wet legs and feet. All I cared about was the look of happiness in his eyes and the pride I felt because I put that look in them.

"I love you," Josh said softly with a nervous smile on his face.

His words shocked me and my brain stopped functioning for a few moments. It was long enough to worry Josh about my reaction and my next words didn't help. "Damn it, Josh."

"What did I do?" he asked, pissed that his declaration was met with such a pathetic response. He tried to wiggle out of my arms, but I wouldn't let him go.

"I was just about to say the same thing," I told him.

"You were going to announce that you were in love with you?" he asked, but I could tell by the smile on his face he knew exactly what I'd meant.

"I was going to tell you that *I* am in love with *you*." I shook my head in disbelief. "You always want to be in control, don't you? Always trying to outdo me. I brought you out here for a romantic declaration and BAM," the last part was shouted loudly, "you have to say it first."

"So say it now," he suggested.

"I'm out of the mood now," I teased.

"Oh, I know how to fix that," Josh said proudly, wiggling his crotch against mine.

"I knew there was something special about you the minute we met. I fought it, I denied it, and then I owned up to it. I am so in love with you, Josh."

"Wow," he whispered thickly. I saw tears form in his eyes as he struggled to grasp the reality of the moment.

"Do not pinch me," I warned him.

"Oh my God. You're reading my mind now," he said then burst into laughter. The unshed tears lost their battle with gravity and ran down his cheeks. "What am I thinking now?"

"Easy..."

"I am not, but I can be tricked," Josh said saucily.

I ignored his attempts to laugh off his emotion. "You're thinking that you want me to take you back to our hotel room, lay you down on that big bed, and make love to you until the sun comes up."

"Something like that," he admitted with a sappy look on his face.

So, that was exactly what I did.

EIGHTEEN

Josh

The next two days with Gabe in Miami were picture perfect; I'm talking worthy of a chick flick. We repeated our love for one another several times a day, we splashed around in the water, ate every kind of delicious food imaginable, walked hand-in-hand on the beach each night, and then returned to our room to make crazy, passionate love. We were a movie night away from the biggest cliché there ever was about dating. In fact, I found a mug online with the famous cliché on it and ordered it so Gabe could add it to his mug collection. I was happy to see that it would arrive at my house while we were on vacation so I could surprise him when we returned.

In the meantime, I had a Valentine's Day gift squirreled away in my suitcase for him. Neither of us talked about making V-Day plans and I figured Gabe might be like a lot of men who gave the day absolutely no consideration as being important. I used to be one of them because I never had anyone to celebrate the day with. I decided to keep it low key and tried not to make a big fuss. I bought Gabe a small box of his chocolate covered caramel and pecan candies and a mug that read: BAD COP. I also brought some massage lotion because I remembered just how much he loved my hands all over him.

Gabe had the same idea for Valentine's Day. He gave me a box of dark chocolate covered cherries and the cutest fucking t-shirt that read: I GIVE BLOWJOBS. A blow dryer, a pair of shears, and a comb were beneath the words. Gabe had also brought some massage lotions with him, but the ones he bought were flavored. I had a lot of fun licking that cinnamon-flavored oil off his dick, while Gabe preferred the strawberries and cream on my body. He worked me up for so long that I gave him plenty of cream to go with his strawberries.

Later, I laid my head on his chest and said, "Thank you for making my first Valentine's Day amazing." You see, prior to meeting and falling in love with Gabe, I never would've told anyone just how lonely that day was for me every single year. I worried that I sounded too pathetic and I was always afraid someone would reaffirm that love wasn't in the cards for me. Gabe gave me the courage to be myself and to say what was on my mind without fear of rejection. That was his greatest gift to me and one I planned to cherish for the rest of my life.

Gabe was silent for a long time so I raised my head to look at him. His brow was furrowed and he looked angry. Gabe turned his face to look at me and his expression softened immediately. "Fucking idiots was what they were. It's hard for me to be mad at them when their stupidity made you available when I came into your life." I realized that his anger the moments before wasn't directed at me but at the people in my past who had hurt me.

I enjoyed the time we spent with his folks too. They were a lot of fun to be around and I saw why Gabe turned out to be the amazing man that he had. The funniest moment of the trip had to be when Al recommended we play some poker one night after dinner. Gabe's eyes about bugged out of his head in fear that I'd lose every dime I had. Ha! He silently shook his head no, but I readily accepted the offer.

I was the one who had the last laugh when I ended up with all the chips that night. I smiled at each of their shocked faces, especially Gabe's because it was obvious he was seeing me in a new light.

"Looks to me you're dating a card shark," Al said to his son. I saw the gleam of approval in his dark eyes as he smiled broadly at me. "Well done, son."

"Dad," Gabe said in a warning tone. "You're not taking him to poker night at the American Legion."

"Why not?" Al and I both asked.

"It's just not a good idea," Gabe said. It turned out that poker night was the same night I planned to introduce Gabe to my parents. I promised Al that he and I would whip some ass the next time I came for a visit.

Away from our everyday lives, Gabe and I had time to get to know one another more, delve deeper into our pasts, and share things that we'd never told anyone else. I asked things like, "Did you ever get caught masturbating by your parents?"

"Not so much in the act," Gabe said, "more like they noticed that my hot showers were getting longer. You?"

"Same, except it wasn't the length of the shower that tipped my mom off," I told Gabe.

"What was it?"

"Once I discovered the cool thing my dick did and how good it felt, I wanted to do it all the time. I quickly learned the side effects of too much jerking off and it wasn't blindness." Gabe threw his head back and laughed heartily, a sound I had become addicted to. "I started using my mother's expensive moisturizer to prevent chafing and forgot to put it back one day. I found a bottle of lube in the shower the very next day."

"Your mom sounds kind of cool and understanding," Gabe said.

It was my turn to laugh. "She is cool and understanding, but she takes things to the extreme. Remind me to tell you about my 'coming out' after you meet her."

"Why can't you tell me now?" Gabe asked.

"It will mean more to you after you meet her. Just trust me, babe."

He did and on that fateful Wednesday evening, Gabe got to see exactly what I was referring to when I said my mom took things to the extreme. Now, lesser men might've been embarrassed about their mother's level of excitement for their happiness, but I had come to terms with Bertie's personality quirks long ago.

"Oh, wow," Gabe said in awe as he looked around the living room of my parents' condo. "I've never seen anything like it." I knew he was understating the obvious because the look on his face was priceless as he took in the "Welcome, Gabe" sign in rainbow colors, the helium filled balloons around the room, and the big poster of the two of us on the wall that said Josh loves Gabe beneath it, like that Happy Days spinoff with Joanie and Chachi. I sure hoped that Gabe and I had a happier, longer run than the ill-fated sitcom.

I didn't ask why she wanted a picture of us as a couple, because I knew what she was going to do; I grew up in her house for fuck's sake. Gabe wasn't the only one springing parental surprises that week. I was happy my mom toned down her party outfit though. I worried she'd wear enough rainbows in her outfit to look like a circus clown, or worse, Mimi from The Drew Carey Show. I might not have known the name of the football team from Cleveland, but I knew the famous comedian-turned-actor-turned game show host. My mom was wearing a sunny yellow dress with a rainbow belt. She reminded me of a Care Bear that Meredith used to have.

"Come give mama a hug, Joshy," she said when she saw me.

I narrowed my eyes at Gabe when he mouthed "Joshy" with a ridiculous grin on his face. I gave my mom a long hug and could feel the happiness she felt for me vibrating through her tiny frame. I had finally brought home someone for her to meet, someone that I loved, and another person for her to love too. As whacky as my mother often was, she never embarrassed me. Everything she did was out of pure love for me, her only child. She was my greatest champion, a fierce warrior who was just over five feet tall, and I adored her.

"I'm so happy for you, Josh," she whispered. "I've hoped and prayed for this day for so long." She pulled back and looked up into my eyes. "Introduce me to your guy."

"Mom, this is G…"

"Oh, I know who this is." My mother elbowed past me and hugged Gabe so tight I worried she was suffocating him. "It's so good to meet you," she said, not turning loose of her prey.

"The pleasure is all mine," Gabe told her, patting her back.

"Bertie, turn loose of the young man. You'll cut off the circulation to his lower limbs," my father said when he walked into the room.

My parents were the exact opposite on every spectrum. I'm talking personality, wardrobe, hobbies, and even food. How they managed to compromise and meet in the middle like they did was beyond me. My father once said that my mother made him a better man because she made him appreciate things he never noticed before, like art, music, and even bright colors. *"She lights up a room and doesn't even know it,"* he once told me. *"Well, she lights me up too. She fills me with a warmth and radiance like my own little ray of* sunshine. *If you want to be happy in life you either need to be someone's ray of sunshine or the sky that allows them to shine bright.*" I don't think I fully realized what my father meant until I met Gabe.

Gabe and I were opposite in many ways too and I hoped the example my parents set for me would help me to accommodate Gabe's needs and personality rather than stifle it. Factoring what I had learned about his need to please from his mother, I knew I'd have to work harder to be his ray of sunshine and not a soul-sucking tornado that would take everything he wanted to give and leave emptiness behind. Later that night, I brought it up when we returned to our beach–as I'd come to think of it.

At first, Gabe laughed at my analogy, but then he stopped when he realized I was serious. "I would never describe you as a soul-sucking tornado, Josh. You're definitely a ray of sunshine and sometimes I need to wear sunglasses because you burn so bright."

I stopped and looked at him. "I don't think I can properly express just how much it means to me that you don't ever try to change me–not the way I talk, dress, or sashay my happy ass down the street. You're not only a blue sky, Gabe, you're one that's so vivid and striking that there are no clouds marring its perfection. Those days are so rare, but then again, I think you are too." I think it was a tossup as to who was more surprised by my words.

"I can think of a way you can attempt to express your feelings for me if words have failed you, Sunshine."

From that moment on, Gabe swapped out his nickname for me and started calling me Sunshine instead of babe. Gabe got a kick out of spending time with my parents too and I don't think I ever saw him laugh so hard when I told him about my "coming out" party. I told him it made his "welcome party" look tame in comparison. It was both a humiliating and heartwarming experience, one that I'd never forget for the rest of my life.

On our last night in Florida, we had dinner with both sets of parents. We were practically ignored as our folks got to know one another and talked about us like we weren't in the same room. We just sat there and watched it all unfold as we enjoyed a lovely dinner while Al and my father discussed who should pay for it. Gabe snatched up the bill while those two argued good naturedly, then we quietly snuck away so we could enjoy our last night of vacation before we had to return home.

It was obvious he needed my warmth and radiance even more when we returned to Ohio to temperatures that barely broke the freezing mark after an amazing week in the sun. Neither of us had been eager to return, but we couldn't stay gone forever. I had a business to run and Gabe needed to look like he wasn't guilty of whatever crimes IA thought he committed.

We had so much to do that Sunday when we returned home. The first thing we did on our way home from the airport was stop by the grocery store to get emergency staples. I had planned to do the real shopping the following day, but there wasn't going to be a damn thing in that house to eat, and I was staying home once I got there. I picked up ingredients for a tossed salad and homemade pizza. Gabe added cupcakes from the bakery.

Gabe helped me carry the luggage and groceries upstairs then left to pick up Buddy from Adrian and Sally Ann's house. I spent a good amount of time fussing over my own feather and fur babies who were happy to see me even though I knew that Meredith and Chaz took good care of them in my absence. I let Jazzy out of her cage to run and play while Diva weaved in and out of my legs.

Savage squawked happily, "Fucknugget! Fucknugget!" I had worried that Savage would revert back to his destructive habits while I was gone, but Meredith assured me that she would keep a close eye on him and even stay over if he looked to be freaking out over being left alone at night. The way he bopped his head and moved from side to side told me that he had done just fine.

As much as I enjoyed our trip, it was good to be home among my familiar things and my babies. I looked forward to spending some quiet time in my salon the following day and getting back into my normal routine, but until then, I had a lot of laundry and things to do. I knew that Gabe would do his part and help, but it didn't take more than one person to load the washing machine.

I sorted the dirty laundry into piles on the washroom floor and returned the luggage to the walk-in closet in my bedroom. When I exited the closet, I realized that there was something on my perfectly made bed that didn't belong. A bouquet of decaying red roses and an envelope was placed in the center of my pillows. I knew in my heart that the gift wasn't left there by one of my friends to welcome me home. My first thought was to remove the offending items from my bed, but I knew I wasn't allowed to touch it. I just stood there staring.

In fact, I was in the same spot when Gabe and Buddy returned. "Sunshine," Gabe called out.

"In here."

Buddy bounded in and made a beeline right for me. It was the jolt back to reality that I needed and not even the ominous gift could stop me from dropping to my knees to give Buddy the hug and ear scratching he needed.

"What the fuck is that?" Gabe asked when he walked into the room. He went over to the bed and leaned over to get a closer look without touching the evidence left behind. "Goddamn it." He pulled his cellphone out of his pocket and called the police station.

Next thing I knew, my home was filled with officers–twice the amount that showed up for the tire slashing. I'm telling you I saw people I didn't even know lived in our town or worked on the force. My house was dusted for fingerprints, photos were taken, the offending items were handled with latex gloves, and Gabe had Meredith and Chaz come over to speak with the police so they could try and figure out when the items were left behind. I wasn't included in any of it; Gabe sat me on the couch and I was left there until the last person left my home.

The quiet night at home I had planned with Gabe was shot to hell. I watched as his body got tighter and his face grew more tense as the minutes ticked away. Gabe had read whatever was in the envelope and I could feel him trying to build a wall between us. I wasn't about to let that happen.

Gabe stood with his back to me for a long time as he ran his hand through his hair. I figured he was searching for the right words to say, but that gave me time to prepare some of my own. Gabe dropped his hand then turned to face me. The devastated look in his eyes shredded me. Whatever he was thinking was hurting him so bad and I was certain I didn't want to hear his thoughts spoken out loud.

"No, Gabe." I shook my head. "You don't get to make me fall in love with you then crush my heart. You're not allowed to say things like your world revolves around me then walk away. You don't get to call me your Sunshine then end us."

"It would only be until this guy is caught," Gabe said.

"No," I said in my most resolute voice.

"You don't even know what was inside the envelope," Gabe told me.

"I don't care." Well, I did care, but I knew that we were stronger together than apart. "This sick fuck just wants to drive a wedge between us and you're letting them win."

"It said: 'If you cared about him then you would've heeded the warning. He will die for your mistake.' I'm already responsible for..."

"Do not say that you're responsible for Nate Turner's death. I'm still not convinced this has anything to do with Nate's death," I told Gabe.

"I might've agreed if the bastard didn't include a picture of a dead Nate Turner that was taken at the scene of his homicide. Whoever this person is means business and for whatever reason they're targeting me. I will not–cannot–let you get hurt because of me. Josh, I would rather break your heart temporarily than see any harm come to you."

"Bullshit!" I knew my heart didn't work that way and I wasn't so sure that I'd forgive him once the threat to me was gone. "Listen very carefully to what I have to say, Gabe, because I'm not playing around here. I've been bullied my whole life and this right here is just a scarier, more intense form of bullying. I. Will. Not. Have. It."

"Sunshine…"

"No! You don't get to tell me you're going to break my heart and in the very next breath use the cutesy name you have for me. We're going to be a team and work through this like the example our parents set for us." I rose to my feet and went to him. "Gabe, I love you. Please don't give up on us."

Gabe closed his eyes and I had hope that maybe he was coming around. When he reopened them, I didn't see the conviction I had hoped my words would stir inside him, but neither did I see desperation for me to understand him. I held my breath while I waited to hear what he had to say and he waited so long that I became dizzy.

"Things will need to change around here," he said firmly.

"Okay," I readily agreed, but then thought about it. "What kind of things?"

"You're getting an alarm installed on all of the doors and windows. You will no longer allow the back door to remain unlocked during business hours. It stays shut and locked at all times. You have plenty of neighbors to the front of your house and business, but none in the back since no one has moved into Bianca's house. You will have a door and a lock installed at the bottom of the stairs so that you can keep people from wandering upstairs while you're busy in the salon." Gabe had held up a finger with every demand that he made. "Those flowers weren't there a few days ago when Meredith enticed a pouting Diva from beneath your bed with a treat. I think the flowers were already dead and were brought up during salon hours yesterday since Saturday is your busiest day. Someone probably came through the back door and headed right up the steps to your home."

None of his demands were unreasonable or too intrusive and in fact made a lot of sense. Blissville wasn't the same town that I grew up in and it was past time that I accepted it. Extra locks and security versus no Gabe. There really was no contest.

"Fine, but it's going to be a snazzy door down there, Gabe. I won't have the ambience and atmosphere ruined by an ill-matched door that sticks out like a sore thumb."

Gabe pulled me to him, wrapped his arms around me, and held me tight. "God, I love you, Sunshine."

NINETEEN

Gabe

I STAYED UP HOURS AFTER JOSH FELL ASLEEP AGAINST MY CHEST. I worried that I let my heart make the wrong decision. I meant what I had said that I'd rather hurt him temporarily so that he stayed alive, but I saw in his eyes that forgiveness might not be forthcoming if I walked away from him, even if it was in his best interest. I caved because I wanted to and for no other reason. I could only hope my actions wouldn't hurt him or do anything to dim his brightness.

Sleep, when it came, was fitful and filled with disturbing

dreams. I saw Josh's beautiful face marred with blood and a bullet wound instead of Nate's. I saw Josh yelling my name and reaching for help that would never come in time to save him. I jerked awake at least ten times in the three hours of sleep I managed to get. Each time, Josh slept soundly nestled against me with his arm and leg thrown across my body to prevent me from leaving him.

God, the thought of breaking his heart killed me, but I wasn't convinced I had been wrong. I was overcome with the need to get as close to him as I could. I needed his flesh against mine everywhere. No matter how scary life was in that moment, there was one constant: I was a man and I had morning wood. I knew I wasn't going to fall asleep again so I rolled Josh to his back and woke him with kisses all over his face and neck until he was fully awake and as aroused as I was.

Josh rolled the condom down my dick after I prepared him then I slid inside him; it was as natural as breathing. I saw in his eyes just how uncertain he was about our relationship and I hated that I put that doubt in his eyes. He worried that I was telling him goodbye with my body before I said it with words. I had told Josh I was staying and I wouldn't go back on my word. "No way I can live without my Sunshine," I said. My words and the way my body moved were an affirmation of my commitment to him–to us; not a goodbye.

I was rewarded with a brilliant smile that banished the clouds of doubt from his pretty hazel eyes. *How had I thought for a second that I could live without his smile every single day?* I promised to kick my own ass if I allowed myself to think it ever again.

Morning sex was usually pretty fast and hungry, and that morning was no different in that aspect, but we held each other tighter and kissed longer because I had almost done something stupid that would've compounded a bad situation. I had a feeling that Josh would get even with me for my flawed thoughts at a time and choosing at his convenience, but I had too much on my mind to worry about it. I'd pay the price and be glad for the opportunity.

I stayed in the shower after Josh got out and dried off, hoping to wake up. Josh surprised me by opening the door and handing me a cup of coffee. He was wearing a wide grin on his face and looked pretty pleased with himself to a level that said it had nothing to do with bringing me coffee.

"Check out the coffee mug. I ordered it while we were on vacation and it arrived already," he said.

I looked down at the mug and it said: **I enjoy movie nights, long walks on the beach, and cuddling.** "Oh my god. Our vacation was a movie night away from a cliché," I told him.

"I know!" He leaned his head in for a quick kiss. "It was absolutely perfect."

It was too. I had never enjoyed myself more than I did with him that week. We laughed and had some great times, which made what happened yesterday so much harder to swallow. I got a glimpse of my future with Josh and I couldn't let it get ripped away.

I stood beneath the hot spray enjoying my coffee until the water ran cold. Josh was already on the phone with an alarm company by the time I got out, dried, and dressed. "It must be my lucky day," he said when I came to him for my goodbye kiss. "They had a cancellation and will be here to install the system today."

Having someone threatening to kill him didn't make him lucky, but it was fortunate that the appointment was open. "Keep the doors locked and text me your grocery demands," I said then thought about it. "Better yet, I'll be home at a decent time and we can go together."

"You'll protect me at all costs, even if someone tries to take the produce I want." Josh held his hands in front of him to form a pistol and playfully hit a pose that made him look like a modern day Charlie's Angels. It was exactly the lighthearted thing I needed to put a smile on my face and remind me just what I was fighting for.

Adrian arrived the same time as me and he pulled me to the

side before we went into the station. "Damn, Gabe. I heard about the threat left at Josh's house."

Even though I hadn't called him, it was possible someone else on the force did, but I was betting he heard about it at the diner. So help me God, nothing was a secret in Blissville. "What did you hear at the diner this morning?" I asked.

"That someone killed his cat and left it for dead for him to find on his bed," Adrian said, confirming my suspicions were correct. "How come you didn't say anything when you picked Buddy up last night?"

"First, it wasn't a dead cat, it was a bouquet of decaying flowers, a note, and a picture of a dead Nate Turner," I told Adrian. "Second, I didn't know about it until after I got home. I made one call to dispatch, and next thing I knew, everybody and their brother–minus you–was in our home dusting for fingerprints and stuff."

"Home," Adrian said then smiled. "You said 'home' and not Josh's house."

It was the second time I said it that morning, but Adrian was the first to point it out. Either Josh didn't hear it or he ignored me when I told him I'd return home from work early. I wasn't sure how to respond to Adrian so I just shrugged my shoulders.

Another random thought occurred to me while I stood in the frigid temperature with Adrian. Josh was meticulous about his home and salon, particularly with cleanliness. Under normal circumstances, he wouldn't have gone to bed until the last black smudge from the fingerprint dusting had been eliminated. It just showed how much I had upset him the night before that he ignored the mess. It was a mistake I wouldn't make again and I wished I was home helping him clean.

"Adrian, something really bad is going on and I honestly can't wrap my head around it." I told my partner about the photo of Nate, the note in the envelope, and the gut feeling that whoever killed Nate thought I knew a hell of a lot more than I did. But why?

"That's a damn good question," Adrian said. "Maybe Captain Reardon will get some answers for us. It would sure help to know what the hell Nate was caught up in."

The captain wasn't in yet, which was unusual, but not unheard of. We had some open cases to work, the largest being the cache of drugs found at the high school, so I tried to focus on them until Captain Reardon showed up. As the minutes ticked by, however, I found it harder to concentrate because the captain was never late to the station.

It was almost noon before he walked through the front doors of the station. A gust of wind caught the bottom of his long trench coat and parted the fabric to reveal the captain had worn his dress blues. He looked at Adrian and me and jerked his head toward his office. We rose to our feet and followed immediately.

"Have a seat," he said firmly, hanging up his coat. I exchanged a look with Adrian while we waited for the captain to take his seat behind his large, mahogany desk. "I drove to Cincinnati this morning since I wasn't having any success on the phone." His choice of wardrobe finally made sense. Someone who looked as powerful and commanding as he did would be hard to ignore.

"What did you learn?" I asked, hopeful it was something that would bust our case wide open.

"I learned a lot of little things, but I'm not sure yet how they all tie together, if they even do," the captain said. I could tell he didn't want to get my hopes up, but I needed something to put my mind at ease. "Let's start with the biggest piece of the puzzle, which is whatever Nate might've been tied up in that instigated this mess. Nate and his nightclub were being investigated for prostitution. I learned that CPD had undercover officers working inside the nightclub to try and bust him." Reardon pointed his finger at both of us and said, "None of this leaves my office."

"Yes, sir," we both said.

"According to my contact, CPD's sting had only been underway for a few days, maybe a week, when Nate received his first threatening email. Whatever illegal operations he might've been running in there stopped immediately. The cops were removed after a week or so of no activity. In fact, they were gone by the time he called you."

"Okay, so why did Nate think that calling the cops made things worse, as if they were involved?" I asked.

"I'm only speculating here, because Nate's not here to confirm or deny," Captain Reardon said. "My contact said that the detectives assigned to the case tried to squeeze information out of Nate. They made it known that he had been under an investigation and said they would protect him if he gave some names. CPD got the impression that Nate was taking money from someone to allow the illegal sex acts to take place in one of his back rooms. They believed that Nate was a small player in the prostitution ring syndicate. They hoped he would turn on the guy next higher up than him and that guy would do the same until they got to the top. Nate denied the allegations of prostitution and said he didn't know anything about a syndicate. A few days later, he called the detectives and requested to close his case."

"There was approximately two months between the time I met with Nate in his office and the time he was killed. Do we know if the threats were stepped up during that time? Was his home searched?" I asked.

"There's a bit of a battle between the Cincinnati Police Department and the Carter County Sheriff's Department over who should be investigating this homicide. CPD said it's their case because they said Nate was killed because of the threats that they were still investigating. CCSD said the incident happened in their jurisdiction so it was their case. CPD did search his home and business, but nothing was found. His business partner…"

"Business partner?" I asked.

"He had a silent business partner, a Mr. Marlon Bandowe. Mr. Bandowe is a member of a very conservative family and didn't want his involvement in the gay night club made public. Mr. Bandowe handed over the financial records and the business agreement between them. It turned out that the majority of the money to start the enterprise was provided by Bandowe, I'm talking a seventy-thirty split. Therefore, the profits were split by the same percentages. Nate's thirty percent was a decent chunk of money, but not enough to account for his lifestyle."

"Do they think he was skimming off the top from whoever was running illegal activities?" Adrian asked.

"He did something to bring their attention down on him and that would be my assumption," the captain said. "You see, the detectives kept investigating the threats even after he told them not to, so I don't think there was any improper conduct on their parts. CPD was able to locate the person sending the emails by tracking the IP address. Unfortunately, when they showed up at his apartment to ask questions they found him dead from a gunshot to the head." Reardon blew out a frustrated breath. "He'd been dead awhile and none of the prints pulled from his apartment led them anywhere."

"A dead end," I said softly.

"Literally and figuratively," Adrian said.

"How does any of this tie to Nate being in our county or Josh getting threatened?" I asked.

"Honestly, Gabe," the captain said hesitantly, "you're the only common denominator in the equation."

"Fuck!" I stood in the captain's office and paced. "Why the hell did Nate have to choose me and what the hell do these people think I know?"

Adrian rose out of the chair and came to me. "We'll figure this out, partner."

"Look, Gabe," the captain said, "why don't you go on home for the rest of the day. Take an extra day to rest."

I didn't want to take the time at first because going home and taking a nap wouldn't solve the case, but I felt exhaustion and stress weighing me down. I hated the thought of Josh cleaning that mess alone or dealing with the alarm installers because those were both irritations that loving me brought into his life. "You'll call me if this breaks?"

The captain assured me that he would and his word was enough for me. I smiled when I saw the vehicles parked behind Josh's house. Why did I think he would be alone after what he'd gone through the night before? In fact, the more I thought about it, I was surprised they hadn't showed up sooner.

I was happy to see that I had been locked out. I called Josh on his phone and he came down to let me in. "I came back to help you clean," I told him as we headed upstairs. "I should've known the cavalry would be here already."

When I got upstairs, I saw that Willa was there with Chaz and Meredith. They were scattered through the house, all of them dancing a bit to the music playing as they cleaned off the black dust and smears.

"You have amazing friends, Sunshine," I said, hooking my arm around his neck and pulling him close.

"I have a lot to be grateful for," Josh replied. "Namely that you get to deal with the alarm guys when they get here in the next hour. If you're a really good boy I'll bake you another pie tonight."

I put my mouth to his ear, "How good do you want me to be?" I saw the shiver work its way through his body.

"Don't be distracting me with your sexiness," Josh told me. "I do have an errand that I'd like you to run, if you're willing," he added.

"What?"

"I found the door I like on the home improvement store app. I was hoping that maybe you could order it for me and have it delivered. I don't mean pay for it," Josh said, reaching for his wallet.

"Let me do this for you. It's the least I can do." I saw the argument in his eyes and knew he wanted to argue.

"Let him buy you the damn door," Willa shouted. "Pick your

battles, baby."

"Fine," Josh said with a huff. Then a smile worked its way across his face as he dug out his keys from his pocket. "One more thing," he said, then bit his lip nervously. "Will you make a copy of these two keys?" They were the keys to both doors downstairs. "For yourself."

I knew he wasn't asking me to move in and that his suggestion was more for convenience than anything, but it made me deliriously happy. "I can do that."

TWENTY

Josh

Not that I wanted it to become a habit, but trying to kill me, bringing me in for questioning, or threatening to kill me was great for my business. I had the ladies lining up for days in the guise of buying products in the hopes of finding out the juicy details of my late-night visit from Blissville's finest–well, the police department. My late-late-night activities with Blissville's finest, my Gabe, was going to stay private.

"I'm starting to see a trend here," Meredith said one night after the salon closed. "This keeps up you might want to stock up on some extra inventory. Hell, you might even want to rent a storage unit to keep it in."

"Girl, you know it."

"Not that I want you to get threatened or hurt, it's just you might as well make a little profit out of the madness."

Some might think it was wrong of me to capitalize on the town's curiosity, but I thought they were wrong for being nosey. Besides, I wasn't the only one to make some cash off the townsfolk. I sold out of every single item that Marabeth made specifically for me. It was so exciting to call her and let her know that I sold completely out of the Jazz's Spice-N-Sass line she had created for my salon. Better yet, were the people who came in a few days after their first purchase looking to buy items in the line they passed over on their first visit. It was an arrangement that benefited both Marabeth and me very well.

The changes Gabe insisted on were a bit of a nuisance at first, but I adapted. It was doubtful I would confess just how much I liked the ornately carved door at the bottom of the staircase that led to my home though. I liked having some kind of advantage over Gabe. I thought it would make the sitting area looked closed in, but the fancy-ass door I chose looked like it had been there since the home was built. I'm not sure how Gabe did it, but the door was delivered and installed in two days, which was unheard of in my neck of the woods.

The biggest change, and also my favorite, was Gabe having a key to let himself into my house anytime he wanted. I didn't miss the reference he made to my house as "home," but I couldn't be sure if it was a slip of the tongue or he genuinely thought of my home as his. I loved when Gabe slipped me the tongue, but I wasn't sure how I felt about the latter.

As much as I loved and craved his nearness, I worried that it was too soon. Hell, I grew some giant–but never hairy-balls and told the man I was in love with him. That was a huge step for me and all that I was ready for at the moment, but I acknowledged that the time for me wanting to take the next step with him was getting nearer every day. Besides, I wanted Gabe by my side because he wanted to be there, not because he thought it was necessary. That wasn't very romantic, and I'd call anyone a liar if they accused me of it, but I was starting to get pretty sappy when it came to Gabe.

I even went so far as to put an aqua blue streak in the front of my hair to match the pair of underwear that he favored the most. Not only did he like the colored streaks I sometimes wore in my hair, but he'd be reminded of how much he liked taking those sexy little undies off of me. It was no coincidence that I was wearing the exact pair of briefs when Gabe saw the streak for the first time.

"I like it," Gabe said, running his hand through my hair. "It's the same color as those Andrew Christians I like so much."

"Really?" I unbuttoned my jeans and opened the fly to reveal the bright color I wore beneath. "Hmm. I guess you're right." My little stunt had the desired effect and we were much later getting to the diner to eat than originally planned.

I learned that as high maintenance as I was, compromising and adjusting actually came easy to me. Gabe was extremely easy to please and very cooperative, but I had to remind myself not to take advantage of his pleaser personality. Perhaps I overcompensated too much, because I drew Gabe's ire when I ordered pizza without any mushrooms.

"For fuck's sake, Josh," he exclaimed when the pizza arrived mushroomless. "I never said anything about the mushrooms to my mom because she worked hard and they were easy to pick off. There was no deeply-rooted motivation for it like she thinks. I will not lie and say that I didn't have issues with being adopted when I was a kid, but the mushrooms were not an example of me trying to avoid getting booted from the family."

"If you say so," I said complacently, just wanting to eat my pizza in peace by that time. I had to admit it sounded awfully similar to the "yes, dear" my father used on my mother in similar circumstances. Gabe was just as pissed as my mother had been.

Gabe threw his hands up in frustration. "I made you chicken Marsala and one of the key ingredients is mushrooms."

I put my pizza down on my plate and turned to face him. I was New Josh and I didn't have kneejerk reactions to things like little fights over mushrooms. I took in the pinched and tired expression on Gabe's face and realized that our little tiff had nothing to do with mushrooms.

I removed his plate from his hand then set it beside mine. "Gabe," I said, crawling on his lap. "Maybe you tell me what's really upsetting you. And don't tell me it's about the mushrooms or anything else. I know you're not really mad that I didn't put any mushrooms on the pizza." Even though I knew I was correct, I thought it might not hurt to be so obvious next time. "So, what's going on with my man today?"

I slipped my hands in his dark hair and massaged his scalp and, just like that, he melted into the couch and gave up all his secrets. "There's been no new breaks in either case and Rocky Beaumont is threatening to sue the department if Nadine finds out he's been sleeping with commissioner Wallace. I don't know why he thinks we…"

"Wait a damn minute!" I waited for Gabe to open his eyes and focus them on me. "Are you saying Rocky likes the D?"

"Um…" I could tell the wheels were spinning as he tried to come up with a way to backtrack or imply I misunderstood.

"No, nuh huh. I heard exactly what you said." I dropped my hands from his head to my waist as I sat in disbelief of what he just said. "You never told me?"

"You know I can't talk…"

"…About open cases," I interrupted again. "Wanda confessed to trying to kill Rocky so his case is closed." I still couldn't believe my Sunday school teacher was capable of murder and attempted murder. "Why didn't you tell me? I know it's not because you think he's a swell guy. You practically growl and snarl whenever you see him around town." Then it felt like a crushing blow to my heart when I realized why he hadn't told me. "You still don't trust me," I whispered softly. I moved to slide off his lap, but he grabbed my hips and held me to him.

"Not true," he argued. "I do trust you and I know damn well outing a guy–even someone as vile as Rocky–isn't something you would do. There is an open case that could involve Rocky and I should never have said anything to you."

"What case?" Then I thought about it. "Oh, you mean Georgia's house getting broken into and ransacked."

"Yes, that one. Rocky had a lot to lose if those photos ever came out. Perhaps he did hire someone to look for them while he was safely out of town. It's doubtful, but I had no business saying what I did. I won't ask you to keep it quiet because I know that you will."

"Damn straight," I replied, feeling mollified. "You better not let anyone rub your scalp around town because you sing like a damn canary," I said joking. "Hey, I know," I said with wide eyes, "maybe the police department can hire me to come in during interrogations and give head massages until the perp confesses."

I could feel Gabe's muscles tightening against my body and it was obvious he was getting jealous thinking about my hands in other men's hair. "I don't think so, Josh. I'm the only one who gets scalp massages from now on."

"My clients will have a big problem with that, babe. I'm famous for my massages." The leering grin he gave me said he was remembering the special massage I gave him in my salon. "Not that kind of massage," I clarified. "That one only belongs to you. I was referring to the massages I give while I shampoo hair."

"Well, I wouldn't want to upset the ladies…"

"And Kyle," I amended.

"Excuse me?" Gabe asked angrily.

"I cut Kyle's hair too," I told him. "Sometimes he comes in for a quick dry trim in the morning and other times he wants the shampoo and scalp massage thrown in."

"I just be he does," Gabe snapped.

"Hey," I threw up my hands, "it's not like that. There's never been a spark of anything there. Wait," I said as I realized something. "Didn't you know I cut Kyle's hair?"

"No," Gabe admitted softly. "He never said and I never asked."

I thought his lack of knowledge about his ex was kind of sad, but I wasn't going to bring it up. They were exes for a reason and I was the beneficiary of that fact. Instead, I shifted my mind onto something else that had been on my mind involving Gabe and hair.

"I don't suppose you'll let me cut your hair," I said to Gabe. His eyes widened and I quickly amended, "Trim. I meant to say trim your hair." I thought maybe he was trying to grow his hair out, but the spooked expression on his face told me there was a lot more at play. "Oh my, you have tonsurephobia."

"You watch your mouth," Gabe said, but the rapid way he blinked his eyes told me he didn't have a clue what I was talking about.

"A fear of getting haircuts," I told him.

"That's a thing?" he asked in disbelief. Or, was it relief?

"It's definitely a real thing and I think you have it," I told him. "Did you have a traumatic experience as a child?" I could tell by the way he bit his lip there was something in his past. "I promise I won't laugh at you."

"Okay," he said after long moments of searching my face for sincerity. "My mom took me for a haircut at this new place when I was like five or something. It had a carnival theme to it with bright balloons and colors everywhere, sort of like the party your mom threw for me. I was so excited because they had special chairs designed for kids." Gabe swallowed hard and I bit my lip so not to giggle because he was so damn earnest and cute. "We roll up to that joint on opening day and it was a fucking circus inside and I don't mean the place was busy, I mean it was packed with clowns." The hard shiver that worked through Gabe shocked me.

"I'd never seen a clown before then and I was overcome with this insane fear of them. I passed out cold when one of them came bouncing over in those damn big shoes and reached for me. Next thing I knew, I'm waking up in one of those kiddie barber chairs and see myself in the mirror. I don't know why, but there was a barber standing behind me with a pair of scissors in his hand. Maybe he came running over when he heard the commotion, but all I knew was that I had blood streaming down the side of my face and he and MoMo the clown were both standing behind me."

"Babe, you're coulrophobic too?" I asked sympathetically.

Gabe rolled us over suddenly and pinned me beneath him on the couch. "Are you questioning my manhood?" he asked.

That I couldn't take seriously and burst into laughter. "It means you're afraid of clowns," I told Gabe. "Hell, no wonder you're afraid of haircuts." I raised my hand and rubbed my fingers over his brows. "I promise you that I'm not at all scary and I won't make sudden moves at you with my shears." My words were spoken tenderly without a hint of humor in them because it wasn't funny. It broke my heart to imagine a terrified five or six-year-old Gabe.

"Okay."

Gabe and Buddy followed me down to the salon. Buddy was curious because he hadn't spent much time down there and I thought maybe he sensed Gabe's distress. I led Gabe to the washroom and took extra time to shampoo and massage his scalp to loosen him up. He seemed to be doing okay when he sat down in my chair. I had to admit that I liked seeing the cape with my salon logo on it wrapped around his broad shoulders. It felt a lot like I was marking my territory without pissing on his leg, which was gross and not at all my kind of thing.

"Ready, babe?" I asked.

"Yep," he said confidently.

"Coming in hot," I warned, as I raised my hand that held the shears.

I took my time and talked to Gabe the entire time to keep his mind on a friendly conversation rather than what I was doing. He talked a lot about his childhood and I noticed that none of the stories were about scary clowns, but almost all of them included the brother he idolized.

"How do you know all that stuff about phobias?" Gabe asked me at one point.

"Psych one-oh-one," I reminded him of how he teased me.

"You seriously took those classes?" he asked.

"I loved psychology and learning about what makes people tick. It would've been my minor degree."

"You were going for accounting and psychology degrees?" Gabe asked. "Were you going to council your clients when they got depressed about the taxes they owed?"

"My father was an accountant and I thought that following in his footsteps might make me more respectable, especially to men that I wanted to take me serious. The psychology was my attempt to understand why people were so cruel to one another."

The smile slid off Gabe's face when he heard my explanation, but I didn't want to see sadness or pity in his eyes. I wanted to see laughter and happiness in them so I bent over his upturned face and kissed him softly until the moment passed. When I pulled back, I was happy to see his love for me twinkling in his dark eyes.

After I finished his haircut, I shaved the back of his neck and dusted it with powder. "I don't suppose you'd let me shave your face, would you?" I asked.

He looked up at me with such trust in his eyes and said, "I'd almost let you shave my balls, Sunshine."

"Almost?" I asked but laughed hysterically. That wasn't a

privilege a man gave lightly, if at all. I was madly in love with Gabe, but I wouldn't let him near my boys with a razor. I left him in my chair so I could get the shaving supplies that I hardly ever got to use.

I gently placed a warm, hot towel on Gabe's face so it would open his pores. I could tell by the happy humming that came from his throat that he was enjoying it. Once I had the shaving cream lathered up, I removed the towel, and spread it on his face. I was so proud of myself for not cracking jokes about my cream all over his face, although I was certain I would bring it up at some point.

I had been trained in the art of straight razor shaving, but I hadn't done it many years, so I used a standard razor on Gabe's handsome face. It was something I would love to do for him in the future though. *Look at that.* I thought of Gabe and the word "future" in the same sentence and didn't freak out. I took my time and gave him a close shave, loving that I would feel the softness of his face against mine once we got upstairs.

Gabe rose from his chair when I was finished and pulled me into his arms. "Thank you, Sunshine. I love my haircut and shave."

"That'll be forty-five dollars," I told him.

His eyes widened and he said, "Uh oh, I forgot my wallet. Can I work it off somehow?"

"Absolutely." I turned and put an extra sway in my hips as I made my way to the door that led upstairs. "There's dishes you can do." I started to run when I heard him coming after me, but I didn't run too fast or too far. Sometimes it was so much better to be caught than to keep running.

TWENTY-ONE

Gabe

Josh never failed to surprise me and, luckily for me, ninety-nine percent of them were great ones. I honestly expected him to laugh at my issues with haircuts and clowns. I didn't expect him to know the names of the phobias or help me through them—well the hair one, anyway. It'd take a hell of a lot more than a hot body and some sweet kisses to get me over the clown one.

Having him wash my hair felt almost as good as a full body massage. I felt the tension wash down the drain along with the shampoo he rinsed from my hair. His fingers felt like magic and I could see why there was never an open slot in his appointment book. He made me forget about the cases and my fears and helped me to just enjoy the moment. He truly was, and I hoped would always be, my Sunshine.

I so badly wanted to find out who was making threats against Josh and why. There was no clear connection to any of it. Sure, Nate had called me one time, but it wasn't like we'd been meeting on a regular basis or that he told me anything of importance. There was no need to threaten me. Unless they thought I knew more than I did because Nate told them so. To what end? Buy him more time, but to do what? He didn't escape; he ended up dead in my county. I felt like the idea had merit, but I wasn't sure what to do with it.

"I imagine the CPD has scrubbed his computer clean and the sheriff may or may not have obtained copies," Adrian said when I mentioned it the following morning while we made ourselves coffee. "Nice haircut, by the way. You get that at the Clip-N-Save?"

"Is that a real place, Adrian? It sounds a lot like a coupon cutting group instead of a barber," I told him skeptically. I pretended to hand him a coupon. "Here's a fifty cents off peanut butter. Do you have any for toothpaste?"

"You're going to need one for boot retrieval out of your smart ass," Adrian countered. He fought to keep the smile off his face, but lost. "You're sounding an awful lot like your boyfriend these days."

"And that's a good thing," I replied because it was true.

"You're quoting Martha Stewart now?" Adrian asked.

"What's a straight guy like you know about Martha Stewart?" Teasing Adrian was one of my favorite parts of the job, and although I harassed him long before I met Josh, the barbs had gotten sharper.

"The kind who has a wife who adores the woman. Hey," Adrian said, puffing up his chest, "I'm a modern man. I'm in touch with my feelings, I'll watch cooking shows with my wife, and I'm not afraid to cry."

"Cry later," said a firm voice behind us. Adrian and I spun around to face our captain. His expression was moderately softer than his tone of voice. "I need you two in my office. Now." We set our cups down and followed behind him without another word. We could make a fresh cup later, but whatever the captain had to say couldn't wait.

"I don't ever discuss my personal life here at the office and I don't believe this is news to either of you," Captain Reardon said. I thought he was chastising us for our little chat at the coffee pot, but his next words erased that. "I'm not fond of my father-in-law and I don't believe it's news to anyone around here either." It was news to me just a few weeks ago, but I kept my mouth shut. "He's not been very forthcoming about anything his department has discovered in the Nate Turner homicide investigation. Well, I got a call just now and he's changed his mind. You see, my wife and daughter–his daughter and granddaughter–are very fond of Mr. Roman and they don't like the idea that he's being threatened, and Big Papa," the captain rolled his eyes on that one, "could be hindering our part in keeping Josh safe."

Relief flooded through my system. "He's going to work with us?" I asked hopefully.

"He wants to see us in his office at noon." I could tell the time and location didn't sit well with the captain, but the sheriff had us by the balls and he knew it. He wasn't required to share details of an ongoing case with us so I was grateful for anything.

"Be ready to leave at quarter till noon. I'm not about to get there early and then sit forever in his lobby while he holds his power trip over my head. It's not going to happen."

"We'll be ready to go, sir." I rose to my feet and Adrian did the same. We thought it was best to let the captain work through whatever he was feeling in private.

"Gabe," he called out from behind his desk.

"Yes, sir?"

"Martha Stewart belongs to everyone," he admonished.

"Yes, sir."

We hadn't been in Captain Reardon's office for very long so our coffee was salvageable. I took a big swig and nearly spit it out. "Who the fuck put salt in my coffee?" No one looked up from their desk to confess or rat out anyone else.

"Paybacks," I called out as I poured the remaining coffee in the sink then made a fresh cup.

"Thanks for saving me, partner," Adrian said as he did the same.

I had just sat down at my desk when the phone rang. "Detective Wyatt," I said into the phone.

"Detective, this is Myrna Evans calling. I'm the editor-in-chief with the Blissville Daily News and I'm calling about a disturbing package that was dropped off through our mail receptacle." I sat up straighter in my chair. "It's a photo taken of you and Mr. Roman in his shop and the message reads: 'The police didn't take me serious, but maybe you will. Josh Roman is going to die.' Now, I'm not sure what's going on…"

I cut her off before she could finish. "I'm coming over," I said then hung up. I picked up my coat and Adrian did the same without question. I was sure the alarm he heard in my voice told him enough. "I tried to end things with him so that whoever this is would back off," I told my partner once we were in the car. "If something happens to Josh…"

"Nothing will happen to Josh," Adrian said. He took a long breath and said, "Look, something isn't right here. There's something different about the M.O. on this one, partner. If the person thought you were involved they'd be threatening you, not Josh. Nate didn't mention anyone he cared about getting threatened to you nor does it appear he did to the CPD. That's not the only thing that bothers me," Adrian said.

"What else, buddy? I'm grasping at straws here."

"Okay, I don't mean this to sound as bad as it's going to, but here goes. If this person was really intent on hurting Josh, then they would've done it by now. Instead they issued a warning, then a second warning, and now a third warning? Come on. It's like those movie villains who never stop talking." Adrian deepened his voice into his best villain voice and said, "I'm going to kill you, but not until I tell you everything I did wrong from the third grade until now. In fact, chances are you might die of boredom before I pull the trigger."

As tense as the situation was, I couldn't help but laugh at Adrian and acknowledge the truth in his words. Being objective when it came to Josh's safety, was the hardest thing I'd ever tried to do. I realized that breaking up with him wasn't the answer, but I wondered if he'd let me put him on a plane and send him to his parents.

We showed our badges to the receptionist and she directed us where to go. Myrna Evans' office was similar to something you'd see on TV. The wall between her office and the reporters' cubicles was made of glass so she could keep an eye on them.

I knocked on her glass door and she waved us in then rose to her feet. "Detectives," she said, greeting us. She gestured to the items she mentioned on the phone that were on her desk. Sure enough, there was a picture taken from the night before in Josh's salon. It was of the kiss we shared after Josh had confessed why he'd chosen the majors he had. His words gutted me, but the love and passion in his kiss stitched me back together. At first, I could only stare at how beautiful and happy we looked. We were opposites in our builds, our coloring, and even our personalities, but we meshed. *Dear Lord, did we mesh beautifully.* Buddy was curled up at my feet to protect me in case Josh tried to cut my hair in a cut that didn't flatter me, or so Josh had said.

"You should frame that one and hang it up," Adrian said beside me.

"It's a lovely picture," Myrna agreed, "but the message that came with it isn't."

"Off the record?" Adrian asked. She nodded and he said, "We are taking this very seriously."

"I'd hate to see anything happen to him," she said. I expected her to say something like she didn't want to find a new hair stylist, but instead she said, "He worked here during high school and he was such a delight to be around." I was glad to know that people saw Josh as more than someone who styled their hair.

"He is that," I agreed. Adrian and I slid latex gloves on then placed the photo, message, and the envelope in an evidence bag. "We'll need you to come down to the station to be fingerprinted," I told Myrna, "so we can determine if there are any prints besides yours on these items." Myrna agreed to stop by the station on her lunch hour.

"Partner, this seems personal; like someone doesn't want you with Josh," Adrian said as we left the newspaper office.

Billy Sampson's face came to mind and I couldn't discount the fact that he was appearing at places that either Josh by himself or the both of us were. Josh was adamant that he left the grocery store without the diapers he said he was buying and I had a hard time believing that he was retrieving things from a storage unit at the exact same time that Josh and I went to see Charlotte. There was too much coincidence for my liking.

"I'm going to call the newspapers in Cincinnati to see if any of them received threats about Nate's life," I told Adrian. I silently made a note to call the office manager of the storage unit and find out if Billy did own a unit there or he followed us. I could pretend to be him and ask when my next bill was due and see if I got a response.

The captain was waiting for us when we got back to the station, coat on and ready to go. He surprised both Adrian and me by getting in the back seat of my car. Adrian shrugged and rode up front with me out to the sheriff's department. Once we arrived, the captain's countenance changed completely. He'd always been very professional, but he looked like a total hard ass when we walked in.

"I'm here to see Sheriff Tucker," he announced crisply to the desk sergeant. Hell, I was ready to salute him.

"He's been expecting you," she said politely. "I'm sure you know the way." I heard a buzzing, followed by the sound of the door unlocking.

The captain pushed the door open and we followed behind him like little chicks to the back of the department. Before we reached the sheriff's door, it flew open and the somewhat jovial guy I had met weeks ago was replaced by a brittle, angry man. Wow! These two had serious family issues.

"You're late," Sheriff Tucker declared.

"We're right on time, sir," Captain Reardon replied. The growled emphasis on the word "sir" made it obvious that he wasn't feeling the respect the word implied.

"If you're not fifteen minutes early then you're late. That was something my daughter knew before you came along," the older man snarled. I figured his daughter's supposed tardiness might have more to do with being a busy working mom, but I wasn't going to open my mouth.

"We're here to talk about what you know, if anything, about Nate Turner's homicide and how it might relate to the threats being made against Josh Roman," Captain said. I liked his no-nonsense attitude because I wasn't in the mood for their pissing contest.

I heard a loud ruckus and shouting in the main room and opened the door to look out. I was a cop; it was automatic to look into situations involving angry voices. I saw Billy Sampson dressed in street clothes heading to the front door with a cardboard box in his arms.

"Fuck you all," he yelled as he left the station.

"What's that all about with Deputy Sampson?" I asked the sheriff, careful to keep the disdain from my voice.

"Former deputy," he corrected. "He'd been acting erratic lately, missing work, and being belligerent. I suspected drug usage, but I didn't know for sure until his random drug test came back positive."

I nearly snorted out loud. Random drug test, my ass.

"What kind of drugs?" I asked.

"He tested positive for quite a few of them," the sheriff said. "We offered to put him on leave until he completed a rehab program, but he refused. He denied he'd had the drugs in his system and said we were trying to railroad him out of the department, but couldn't say why we would want to do that." He shook his head. "It's really sad."

"Sir," I said kindly, "we have an evidence locker full of drugs that were found in the school system where his mother works. I think that's a tad too coincidental. Perhaps we'll find that these drugs came from the same batches if we test our drugs against the ones in his system."

Sheriff Tucker thought about it for a long time before he said, "Okay, we can do that."

"Now what about the Turner case?" Adrian asked.

"Well, boys, I'd like to be able to tell you that we had something to go on, but we really don't," Tucker said. I noticed that we got more out of him than snarled responses if Adrian or I asked a question, rather than the captain. "No fingerprints other than Nate's were in the car, we sent a sample of the paint transfer left on the bumper from where the other car struck his to the state lab in Columbus for analysis, but nothing has come back yet. The CPD didn't have any leads for us. I hate to say it, but unless something breaks loose for us, Nate Turner might end up as a cold case."

As the brother of someone whose killer was never brought to justice, that didn't sit well with me. We thanked him for the information and he promised to email a copy of Billy's drug test results to us so we could compare. None of us wanted to think an officer of the law was involved in a drug ring, but we couldn't rule anyone or anything out.

"Sir, can I ask you a personal question?" Adrian asked once we returned to my car.

I glanced up in the rearview mirror and saw the captain sneer, but he groused, "Yes."

"What the hell did you ever do to make the sheriff dislike you so damn much?" Adrian asked.

It took the captain a few seconds to acknowledge the question, but then he said, "I went to the University of Michigan."

I recalled seeing Sheriff Tucker's large Ohio State University diploma hanging on the wall and smiled. "Ahhh, that explains it," I said.

TWENTY-TWO

Josh

I admit I was a bit freaked when Gabe told me that my nemesis had sent a photo of Gabe and me to the paper with a threatening message. I mean, I didn't want shitty pictures of me being sent to the paper. I had an image to uphold in my town. Then Gabe told me what a good picture it was of us and I went from being alarmed to wanting a copy for us. Gabe promised I could have it once it was no longer evidence. I planned to frame the photo and set it at my station for everyone to see. I could tell he was frustrated with me and my lack of concern for my safety, so it was quite refreshing to hear that Adrian was thinking along the same lines as I was.

I took the threat seriously, at first. Hell, whoever it was trashed my pretty Princess and it pissed me off. Other than that, it had been photos and a few vague threats. If someone really wanted to hurt me, like Oscar Davidson did when he realized I'd given a description of him to the police, they wouldn't send one warning after the other. Oscar gave me no warnings; he broke into my home and would've killed me had Gabe not shot him. I applied the same logic to the new disturbance in my once orderly life and found comfort.

I still shivered hard every time I thought about Oscar Davidson, which became less frequently as time passed by. He wasn't coming back from the grave to kill me and whoever was sending these so-called threats didn't really want to kill me either. I don't know why I was so certain, I just was. Also, as sure was my belief that Billy Sampson was behind it all. The timing was just to convenient for me.

It wasn't arrogance on my part that Billy was jealous of Gabe and me or that he wanted me all to himself that was guiding my beliefs, it was just my vast experience with bullies–namely him. First, it was my theory that Billy would fall into his old habits–not that I believe he'd outgrown them–once he returned to Carter County. Second, seeing me happy would piss him off. I lived my life happily in the open while he pretended to be something he wasn't. That had to really pinch his pecker. Throw in the fact that he was using drugs and you had an unappetizing recipe for harassment.

I could tell that Gabe was starting to come around and think like Adrian and me. It didn't make him feel better because he felt the drug usage made Billy even more unstable. He was holding out hope that the drugs in Billy's system matched the ones found at the school so that he could be brought in and questioned. According to Gabe, it could be weeks before he got the results back because nothing happened quickly for small town law enforcement agencies when they had to rely on overburdened and underfunded state labs. He reminded me that real police work didn't look anything like the CSI shows I had loved so much.

The only thing I could do was be more aware of my surroundings. The weather had been too cold and the sidewalks too slick to run outside and I'd been forced to run on a treadmill at the gym. March was right around the corner and, even though it was a tossup month–meaning all four seasons could occur in one day–it was a big step in the right direction to getting back out in the fresh air to run. I would, however, miss hearing the grunts that escaped Gabe when he lifted weights.

Just knowing he was hot and sweaty in the same room as me made it hard to keep my focus on my pace and breathing when I used one of those preset options on the treadmill. Fuck, it had me running on an incline so steep that I looked like that cliffhanger game on The Price is Right. The last thing I needed was the annoying-ass music they played during that game in my head, but it's what I got. Instead of going over the edge of the cliff like the mountain climber in the game does when a contestant can't guess the price of the items correctly, I was in jeopardy of face planting on the treadmill in a crowded gym. I made a mental note to bring earbuds to the gym with me the next time so I could tune out Detective Sex Sounds, focus on my running, and avoid getting an inconvenient hard-on.

I never ran with earbuds in my ears. Once, I came out to my parents–as if they hadn't already known–my father took me aside and had a very serious conversation with me. He told me that, although moms and dads all worried endlessly about their children, parents of minorities had added concerns. He explained that some people would hate me just because I existed. That may seem like a horrible thing for a father to tell his son, but his exact words to me were, "I can't allow my boy to become a heartbreaking statistic. If something happened to you, it would kill your mother and me. Pay attention." By then, I'd already experienced plenty of hateful things said about me and to me, so I knew what he was talking about, yet, I had never been physically hurt in any way. It took me years to understand that verbal abuse was equally as damaging, if not more, than physical abuse.

I took my dad's words to heart that day. Some people might've had the impression that I was a flighty person without a care in the world, but that was the furthest thing from the truth. I was usually hyper aware of my surroundings and had developed a Danger, Will Robinson radar. It was going crazy one night when I took the trash out after the salon closed. Gabe normally insisted on doing it, but he was on the phone with his mom and I wanted to get it over with so I could go upstairs and enjoy the rest of my night.

I wasn't scared when I felt Billy's presence because I knew that Gabe was a loud scream away. Even so, I wanted to deal with Billy on my own once and for all. The motion detector lights that Gabe installed on the corners of the garage came on as I was putting a lid on the trash can. My heart sped up, but my mind remained calm.

"He must not really give a shit about you," Billy snarled from behind me. "Either that or you're really fucking stupid. I think it's a little bit of both. Someone's threatening to harm you, yet, here you are in the dark all by yourself."

I slowly turned around and faced Billy. I was shocked at how sick he looked. There were large bags under his eyes, his pupils were blown, and he shook all over like he couldn't wait for his next fix. "Let me guess, you were just in the neighborhood?" I asked sarcastically. We both knew better.

"You might say that," he told me. The sneering smile slipped from his face and all I saw was unbridled rage. "I never knew you were such an exhibitionist, Josh. Do you like leaving your bedroom curtain open for people in the neighborhood to watch you and your detective having sex? Is that part of your gay agenda?"

There was so much wrong with what he had said that I wasn't

sure what to address first. I decided to take them in order so that I didn't miss anything. "I've never been an exhibitionist and the only home on this block with a view into my bedroom window has been vacant for months." I cocked my head to the side and added, "That means your perverted ass has taken advantage of the situation. You've been watching me and Gabe through my window just like you've been following me around and leaving those stupid photos behind as a warning. The newspaper stunt was over the top, Billy."

I won't lie, it made me sick to my stomach to realize that someone so twisted saw something that was so beautiful and pure with love. I needed to move on or risk not finishing what I had to say about his hateful comments, although I figured it was like talking to a brick wall.

"And, wanting to be treated equally and accepted as who I am isn't an agenda, Billy. I love Gabe and he loves me. We just want to live peacefully and be able to enjoy the same things that straight couples do."

"You're disgusting and I hate you," Billy snarled, taking two steps closer to me.

"Oh, I don't think you hate me at all. I think you hate yourself. It's too bad that you hide behind lies and drugs. Besides, if you hated me so much then you wouldn't be trying to break Gabe and me up with your stupid Nate Turner copycat shit. No one is falling for that stunt; we were just waiting for you to fuck up and tip your hand. Sort of like right now."

"Shut up," Billy said between gritted teeth. "You don't know anything about me."

"Oh, I know plenty. I hate to break this to you, but you're not that special or unique. You're no different than any other guy who's ashamed of who he is and who he loves." I'd been accused of not knowing when to shut my mouth once I started slinging snark everywhere and that could probably be classified as one of those times.

"I said shut the fuck up." That time Billy screamed the words.

I knew it was loud enough to get Gabe's attention, but I couldn't be distracted by that. I saw in his eyes that he was ready to act on his aggression and I was ready for him.

Billy took a step toward me while he reached for me. I brought my knee up and racked his balls hard enough to send them bouncing off his internal organs like a pinball game. "Fuck!" he roared. When he doubled over to grab his nuts, I brought my knee up to his nose. I heard the sickening crunch of cartilage breaking, followed by the gush of his hot blood all over the knee of my pants before I was able to pull back.

Billy fell to the ground howling and writhing in pain, unsure where to grab–his aching nuts or his gushing nose. Gabe came running out of the house with his gun drawn, but holstered it immediately when he saw that Billy was prone on the ground. He reached for his next best weapon instead, his cellphone. "I need a car sent to Josh's house," he told the dispatcher. "One car," he clarified, "and probably an EMT."

Luckily, only one squad car and one ambulance responded like Gabe requested. The EMTs stayed long enough to staunch the flow of blood from Billy's nose then he was hauled away in the back of a squad car, crying and snotting about the pain he was in. I had zero sympathies for him.

"Remember how Laura told me that Billy had disappeared for a few days?" I asked Gabe, after we were alone again in the warmth of my home.

"Yeah," Gabe replied, looking me over. "Get these jeans off," he said rather forcefully.

"I'm not really in the mood right now," I replied sardonically.

"Josh, you have his blood all over you," Gabe said.

In all the excitement, I had forgotten that he bled on me. I followed Gabe to the bathroom and peeled my clothes off before stepping inside the shower.

"Can we get back to the bombshell Billy dropped before I

kicked his ass?" I asked Gabe.

"His nuts," Gabe corrected absently as he began washing me. It was obvious that Gabe was focused on fussing over me and I wasn't about to refuse his soapy hands on my body.

"I still knocked him on his ass," I argued.

"True."

The hot water and Gabe's hands melted the last bit of tension that remained in my body. I knew that a heavy exhaustion would follow when the adrenaline from Billy's failed assault faded. I needed to tell Gabe what I learned before I fell asleep because I didn't want him to be caught by surprise if it came out later when Billy was being questioned.

"Billy's been watching us," I told him.

"I'm glad you were right about him being the one behind the pictures. As disturbing at it was, he's not nearly as dangerous as whoever killed Nate. They weren't playing around," Gabe said.

"It's worse than you realize, Gabe. He's been squatting at Bianca's and watching us through my bedroom window. He…"

"That son of a bitch," Gabe growled. He balled his fists at his side and his chest bellowed as he breathed hard with fury. I wasn't worried that he would hurt me, but I thought my carefully chosen bathroom tiles were in jeopardy of getting punched.

I covered his fists with my hands in an attempt to calm him and save my tiled wall. "It's my fault," I told Gabe. "If I hadn't been so enthralled in seeing the light from the full moon on your skin…"

"Stop," Gabe said, shaking his head. I wasn't sure what he wanted me to stop until he spoke again. "You're not to blame for any of this," he said, cupping my face. "You're not the only one who was seduced by the light and shadows the moon brings out in your room. He was the wrong one, not us."

Gabe kissed me fiercely in the shower and made me forget all about Billy and his hate. We turned off the shower, toweled off, and made love in the moonlight once more. I held tight to Gabe's body as he moved inside me, loving every expression that crossed his face and word of devotion that left his lips. What we shared was the greatest of gifts a person could ever receive in life.

Later, a thought occurred to me as I laid my head on his chest and listened to the comforting sounds of his steady heartbeat. "Gabe?"

"Yeah, Sunshine."

"In the past few weeks, you've referred to this place as your home, but tonight you called it my house. Which is it?" I bit my lip in the dark while waiting for him to answer the question. I don't know why it mattered so much or why I needed an answer in order to fully rest, but I did.

"One represents the reality of our situation and the other represents the future I wish to have." Both the timbre in his voice and the meaning of his words caused me to wiggle with joy against him. "You better settle down there before you wake my dick back up," Gabe warned. "You're going to need a good night of sleep for the day you'll have tomorrow."

I thought about it for several seconds, but that's all my mind needed to conjure up a billion things. I didn't miss a birthday, anniversary, and I knew for a fact we didn't have dinner plans because it was one of my late nights at the salon. "What's tomorrow?"

"Babe, the cops *and* an ambulance were here tonight. It's going to be wall-to-wall with people in your salon tomorrow."

TWENTY-THREE

Gabe

Relief didn't begin to describe the emotion I felt when I found Billy crumpled on the ground from the beat down Josh gave him. I felt even better when I learned from Josh that Billy basically admitted in a roundabout way that he was the one behind the pictures. He didn't come right out and say it, but he didn't deny it when Josh confronted him either. All of that faded when Josh told me about Billy squatting in Bianca's house and watching us through his bedroom window. Josh had tried to blow it off like it didn't bother him, but I knew better. Billy was a hurtful reminder of his past and someone he wouldn't want to spoil something that we cherished together.

Damn that Billy! I fucking hated that he saw Josh in a light that I was positive others had never seen, especially not him. With me, Josh was free to be himself without fear of judgment or scorn. With me, Josh let down his guard and showed me everything he felt. With me, he wasn't afraid to be vulnerable. He radiated lightness that threatened to outshine the moonlight he loved so much. Those things were for my eyes only, and Billy Sampson violated that. For that reason alone, I was glad Josh kneed him in the balls. From the sounds that came out of Billy, he would need to have them surgically reset.

For obvious reasons, I knew I wouldn't be involved when Billy was being questioned or during the search of Bianca's house for evidence he might've left behind there. I was fine with that for a few reasons. One, I wasn't going to give his lawyer a legitimate defense or a jury a reason to toss out the charges against him due to my relationship to the victim. It was a line cops should never cross, but it was harder than people realized to take a step back and let others take the lead when it involved someone you loved. Two, I trusted my team, which made being relegated to watch the interview through the monitors under supervision tolerable.

Captain Reardon gave up his chance to play bad cop, which I secretly thought he enjoyed a lot, to keep an eye on me so that I didn't fuck up the investigation. Not only was Billy a suspect in Josh's harassment, but he used police evidence to do so when he put that picture of a dead Nate Turner in that envelope and placed it on Josh's bed.

Adrian took the lead and Officer Wen played the role of bad cop in my absence. I couldn't help but gloat when he limped into the interview room. Billy was brought in, looking more haggard than a college co-ed coming off a weekend bender. Both of his eyes were black and his nose was swollen from where Josh broke it. He was covered in a sheen of sweat and grime that made my nose twitch. "I hope they let him brush his teeth before he was brought in." I was taking a page from Josh's playbook and cracking jokes to cover my nerves. The guys had just returned from executing the search warrant and I was curious to know what they discovered in Bianca's house.

"Not likely," the captain replied. "See, it's not so bad being on this side of the monitor sometimes."

"Billy, I know you've been read your rights, but I'm going to read them to you again." I listened to Adrian read them off to Billy and then sat a little closer when Billy waved off his rights to an attorney. "You're being arrested for the stalking and harassment of Joshua James Roman, breaking and entering at the residence located at two twenty-five Elm Street." Adrian took a pause and looked down at his notes. "You're also being arrested for tampering with evidence and impeding an investigation. The DEA will be here later this afternoon to formerly charge you with possession of drugs with intent to distribute, and suspicion of drug trafficking. Are you sure you don't want a lawyer present?"

"Holy fuck!" I said in disbelief. I looked over at the captain.

"That's fucking bullshit," Billy roared. He tried to pull free from his bonds, but he didn't get very far. His hand and ankle cuffs were connected to a chain that was anchored in concrete. "What drugs?"

"The huge stash of drugs we found with your personal belongings in the house on Elm Street," Officer Wen said. "Forget about the drugs for now because the DEA will be asking about them. We want to question you about your harassment of Josh Roman and find out what you know about Nate Turner's death."

"What?" Billy honestly sounded shocked.

"We're not playing around here, Billy." Okay, Adrian was playing bad cop too. "You were the person who discovered Nate's disabled car along the side of the highway. We just want to make sure you weren't the one who put a bullet in his head."

"I didn't kill anyone," Billy said with his hands up, it seemed as if all the fight had drained from him.

"So we're not going to find the gun that killed Nate Turner in your truck, home, or storage unit?" Wen asked.

"No," Billy said.

"Do you admit to stalking and harassing Josh Roman?" Wen asked.

"I do, but not for the reasons *he* thinks," Billy said defensively. "I only did it to cast doubt about Detective Wyatt's character once I learned about his history with the dead guy. I hate that dickhead." The feeling was mutual.

There was no way that Billy would admit to being obsessed with Josh, but I knew differently. I might've bought the smoke and mirrors thing if he hadn't taken up residence in the empty house across from Josh so he could watch us having sex. I saw the possessive gleam in his eye the time I found him standing in Josh's kitchenette. I suspected the investigators knew the truth but chose not to call him on it. He'd be more likely to cooperate because of that decision.

"So, for my benefit, I want to recap what you've said to us this morning and you tell me if I misunderstood you," Adrian said. "The Feds will be here soon so I want to wrap up things on my end before they take you away."

"They weren't my drugs," Billy said defensively. The panic he must've felt was making his voice rise in pitch. "I know fucking well this is some kind of conspiracy. There's no fucking way I tested positive for drugs on my *random* drug test and I never had any drugs in my possession while I was at the house on Elm Street. Those drugs were planted there *after* I was arrested. Someone is making me the fall guy for their drug business." He might've been more convincing had his body not betrayed the obvious signs of withdrawal.

"You'll need to tell that to the Feds," Wen told Billy.

"Billy, I need you to focus on what I'm asking," Adrian told him. "Did you begin harassing and stalking Josh Roman to put attention on Detective Wyatt's connection to Nate Turner, and did you make it look like it was the same person who stalked, and later killed, Nate Turner?"

"Yes."

"Those are all the questions we have for you at this time," Detective Wen said. He motioned for the guards to come get him and take him back to his holding cell.

"What's with situation with the DEA?" I asked the captain when the interview was over.

"The drugs found on Elm Street and the ones found in the school were packaged in the exact same way. I am positive once the Feds run tests that they'll confirm they're from the same batch," Captain Reardon said.

"Do you think it's at all possible that Billy and Nate were trafficking the drugs together and it had something to do with Nate's death? Is Billy Nate's killer?"

"The only thing we can do is talk to the CPD and find out what they know, if anything, about drugs being trafficked through Nate's club. If the guy was into prostitution to make extra cash, then I don't think drug running is too farfetched. The two often go hand in hand. The more we know about Nate the more it will help us find his killer," Captain Reardon replied.

"I realize that Nate's club was on the river, which would be appealing for trafficking, but there's something this county has that makes it even more enticing," I said. "Think about how many major interstates and highways run near here. I need to dig deeper into Billy's past to know what he's been up to before he returned to Blissville."

"You can't be involved in that investigation," the captain reminded me. "I've already talked to the sheriff and we're going to pool resources and form a task force between us and CPD to solve Nate's homicide. There's nothing that truly ties Nate to the drugs. We're going to go with the assumption that the two incidents are separate. So, you're going to lead our task force unless we do find a connection to Sampson. I'm going to let the DEA handle the investigation regarding the drugs found in Billy's possession and the school locker. They have resources that we don't have. Billy can scream that they aren't his drugs all he wants, but all the DEA is going to see his connection to a woman who has access to the school."

"Yes, sir." Captain Reardon rose to his feet, but before he could leave I asked, "Can I ask you something, sir?"

"Yes, Gabe."

"For my own sanity and assurance, can I see the evidence that was collected from Bianca's home on Elm Street?"

The captain thought about it for a minute and then nodded. "You can see pictures of the evidence," he amended.

It twisted my guts to see how obsessed Billy really was with Josh. There were two dozen photos taken of him, but luckily none of them were the two of us having sex. It was doubtful Billy wanted a photographic reminder of just how far Josh had moved on. In the solo pictures of Josh, he could convince himself that he was just waiting for them to resume whatever fucked-up relationship they'd had in the past. It was also pretty obvious to the cops who did the search that Billy's claim about just using the situation to his advantage was a lie because mixed with the photos of Josh on the bare mattress was an open bottle of lubricant.

It was a good thing the captain hadn't let me see those photos before the Feds took Billy away because I wasn't sure the rage I felt would've been quieted by my sense of right and wrong. I seethed at my desk for hours, ignoring everyone around me as I wandered how far Billy would've escalated his obsession of Josh. What had he planned to do the previous night when Josh was outside alone?

I made myself physically sick as I turned the same thoughts and questions over in my mind.

Yet, something in the back of my mind nagged me when I looked at the photos, but I was too damn angry to focus. Then it hit me. There was a silver pair of scissors in the photos of evidence that were similar to the pair that Josh had given Georgia when she'd replaced his old pair with a pair of blue ones when he opened the new location of his salon.

Back when Georgia was killed, I assumed that stylists only had one pair of scissors they used, but I knew better after the recent haircut Josh gave me. Josh had a black leather case that unwrapped to reveal several sets of shiny blue scissors in various sizes, each of them with Jazz engraved on them.

"Adrian," I said suddenly and loud enough to startle him.

"Yeah?" he asked, clutching his chest.

"Come look at this," I told him.

Adrian came around to my desk and looked at the picture. I pointed to the scissors and said, "I can't tell from this picture, but do those look engraved to you?"

He squinted then replied, "They sure do."

I picked up my desk phone and dialed the salon because I knew Josh wouldn't answer his cellphone if he was in the middle of a color, cut, or style. "Hi, Chaz, it's Gabe." He was happy to hear from me and wanted to chat but quickly realized, by the tone of my voice when I asked for Josh, that I was all business.

"Hey, babe," Josh said into the phone. "What's wrong?"

"How many pairs of scissors did you give Georgia when she gave you the blue set?" I asked, getting straight to business.

"Two," he replied slowly, as if confused why I would ask. "The set she gave me was several steps up from my old ones."

"That's what I thought. Thank you, Sunshine." I hung up the phone without saying goodbye and looked at Adrian. "I think we know who ransacked Georgia's mansion." It looked like Billy helped himself to a little souvenir in the process. "Now we just need to figure out why."

Unfortunately, the only person who knew the truth had left with the DEA hours before and I worried that we'd never get another shot at talking to him.

TWENTY-FOUR

Josh

I LOOKED AT MY CORDLESS SALON PHONE IN DISBELIEF WHEN I heard a click followed by a dial tone. How dare he call me up, get me excited with the sound of his voice, call me by my special name, and then hang up without a goodbye? I wasn't having any part of that rudeness and my mind began spinning a plan that would make him think twice before he hung up on me again. Hmmm… sexy music, my sexy beast handcuffed to a chair, and a seductive torture he'd never ever forget. Oh, the possibilities were endless.

I handed the phone to Chaz who raised a brow that I could only answer with a shrug because I had no idea what was going on, but he could bet his ass that I would find out. My ears picked up bits and pieces of the conversation going on between the four clients in the salon. I stopped what I was doing and stared in shock at what I heard.

"It's more about the texture for me more than the actual taste," Esther said sitting in Meredith's chair.

"Yes, Esther," Jessica said from Marci's chair, "not to mention how thick it is no matter how much I whip it before I put it in my mouth."

"I know! I swear, I gag on the thickness of it sometimes," Missy said from Heather's chair.

"I hate it when it's chunky," Alice said with a shudder from my chair.

Meredith looked up from straightening Esther's hair and laughed when she saw my expression. "They're talking about Greek yogurt, baby."

"Oh," I said in relief, "I thought you all were talking about cum."

Seven sets of eyes widened in shock, make that eight because I couldn't believe I said that out loud. I blamed Gabe for forgetting my filter and decided to add time to his torture before I let him come later that night. In the meantime, I had an apology to make for my crude words, "Ladies, I apologize..."

They all burst into laughter, some of them so hard they had to wipe their eyes. "Sweetheart, we hear the way your bird talks. We know he got it somewhere," Alice said when I resumed my position at the back of her chair so I could continue cutting her hair.

"Don't you blame me for that bird," I told them. "He was like that when I got him. Hell, he makes *me* blush."

"Dirty Bird! Dirty Bird!" It was like he knew the exact time to chime in.

"See," I said to my clients. "He's confessing to corrupting me, not the other way around."

I could tell they weren't convinced, but that was fine by me. I was just happy I didn't offend anyone with my bawdy talk about cum. I felt the little hum of anticipation throughout my body as I silently strategized exactly what I was going to do to Gabe. In fact, by the time it came time to put my plan into action, I felt like I was the one who'd been tortured all day. I feared that I'd embarrass myself by coming too soon. I went up to my attic studio and set everything up and waited for my man to come home.

"Sunshine, where are you?" I heard Gabe call when he got home.

"Up here," I called out. "Lose some layers before you come up."

"Alright," I heard Gabe say excitedly. "And here I thought I would be in trouble for hanging up so abruptly." Yeah, I couldn't keep the smile off my face as I heard him charging up the steps. He skidded to a halt when he saw me standing there in the beam of light I had aimed at the pole. The jock strap I had chosen was black mesh and the way his mouth popped open said he liked what he saw. I raised my arm so he could get a good look at the handcuffs I held in my hand. "Oh damn," he whispered huskily, "I might not survive this night."

"Have a seat," I said pointing to the chair.

Gabe did as he was instructed then I walked behind him to secure his hands with the flimsy cuffs I'd received as a party favor or some shit. I walked around to stand in front of him and I felt his eyes all over my body as surely as if he touched me with his hands. Heat and desire radiated off him and we hadn't even started yet.

I removed his tie and belt then opened his shirt and pants. I didn't release his cock from his underwear because I worried that I wouldn't finish my plans for torture, but I did revel in how hard he was for me already. I couldn't resist kissing his lips just once before I hit the play button on the remote to start Luke Bryan's "Strip it Down." I figured I'd spin on my pole and tease him awhile before I rode his cock to the same rhythm.

I mounted the pole and performed my favorite spins and moves. Feeling his sexy eyes on me and knowing how turned on he was only spurred me on more; it made me more daring with my spins to go higher and hold on longer. I found myself doing sexy dances using the pole that I'd never dream of performing for anyone other than him. Through it all was the smug awareness that the best was yet to come when I had him deep inside me.

Unwilling to wait any longer, I sauntered over to the drawer where I stored the supplies the last time we visited the attic. I could see his pulse hammering in his throat as I neared him, but he looked too stunned to speak.

"Take these cuffs off me," he said gruffly, proving me wrong.

"Not yet, baby." I leaned over and bit Gabe's bottom lip then gave it a good tug.

"I am being punished," he growled.

I turned my back on Gabe and lowered myself until I straddled his thick thighs. "You call this punishment?" I asked, rubbing my ass against his erection.

"It's torture when I can't touch you," he replied. We both knew he could break loose of those cheap cuffs if he wanted to.

I wiggled against his groin until I felt the dampness of his pre-cum on my bare ass cheeks. Then I knew it was time to crank up the cruelty. I leaned forward and balanced myself with one hand on his knee while I reached around and stretched my ass with two fingers from the other hand. The growls and snarls that rumbled from Gabe's chest told me how badly he wanted to grab me and fuck me. Yet, he kept his hands to himself and let me have my way. I didn't think it was possible to love him any more than I did in that moment.

"You can't keep me tied down forever," Gabe said when I turned to face him.

"Don't plan on it, Detective." We both knew mine was a

figurative response to his literal remark. It should've shocked me how much I wanted to be tied to him forever, but I gave up fighting my feelings some time ago.

Gabe eagerly raised his hips to assist me when I began pulling on the waistband of his trousers and boxers to remove them. "Kiss me," he urged while I prepared him.

"Not yet." I would be a goner if I did.

Instead, I turned and presented my ass toward him again. I heard him whimpering softly because he knew I was about to bust out the reverse cowboy I had been boasting about almost since we met. I straddled his thighs once more and lowered myself onto his cock until he was buried completely inside me. I let my body adjust to him while I caught the beat of the music, then I began to sway and rock up and down his cock with my arms in the air. I used my thighs, my abs, and my hips to turn the reverse cowboy into a piece of art.

"I need to touch you, Sunshine," Gabe said. "Please let me touch you."

I savored every pitch and roll that made his cock rasp over my sensitive opening and the broad head of his cock nudging my prostate until I shook with the need to come. I didn't want to come yet, so I slid his cock out of my ass then sexily ground it against his cock in rhythm to the music.

"I need you," he pleaded with me.

I inserted his cock in my ass again and alternated the tempo of my movements to rev him up then wind him down. I couldn't tell which one of us shook the hardest with the need to come, but I knew who was going to blow first. I rested my back against his chest, which brought my neck and shoulder in close proximity to the part of his upper body he could control–his mouth. Gabe bit down into the corded muscle of my neck and I shot all over myself. I kept riding him until my balls were empty.

Gabe's body shook hard beneath mine and I felt his dick pulsing hard in my ass. "Can I touch you now?"

"Yes," I agreed, mostly for selfish reasons. I didn't think I had the strength left in my body to finish him.

Gabe broke the handcuffs with a quick tug and brought his hands around me to cup my face. He held my face turned toward his so he could ravage my mouth with one hand while the other held my hips still so he could thrust up into me.

"I'm going to find a way to pay you back for this stunt," Gabe growled after he broke our kiss. "Do you hear me?"

"Yes."

"I don't know when or how, but I'm going to strike when you least expect it. I'm going to give you so much pleasure you think you might die from it."

"You mean like now?"

"Always with that smart mouth," Gabe groused, the slapping of his hips against my ass punctuated his every word. He rose to his feet like I weighed nothing then gingerly pulled his dick from my ass before he turned me around to face him. He then hoisted me up to straddle his waist and I lowered myself back down on his dick. "Hang on tight, Sunshine."

Gabe grabbed my ass with both hands and began to fuck me fast and hard. Sweat popped out all over his body making it hard to hold onto his biceps as he bounced me up and down his cock. I loved the animalistic sounds that Gabe grunted as he neared his orgasm and I loved even more that I was the one who brought that out in him.

He held me tight to him when he spilled inside the condom and I clung to him as if I was afraid he would disappear. Truly, the threat against me was over and he and Buddy could return home and rest assured that I would be fine. I didn't let my mind go there because it would ruin my night with him. Instead, I focused on the loving way he pulled out of me and lowered me to my feet.

"You good to stand?" he asked. I nodded that I was because

I was still trying to catch my breath. "Good, then how about you carry me?" He raised his big leg up as if he was going to climb into my arms.

"Huh uh," I managed to say, shaking my head. "Not on my best day."

"You calling me fat?" Gabe asked, sounding all huffy.

"No, just thick."

"I got all the thick you can handle right here," Gabe said, grabbing his goods.

"Ain't that the truth," I said, limping playfully as I shut off the music and made my way to the top of the stairs. "Maybe we should give my ass a break and take yours out for a drive." I looked over my shoulder to see what kind of reaction I'd get from him.

"Okay," Gabe said without hesitation as he pulled up his pants. There was only one time I engaged in anal play with him and that was when I gave him a massage. I never asked about his position preference and dared not allow my brain to conjure up the things he and Kyle got up to when they were together.

"Oh," I said softly. Truthfully, I had only ever bottomed before and the idea of topping Gabe intimidated me.

"Didn't expect that answer, did you?" Gabe walked to me and cupped my face. "I'd welcome the feel of you inside me, Josh. In fact, I crave it."

"Oh." I wanted him to be happy and if penetration was something he wanted then it was something I'd give.

"You look panicked," Gabe said, a tender smile spreading across his face. "I'll never ask you to do something that makes you feel uncomfortable."

"No," I said hurriedly, "it's not that. It's just…" I thought about how I could express what I was feeling without sounding pathetic. "No one has ever wanted me in that way."

"I'm not like anyone you've ever known before," Gabe said, causing me to snort.

"You can say that again."

"I'm not like anyone you've ever know before," he repeated.

"Thank God for that," I said, wrapping my arms around him. "Let's get cleaned up and we'll order pizza."

"Don't you dare leave the mushrooms off," Gabe warned.

"Triple mushrooms," I declared, walking ahead of him.

Thirty minutes later we were cuddled on the couch eating pizza and watching the next biggest sporting thing on television. There was always some kind of major sporting event going on. "Tell me again about this big, exciting event that's coming up," I told him. "March Mania or something?"

"March Madness." Gabe looked at me like I had seven heads. "Right now it's conference tournaments, but March Madness is right around the corner."

"Oh boy," I said, dryly. I decided I would need a television in the bedroom once Gabe moved in.

Once, not if. Once. Joshy boy was growing up. My eyes must've widened because Gabe looked at me worriedly.

"What's the matter? Did you remember something important you wanted to watch?" he asked.

"No," I said. "I was just remembering our abrupt conversation earlier and wanted to know why you asked about the shears." That wasn't really what I had been thinking, but it must've seemed reasonable to Gabe.

Gabe told me everything that he could, which wasn't much at all. I just knew Billy confessed to stalking and harassing us and he'd been arrested by the DEA for serious drug charges. Those were things that the police would release to the paper so I was just learning them a few hours early. Gabe shocked the fuck out of me when he finally got around to answering my question.

"Mine? Are you sure?" I asked.

"Adrian and Captain Reardon looked at the scissors and they definitely have your name engraved on them. They're identical to the ones used to kill Georgia, but they're a little shorter."

"Fuck me!"

"I'm chest-thumping proud you think I could go another round after what we just did, but I'm out, Sunshine." He tapped the armrest on the couch. "I gave you everything I had." Lord, Gabe had been hanging around me too much, but I sure as hell wasn't complaining and I definitely didn't want to change it.

"What the hell was he doing with the shears I gave Georgia?"

"Well, I think he was truly obsessed with you and kept them as a souvenir when he found them while ransacking Georgia's mansion," Gabe told me.

The idea that Billy was somehow obsessed with me was something I just couldn't wrap my head around, even though the evidence supported the theory. "Why Georgia's house? What was he looking for?"

"Our theory is that Rocky and Jack weren't the only ones Georgia had pictures of and was attempting to blackmail." Gabe rubbed the back of his neck with his hand and let out a deep sigh. "Guessing is one thing and proving it is another."

I sat quietly thinking about what Gabe said. Georgia had been my friend and I truly missed her, but I was learning things about her that I never suspected. When had that part of Georgia's life started and why? Was she bored? Did she want to hurt others like she'd been hurt? A misery loves company type of thing?

I thought back to the conversations we'd had during the last year of her life and nothing about her blackmailing attempts slipped out, not a hint of anything sinister stuck out in my mind. "The only thing that I can even think of that ties Georgia to the Sampsons is Georgia's failed run at being elected to the school board. This dates back a while, but she was convinced that Delaney Sampson sabotaged her because she caught her husband checking Georgia out during a board meeting. Delaney was best friends with the woman that Rocky dumped so he could chase after Georgia. Delaney didn't want to find herself in the same boat," I told Gabe.

"So you think that Georgia was looking for dirt on Delaney and discovered what Billy was up to?" Gabe asked. He nodded his head after he thought it over. "Nothing surprises me around here."

"I did," I reminded him.

"You were the best kind of surprise there is, Sunshine."

After the game was over, Gabe made no mention of returning to his home and I sure as hell wasn't bringing it up. I snuggled back into his spoon and was grateful to be in his arms, whether it be for a night or… forever.

TWENTY-FIVE

Gabe

For the first times since I moved to Blissville, I was partnered with someone who wasn't Adrian. The captain split us up so that I worked on Nate Turner's case while Adrian looked into all things related to Billy Sampson. Even though the Feds took him off our hands, we had to know if anyone else in our county was involved with the drugs. The Feds were looking to move up the chain of command and wouldn't focus too intently on local connections unless it meant they were a bigger fish to fry than Billy.

To do that, Adrian would need to dig deep into Billy's background and find out what he'd been up to while living in Texas those past ten, or so, years before moving back to Blissville. I told him what Josh had said about Georgia's past fights with Delaney and neither of us were blowing it off because we had both learned the hard way not to underestimate the ladies–at any age.

It sucked to miss out on the interviews with the people who knew Billy best, but I couldn't take the risk that my involvement would give Billy a Get out of Jail Free card. I knew that Adrian would keep me informed every step of the way, just as I would tell him all about what I learned in my case. I already missed working with Adrian and we hadn't even parted ways yet.

"I hope CPD doesn't give you guys any hassle," Adrian said. "I hope Sheriff Tucker isn't sending us lame temporary partners either. I can't get stuck with someone who sucks his teeth or something." It was good to know I wasn't the only one dreading the temporary reassignments, even though we knew they were necessary.

"We're not too lame," said a voice from behind us.

Adrian and I slowly turned away from where we'd been standing by the coffee pot and faced the two men in suits that were standing behind us. One looked amused while the other looked annoyed. I'd never tell Adrian this, but I sent up a silent prayer that Adrian got stuck with Detective Sourpuss. I mean, I had to ride in the car with my new partner for almost an hour to get to Cincinnati. I knew in my heart that Adrian would understand, although I had no plans to confess.

"We're stealthy though," Detective Smiley said. He reached a hand toward me because, hey, I wasn't the one caught saying something embarrassing. Thinking it to myself didn't count. "I'm John Dorchester. I don't suck my teeth, fart or scratch my balls in public, and I can be trusted off the leash." Okay, I really preferred to work with this guy.

"I'm Gabe Wyatt," I told him.

"It's your lucky day, Detective Wyatt," he replied. "I'm," he pointed at his chest with both thumbs, "your new partner."

I could've clapped in joy, but instead I said, "Temporary partner."

"David Whitworth," Detective Grim said before he sucked obnoxiously on his teeth. He didn't bother to extend his hand and neither did Adrian.

"Adrian Goode," my partner said flatly. I was grateful that Adrian didn't try to one-up him by scratching his nuts or farting. "Does that mean you can't be trusted off the leash or that you like it on the leash?" Adrian asked his new partner. I knew he wasn't going to let that comment pass.

"Neither," Whitworth deadpanned.

"Well," Dorchester said, "I think it's time for us to get moving."

"One minute," I told him. I tipped my head for Adrian to follow me out of earshot. Once he did, I said, "Don't let this guy drag you down…" I paused when Adrian's phone chimed with an incoming text.

Adrian chuckled when he read the message and typed out a quick response then put his phone in his pocket before he turned his attention back to me. "Don't you worry about me, partner. You're going to have your own uphill battle."

I thought about Dorchester's personality and was confused about what Adrian was referring to. I had assumed that he had received a text from his wife, but maybe it was something concerning my new partner. "What's wrong with Dorchester? He seems fine to me."

"He is fine, which is exactly what I told Josh when he texted me just now wanting to know if your new partner is cute." Adrian laughed hard at my wide-eyed expression.

"Are you fucking kidding me? You're going to start trouble between me and my guy because you got the jerk for a partner?" I whispered angrily.

"I heard that subtle sigh of relief when you realized you got the good one," Adrian whispered angrily back. "Just for that, I'm not naming my baby after you."

"You've already said that," I reminded him.

"Well, now it's for sure."

"You can't blame me for being relieved. I have to ride all the way to Cinci and back with my partner. Forgive me if I don't want to be stuck with a dud," I told Adrian. "You'd feel the same way." Being stuck in a car with someone was an intimate experience, not the same as sharing a bed, but you were trapped in a small space with them with very little in the way of entertainment to distract you if they were horrible to be around. My phone chimed in my pocket with an incoming text and Adrian and I both knew who it was from. "You're an asshole, Adrian."

I couldn't keep the smile off of my face as I read Josh's message. *Behave! Don't make me piss on your leg before you leave the house each morning. Love you!*

He wouldn't have a moment's doubt if he fully accepted how crazy in love I was with him. He knew I loved him, but I doubt he grasped the depth of it. Hell, I was still coming to terms with it. The text I sent back was short and sincere. *No one can replace my Sunshine. Love you more!*

Adrian and I exchanged a bro-hug and went our separate ways, but I knew I'd be texting or speaking to him throughout the day. I wondered if we were going to have a debate as to who drove, but it was solved pretty quickly when he saw my Charger in the parking lot.

"You drive your own vehicle?" he asked once we hit the road.

"Yeah, but I get compensated for mileage, oil changes, and tire rotations," I replied. "I typically don't rack up a lot of mileage under normal circumstances."

"Yeah, these are anything but normal," he commented. "I was sorry to hear that Sampson was harassing you and your boyfriend."

"It's not your fault," I told him, but something in his voice told me that he felt that way.

"I should've gone to the sheriff when I heard him making homophobic comments about you after Nate was found dead," Dorchester said. "I'm sorry if my silence aided him in making things more difficult for you guys."

Billy didn't harass us because we were gay, he did it because he wanted to cause trouble between Josh and me so he could step back into Josh's life. I wasn't going to say that to him though. Although the truth would most likely filter out into the community, it wasn't going to be through my lips.

"I appreciate your apology, Dorchester, but it's not necessary," I told him.

We spent the rest of the trip talking about the upcoming March Madness tournament, which reminded me of the scornful look on Josh's face when he realized his television was going to be showing more sports. I could've gone home to watch basketball the other night after my punishment, but I wasn't really too eager to return to my empty house nor did he seem eager for me to leave. It was a conversation that we needed to have, but I was hesitant to bring it up. I wasn't sure how well my heart would handle hearing that Josh didn't want to be with me as much as I wanted to be with him.

My first impression of Detectives Weston Jade and Carl Harris was that they seemed like upstanding guys that were willing to work with us, but I had been fooled in the past by a Good Ole Boy routine. IA had cleared them, as well as me, of having acted improperly in regards to Nate Turner's investigation and death so I was giving them the same benefit of the doubt that I hoped they were giving me.

The four of us gathered around a table in a conference room

to go over the case. Jade passed out blue file folders containing the interview notes and photos of evidence from all the agencies involved. "Has there been any evidence or rumors that Nate Turner was involved in trafficking or distributing drugs?" I asked.

"Oddly, no," Harris said. "We'd sent undercover cops into his club plenty of times and there was never any sign of dealing or trafficking out of that establishment."

"We've asked Detectives Seviere and Drake to join us in case you have questions about the undercover investigations they ran. They should be here any minute," Jade said.

I continued to look through their notes while we waited. "What about the silent partner, Marlon Bandowe?" I asked. "What were your impressions on him?" I noted there wasn't much written about the man in the notes, which could mean that he just didn't leave much of an impression or these guys weren't as thorough as I would've preferred.

"Truthfully," Jade replied, "he was just kind of there. He appeared wholesome and… boring." He shrugged indifferently.

"Sort of nondescript," added Harris. "Medium height, medium brown hair, average blue eyes. There was nothing out of the ordinary about him."

"Except his vehemence about people not knowing he was involved with the club. He kept saying that he had only fronted the startup money and wasn't involved in the operation of the business," Jade added.

"Do you think he felt strongly enough about it to kill or hire a killer?" Dorchester asked. "It seemed to me that Nate's killing was very personal and it didn't seem like he was the type to build personal relationships. If he wasn't running drugs or prostitution, then why was he being threatened? Better yet, why avoid the police if he had nothing to hide?"

"All things we ask ourselves daily," Jade admitted. "There are no solid clues to anyone."

"What about his family background?" I asked.

"Well, he was the only child of Charles and Marie Turner. They're both deceased."

"Adopted child," Harris added. "The Turners were already in their late forties or early fifties when Nate was adopted. They were fairly well off and Nate enjoyed a privileged country club and private school life."

"So that explains why his home and personal belongings speak of a larger income than what he earned from the night club," Dorchester commented.

"Yes, he inherited quite a bit of money from his folks when they passed," Jade answered.

"Did they die at the same time?" I asked the detectives.

"No," Harris said then flipped to the page that had the notes about the parents. "Mrs. Turner died of lung cancer in May of 1999 and Mr. Turner died from a heart attack five months later. An online story I found on the couple indicated that he died from a broken heart." So Nate didn't kill his parents for money, he wasn't peddling drugs from the club, nor was he involved in prostitution. What was he into then? Someone obviously wanted him dead for reasons he didn't want disclosed. Why?

There was a knock on the door and two people walked in. First, was a tall redheaded woman and behind her was a man I recognized, even if it had been a year since I last saw him. I swallowed hard when his eyes lit with recognition also. I chewed the inside of my cheek and hoped that working with him wouldn't be awkward.

"Detectives Allyson Drake and Paul Seviere," Jade said in introduction, "meet Detectives Winchester and Wyatt."

"Dorchester," John corrected. "Winchesters are the dudes who hunt demons and stuff on a television show. I'm not nearly as cool or bad ass."

"Sorry about that," Jade said. I wasn't sure if we was apologizing for the mistake that he made or because Dorchester wasn't as cool or bad ass as the Winchesters.

Drake and Seviere came over and shook both our hands. Nothing was said between Paul–now that I knew his name–and me. What was to discuss really? We hooked up at a hotel near Vibe one Saturday night a year ago and never saw each other again.

"It's good to meet you," was exchanged between the four of us and everyone took a seat.

"Detective Wyatt was someone that Nate Turner reached out to when the threats started arriving via email," Harris said. I listened to him explain to the new arrivals the events that took place between my meeting with Turner and him being killed in my county.

"So you think he was coming to find you?" Detective Drake asked.

"That was the original theory," I replied then told them about the drug bust and Billy Sampson's arrest. "Was there any serious rumors or hints that he was moving drugs out of the club? We're just trying to see if the two cases are tied together somehow." The more information I heard about Nate made me think that they were two separate incidents. As much as we wanted to tie everything up with a Billy Sampson bow, we just couldn't.

"None," Seviere said. "Sure, some of the club patrons had their own stash that they brought in, but no one even hinted that there was anything good I could score there. I didn't just show up once or twice and ask either, I'm talking I was there as a regular club goer for more than six months and nothing."

"We didn't find anything during the prostitution investigation," Drake said. "Nothing. If he was breaking the law, then he was brilliant at it."

"Knowing what all of you know about the circumstances, how likely do you think it is that Nate Turner is connected to Billy Sampson's drug bust?" I asked.

"Not likely. Right?" Seviere said then looked at the rest of the group to see if they agreed. It was a unanimous agreement that we were looking at two separate cases.

"So, we push all talk of Billy Sampson aside and focus solely on Nate Turner," Dorchester said.

I had thumbed through the interviews but didn't have time to go through them all in detail before we starting talking. I decided to read them thoroughly at home, but for the time being I wanted the highlights. I started with Dorchester. "Who claimed the body?"

"His lawyer did," he replied.

"What about the interviews you did with his employees?" I asked him. "Did anyone give any reason why someone would want to kill him? Any fights with vendors, city officials who wanted to close him down, or a religious group who protested the immorality of a gay club? Anything?"

"Nothing," Dorchester said. "They all seemed to really like working for him. He had a reputation as a hard ass and a playboy, but his employees didn't see him that way. They spoke highly of him."

I asked some follow-up questions as they came to me, but I didn't learn anything new after nearly two hours of talking about the case. I blew out a frustrated breath and said, "I want to set up interviews with all of them again, but only after I've had a chance to review all of the notes. I'm pretty good at the bad cop thing," I told them. Of course, the last time I played the part I was knocked unconscious, but they didn't need to know that. "Besides, I've been to that club a time or two and I can promise you that not all of his employees loved him."

I'd seen the looks that some of them gave him when he came out of his office. In most instances, people didn't like to speak ill of the dead. In others, they had something to hide. What we needed to determine was if either applied to Nate Turner.

"Can you tell me where the bathroom is?" I asked Jade. "It's a long trip back."

"Sure, it's the…"

"I'm heading that way too," Seviere said, cutting him off. "I'll show you." I knew he wanted to have a private word with me so I wasn't surprised when he said, "I'm not out at work," once he was certain we were alone in the restroom.

"I have no desire to change that," I assured him. "What happened between us was a long time ago and is no one's business."

I saw the relief wash over his face before he smiled at me, very similar to the one he gave me the first night we met. I had a suspicion I knew where his mind was going and I wanted to make my position clear to avoid any more awkwardness than already existed. I looked at my watch and said, "I need to start heading back. I have things to wrap up at the station before my dinner plans with my boyfriend."

"Ah, I don't want to hold you up. I'm sure we'll see each other again before the case gets wrapped up," he said. Although I appreciated his confidence, I figure it was more like *if* the case got wrapped up.

Dorchester and I got on the road as soon as I finished using the bathroom. I was sure that Adrian would be glad to get a break from his new partner, if he hadn't killed him already.

"Let's go rescue your partner from mine," Dorchester said, reading my mind. I was once again grateful for the hand that fate dealt me and hoped that Adrian wouldn't retaliate too terribly.

TWENTY-SIX

Josh

I REGRETTED IT THE MINUTE I SENT ADRIAN THAT CHILDISH TEXT asking if Gabe's temporary new partner was cute. It made me look extremely insecure when I mostly wasn't and I was reasonably certain that Adrian was going to tease Gabe about it. When Adrian told me that the new guy was fine, not cute, then I knew for a fact he was going to tease Gabe, so I bit the bullet and texted Gabe in hopes that I beat Adrian to the punch. Then Gabe sent me the sweetest damn text that made my insides melt.

I sat there at my dining table staring at the change of address card that I picked up from the post office for the longest time. I had filled it out and all it needed was Gabe's signature to make it official. Was I basing my decision to ask Gabe to move in with me on genuine affection or fear? There was no doubt in my mind how much I loved Gabe, but there was still that nagging fear that Gabe would wake up one day, look at me, and wonder what the hell he was doing with me. It was a demon I had to battle on my own because Gabe had never given me a reason to believe that he wanted anyone else. I was his Sunshine.

Then I had to question: was having a healthy dose of uncertainty a bad thing? Wasn't it good that I didn't take Gabe and our relationship for granted or was it arrogant to believe that he could never find someone else? When did a healthy dose of uncertainty turn into something dangerous to a person's psyche? What was the right balance of being confident that your man loved you without strutting around like an ignorant peacock? I had seen confident people's relationships fail just as I had for the insecure ones. Why? I felt it was because the proper compromises weren't met. I wasn't just talking about food and television choices, but personality compromises. Opposites attracted, there was no doubt about it, but it took a lot of effort to make those relationships work.

Gabe was worth putting in the time–we were worth putting in the time. I needed be sure he felt the same way before I made such a big leap. I found myself evaluating things for so long that I didn't realize it was time to open the salon until Meredith came upstairs and found me staring at the form. Hell, I didn't even do my preopen inspection of the salon to make sure it was perfect for our clients.

Meredith sat across from me and reached for my hand. "He is madly in love with you, Josh."

"I know that he is," I replied. *Now*, is the part I left out.

"You're just worried that it's too soon or are you afraid that you're ready and he's not?" she asked softly.

"Both," I replied honestly. "Mere, it'll suck hairy balls if I tell him I want him to move in or I ask him to and he says no." She shook her head like she didn't see it happening. One minute I agreed with her then the next I was right back to having my doubts cast a huge shadow over my confidence.

"I know that you'll find the right words, way, and time to bring it up with Gabe. Even if he says he isn't ready it doesn't mean that he never will be," she reminded me. I nodded my head in agreement then she asked, "Ready to get your day going?"

I folded up the completed change of address card and put it in my back pocket to remind me of a decision I wanted and needed to make on a future I wanted and needed to have with Gabe. I picked up Savage's cage and followed Meredith down the steps. I expected him to spew filth, but instead he said, "Big Daddy loves me." I giggled because Gabe had been working to clean up Savage's language and those four little words reminded me how much Gabe wanted to be a part of my life.

"He sure does, Dirty Bird," I told Savage, as if he knew what the fuck I was saying.

The decision was made, just like that. If I hadn't been sure, then the list of songs the radio played that day would've convinced me to take a chance, to put love first. *Holy fuck,* I was starting to sound like one of those fortune cookie messages.

That day, something happened that never did. I had a cancellation. *Gasp!* Less confident stylists might've panicked and worried that the end was near, but I accepted it for what it was–a client with the flu. I was actually grateful for a little bit of extra time to treat myself to a delicious lunch at the diner.

Oddly, it didn't feel right going there without Gabe, even though I'd gone there without him for twenty-eight years and only a few months with him. I was starting to feel that way about several places, most importantly the place I lay my head down each night. I could quiver in my shoes and worry what would happen when

Gabe left me or I could accept that he was in it for the long haul and take the next step to show him that I was too.

My early morning decision was reaffirmed and I was starved to death. I had just ordered a plate of meatloaf, Brussel sprouts, and baked macaroni and cheese when I was joined by an uninvited, but not altogether unwelcomed, guest. "What's up, Doc?"

"A whole lot of nothing much," Kyle said, taking a seat across from me.

I don't know where it came from or why I couldn't stop the words from spilling from my mouth, but I blurted out, "Were you aware that Gabe didn't know I cut your hair?"

"I'm not at all surprised," Kyle said. The crooked grin on his face told me he wasn't too upset about it, but I felt terrible. It sounded like I was rubbing it in. "We didn't connect the way you two did, not even in the beginning when things were new." Kyle tipped his head and said, "He showed more passion with you in that parking lot kiss then he ever did with me."

I knew his receptionist told him all about the kiss Gabe planted on me in his parking lot, but Kyle sounded like he saw it with his own eyes. "How do you know?"

"Outside camera," he replied. "Alyssa told me about the hot kiss, but I thought she was exaggerating so I had to see it for myself." *Wow, there was no way in hell I could watch a video of Gabe kissing someone else.* It just went to show that they weren't meant for one another.

"You thought she was exaggerating because I wasn't his type?" I asked.

"No, because I had never witnessed the passion from Gabe that Alyssa described seeing. It's true," he said when I just kept staring at him like I had to be dreaming the conversation. "I can tell by your expression that lack of passion isn't a problem you have with Gabe. I could also see the difference in him when he was with you in that video. You light up his entire world and let me tell you something,

Josh, there isn't a thing about you he wouldn't notice or a place you could hide that he wouldn't find you."

"Wow," I said softly.

"I want that for myself someday," he said wistfully, then quickly added, "a relationship, but not with Gabe."

"I knew what you meant." I debated if I should say something to encourage him to ask a certain guy I knew out. I didn't want to do anything to embarrass my friend and I didn't know Kyle well enough to know how he'd receive it. I mean, it was much easier to dole out advice than to accept it. I went with, "You know, you'll never find that relationship if you don't take some chances."

Kyle tilted his head as if he was giving my suggestion merit. "True," he said noncommittally. "Anyway, I got to run, but I'll see you around."

Kyle left and I enjoyed my lunch in peace, grateful that people stopped losing their shit when I ordered something different than what I normally would on any given day. I bought two pieces of chocolate silk pie to go so I could have a celebration dessert with Gabe later then headed back to the salon.

The weather was a balmy thirty-eight degrees when I had left for lunch so I decided to walk. I heard someone calling my name and turned to find Laura Sampson running to catch up to me. *Great!* First I ran into the ex of my current love and then I ran into the current love of my first crush.

"Thanks for waiting for me," Laura said breathlessly once she caught me. "Can you give me a few minutes of your time? I've been meaning to stop by the salon or call you."

"I'm glad you didn't stop by the salon because I don't discuss my personal life there," I told her, but not in a harsh way.

"You just talk about everyone else's," she fired back. She waved her hand to cut me off when I opened my mouth to respond to her allegation. "I know that you don't act like that, Josh. I'm sorry. I'm just…"

"... Reeling?" I finished for her. "Shocked, disappointed, and angry too," I also suggested.

Laura gave me a small smile and said, "Yes, to all of those things, but none of them are directed at you, despite my barb." I wasn't sure what all Laura had been told by the police, Feds, or even Billy himself, so I kept my mouth shut. She had something to say and I was going to let her say it. If she was wrong about something, I could correct her. "I've known about Billy's feelings for you for a long time, since the beginning really."

"I wouldn't call them feelings," I replied. *So much for letting the woman talk. On the other hand, I did say I would correct her when she was wrong.*

"He didn't want to admit it then and he sure as hell doesn't want to admit it now, but I know the truth. You know the truth," she added. "Something has been off with Billy for a long time and I figured that maybe he was coming to terms with his sexuality, I was even prepared for the conversation and had a response ready to go. I wasn't at all equipped for him to disappear, or to find out he'd been using drugs again, and I sure as hell wasn't ready to find out he'd been arrested. I don't know many details—not that I'd discuss them with you—but I know that he had been harassing you. I'm really sorry for that, Josh."

"It's not your fault, Laura," I said, reaching for her with my hand that wasn't holding the paper bag with pie.

"Thanks for saying so," she replied, but she didn't sound convincing. "As for the rest of what I've been told," she closed her eyes briefly before continuing, "I just can't reconcile those things with the man I married and the father of my children. I just want to make sure he gets help."

"I'm sorry, Laura." Even though I wasn't responsible for any of the things that happened, that didn't mean I wasn't sorry for what she was going through.

"It's not your fault, Josh," she said, smiling as she repeated my words. "I just wanted to clear the air so that there wasn't any awkwardness between us."

"Thank you for that, Laura. I won't pretend I was looking forward to this run-in, but I'm glad it happened."

"Take care of yourself," she said as she took a few steps backwards. Then she gave me a small wave and turned around to walk away.

The interaction stayed on my mind for the rest of the day. There she was, a woman who could've been bitter and taken that bitterness on a rampage to hurt everyone in her path; instead, she was trying to comfort me and make me feel less awkward about a situation that she wasn't responsible for. She wanted to help Billy rather than hurt him. I hoped I was a big enough person to feel the same way had I been in her shoes, but I wasn't so sure. It wasn't that I wished harm on Billy for what he did to me, I just wished that I didn't have to see him or ever talk to him again. I wasn't in love with Billy, but Laura clearly was.

The emotional rollercoaster that I had been on since I learned Billy had moved back to town caught up to me. All I wanted to do was go upstairs and crash hard, but that wasn't the card I wanted to play. No, I had a very special card in my pocket that trumped all others.

My exhaustion faded the second I heard Gabe's key in the door at the bottom of the steps. Buddy heard it too and pranced around in circles until Gabe knelt down and gave him the loving he wanted. It reminded me of the time Gabe threw himself down on the floor for a belly rub that led to other things. I launched myself into Gabe's arms and wrapped my legs around his waist as soon as he got up from greeting Buddy.

"Hey there, Sunshine," Gabe said. "You're looking extra…" he narrowed his eyes as he searched for the proper word, "sunshiney."

"That's because I have something in my pants for you," I replied, waggling my eyebrows.

"Oh, baby, I know all about the delights you have in your pants," Gabe said then nuzzled my neck.

"I was referring to a particular delight–at least I hope you think so–in my right rear pocket," I told Gabe. I slid to my feet after he pulled the change of address card out of my pocket. I bit my lip while he took his sweet-fucking-time looking it over without an expression on his face. "It just needs your signature on the bottom," I said timidly.

Gabe threw his head back and laughed. I took a step back, unsure what he thought was so goddamned funny until he reached into his coat pocket and pulled out a blank change of address card. "I was going to get your permission first before I completed it, of course. I spent the last few hours thinking up cute ways to propose the idea to you, but came up flat. You, on the other hand, came up with the perfect plan. You jumped me and told me to reach inside your pants."

I was so relieved that I was speechless, but Savage said it all for me. "Big Daddy's home!"

"Yes, he is," Gabe and I both said at the same time then began our celebration with a toe-curling kiss that led to hours of pleasure. It wasn't until the next morning that I even remembered the pie I bought for us. So, we had celebration chocolate silk pie for breakfast with our coffee.

TWENTY-SEVEN

Gabe

IT FELT LIKE I FLOATED TO WORK THE NEXT DAY. I HAD JUST COME off one of the most beautiful moments of my life, I got to eat chocolate pie for breakfast, and it was a Friday. What more could a man want in life? Had Josh been with me on the road to Cincinnati, he would have rattled off a bunch of snarky things had I voiced my thought, but my guy wasn't riding shotgun that morning–Detective Dorchester was–and I kept my thought to myself.

"You're looking mighty perky this morning," Dorchester

commented. "Must've had a wonderful evening."

"Do you *really* want to hear about my evening?" I asked.

"I wasn't really thinking along the lines of something that personal, but do you think the idea of two guys having sex creeps me out?" he asked. I saw him shaking his head out of my peripheral vision. "My sister is gay so you're not the only person I know from the rainbow community."

"Yeah, but most straight guys think two chicks together are hot," I told him. "As long as they don't want equal rights or to raise a family together," I added under my breath.

"Lesbian sex isn't hot when it involves your sister!" Dorchester's revulsion made me smile and eased the slight amount of tension that creeped in. Maybe someday I'd do less assuming about people's views on the LGBTQ community, but I wasn't quite there yet. "Anyway, I'd like to think I wouldn't be that asshole even if my sister wasn't a rainbow baby. Not everyone is like Sampson."

"You're right, Dorchester. I'm sorry if I came off like a cynical asshole," I replied.

"No apology needed," he told me. "I'm sure your life experiences had a lot to do with it."

He was right, but I decided to change the subject back to the case. "What are your opinions on the Turner case so far? You think anyone interviewed might be hiding something?" I had spent hours looking over the interview notes and making a list of new questions I wanted to ask once we returned to the station.

"We have a guy who was being threatened, but we don't know what for. He said that going to the cops made it worse, but we don't know why. When he worked with the police he wasn't forthcoming, so he had something he wanted to hide or perhaps someone he wanted to protect. He wanted to be saved, but wouldn't do anything to save himself, except for maybe his last act of coming to find you," Dorchester said. "By then it was too late."

It still bugged me that Nate appeared to have been looking for me the night he died. It wasn't that I felt responsible, because I felt I acted in the most professional way with the information he presented to me in his office. I never received his email that reached out to me for help because it was captured by our server for review. Still, a man was dead and just maybe I could've prevented it. I kept those comments to myself because they weren't beneficial to the investigation.

"That sums up my thoughts exactly. What about the task force? Any opinions on them?" I asked Dorchester.

As soon as the words left my mouth, I realized that I hadn't told Josh about my run-in with Paul from the task force and that we'd hooked up once a year ago. I had planned on telling him when I left Cincinnati, but then I got busy reading the reports and interviews and forgot about it. Then I stopped by the post office on my way home and picked up the change of address card. Once I held that in my hand, my mind was too busy figuring out a way to start the future I wanted, not focus on an incident from my past that was barely a blip on my radar.

Paul wasn't even really on the task force, I told him I was in a relationship, and nothing else was required to my way of thinking. I mean, Josh hadn't told me about the guy from college that he said treated him worse that Billy Sampson, which was hard to believe. Hell, I was almost afraid for the college guy's safety once I found out how he treated Josh. I reasoned that telling him would cause more harm than not telling him. *Where could I go wrong with that kind of logic?*

"I think they're all stand-up people," Dorchester replied, bringing me back to the present. "I just think there's not a lot to go on until someone coughs up a lead. It's like a tightly knit sweater that holds together nicely until one tiny string comes loose and then it begins to unravel. We really need to find that loose string."

"Or help it come loose," I added.

When we arrived at the police department, I noticed that some phones had been added to the room we used the prior day. I knew then it was going to be an unglamorous day of making phone calls to try and schedule second interviews with people. If we didn't have luck getting them by phone, then we'd hit the streets and do it in person.

"The hard part will probably be tracking down the employees since they would've found new jobs after Nate was killed," I said out loud to the group after we'd left voicemail messages for almost every person on the list. The only people we reached by phone was Nate's lawyer and his silent business partner, but I guess that really didn't count since we talked to their personal assistants who promised to get back with us with a time we could meet.

"The club didn't close," Harris said casually. "Bandowe hired someone to manage it temporarily until the sale of the business goes through."

"Where is that in the notes?" I asked him.

"I didn't really think it was that pertinent." Harris sounded a touch defensive, which wasn't my goal at all. The last thing I needed was to alienate the people on the task force.

"I apologize if that came out sounding critical," I told him. "I was making sure that I hadn't overlooked something or that I wasn't missing a page. That's all."

Harris relaxed a bit and said, "It's all good, man. It was something that I learned from Paul, not as part of the investigation. The club did close for a while so maybe I should've said it reopened instead of implying that it never closed."

Until evidence to the contrary was discovered, I was convinced the club was at the root of the case. Maybe not because of any illegal activity coming from it, but because of how successful it was. Or, he chose the wrong person to take to his office for a one-off fuck. The emails that Nate received didn't have a religious puritanical feel to them. The one email referred to him having a beautiful cock and it was a shame it belonged to a piece of shit excuse for a man. Had it been from a person who was offended about where Nate stuck his dick then I thought it would've said so, they definitely wouldn't have referred to his cock as beautiful.

"What about the kid they tracked the emails back to? Um," I flipped through the notes until I came to his name. "Owen Smithson? What connection did he have to Nate, if any? Did he have a family member or friend who worked at Vibe or liked to go there? Do we know yet if the same caliber gun was used in both shootings?"

"The M.E. reports both state the gunshot appears to be from a forty-five. The shots were fired from close range and exited their skulls. Neither bullet was found on the scene which indicates it had been removed by the shooter. The details in both shootings are too similar to be a coincidence. The only difference was the location– Owen was killed in his apartment and Nate was killed in his car," Jade said.

"Owen didn't have any connection to Nate or the club that we could find," Harris added. "We looked hard, but there was nothing. It would appear that someone hired him to send the messages and pictures then eliminated him when he'd outgrown his usefulness," Jade told us.

"The only similarity between Nate and Owen was that they were both adopted, but not through the same organization. Nate's adoption was private where Owen was adopted after spending several years in foster care. Neither of their stories would be considered unique if they hadn't been killed by the same person."

"There's something more there," I told them, although I couldn't tell them why I thought so. "Why hire Owen? How'd they find him?"

"He hung out at a cyber café a lot and the guy might've found him there."

"Or woman," I reminded him. *Weaker sex, my ass!*

We hung around the station for a bit longer waiting on voicemail messages to be returned then hit the streets to knock on doors when no one called us back. We only caught a few on our list at home and learned absolutely nothing new. The one good thing I took away from the interviews we were able to conduct was that it didn't appear that anyone was trying to hide anything from us. I got the impression that they really did want us to solve Nate's case.

I looked at my watch and saw that it was too early for the club employees to show up, but it was late enough that I wanted to start heading back home to Josh. It wasn't that we had anything exciting planned, but I looked forward to our night anyway. I quickly learned to expect the unexpected from Josh and whatever happened would be wonderful.

Then a lightbulb went off in my head. The best way to get some questions answered was from the inside. I wondered how Josh would feel about dinner and dancing on a Friday night or even a Saturday if he was too tired after being on his feet all day. I mentioned it to Dorchester to see what he thought about my idea.

"I don't see how it could hurt. You can have a fun time with your guy even if you don't learn anything new," he said.

"True," I replied. He was right, what could it hurt?

Fast forward and I knew exactly how it could hurt. Josh couldn't wait to go dancing with me Saturday night and was even more excited when I told him I'd be doing a little investigating too. I had to ask him to change his outfit three times because each one of them looked like some cheesy undercover ensemble you'd expect to see in a comedy spoof about undercover work. The last one was the worst and it made me think we would end up looking like a modern day Starsky and Hutch. As funny as his first few outfits were, it was the final one that caused me so much pain.

"I'm not changing again," Josh said firmly. He crossed his arms over his chest and glared at me with eyes that grew a darker hue when he was horny or angry. I knew damn well he wasn't horny, as for me… those tight jeans were going to be the death of me. I knew every eye in the room would be on his ass and I didn't like it one bit. "There's nothing wrong with this one."

I realized why his eyes looked bigger and darker. I had never seen him in eyeliner, not even when I saw him that one time at Vibe. I wondered if it was something he only liked to do on occasion or if he was testing me, perhaps both. "You're wearing eyeliner," I said. I would not fail if it was a test. "It makes your eyes look bigger." I walked to him and tilted his chin up slightly so I could have a better look. "Just make sure you keep those beautiful eyes on me."

My answer seemed to appease him and we set off for the club. Josh was right about what he said earlier about there being nothing wrong with his outfit. I just didn't like the idea of the attention he was going to get, but that was my problem, not his. I would just have to step up my game so that he was too busy having a good time with me that he wouldn't notice anyone else, which meant I was going to be forced to dance.

The club was as busy as I expected it would be on a Friday night. The music was thumping loudly, sweaty bodies were grinding against one another on the dance floor, and drinks were flowing at the bar. If it was up to me, I would've marched straight up to the bar and began asking questions, subtly of course, but Josh was eyeing the dance floor like it was a long-lost friend.

I grabbed his hand and began leading him in that direction. "I can't dance worth a shit," I yelled over my shoulder in warning.

"That's okay, baby, you just stand there and I'll dance good enough for both of us," Josh replied confidently.

I anticipated that I would stand near him and kind of move from side to side while glaring at every swinging dick in the place, but that isn't what happened. Josh's infectious happiness and laughter urged–okay, yanked me by the dick–out of my comfort zone and into Fun Land. I stopped worrying about my moves and how lame they were or anything else. All I wanted was to keep that wide smile on Josh's face and the laughter in his life at any cost.

After a long time, Josh crooked his finger for me to follow him and I did. "I think it's time we start interrogating the club staff," he told me.

"We're not going to interrogate anyone, Sunshine. I'm just going to ask about the new management in a non-threatening way." I wasn't in the mood for bad cop. I was in the mood for some quick, honest answers and then take my guy home for some strong loving before we went to bed. If given the choice, I also wanted to sleep in until at least ten the next morning.

"Damn," Josh said in disappointment. "I was hoping to see you in action."

We found a place at the bar, but there was only one stool. I motioned for Josh to take it, but he shook his head. I wasn't going to battle him over who sat on the stool. If he didn't want to sit, fine; he could stand between my legs so I could nibble on his neck while we waited our turn.

That's exactly what I was doing when I heard a familiar voice say, "This must be your boyfriend."

Josh's head snapped in the direction of the voice and I watched with an inward smile as Josh slowly raked his eyes from Paul's toes to his eyes then narrowed them in suspicion. "Why, yes I am and who might you be?" Josh asked sweetly. I was pretty sure I saw him bat his eyelashes a few extra times for emphasis.

Paul extended his hand and said, "I'm Paul Seviere. I work on Gabe's task force."

Josh accepted his hand and said, "I'm Josh Roman. I work on Gabe's nerves."

Paul threw his head back and laughed. "I like him," he said when he was finished. "So, are you guys here on a date or checking things out?"

"Both," Josh said. "Gabe won't let me interrogate anyone though."

"I just want to find out whatever I can about the new management." I told Paul some of my theories and he nodded his head.

"In that case, you might look hard at the former owner slash silent partner. The identity of the new owner hasn't been made public and the employees aren't talking. It's doubtful the interim manager knows much. I guess it's possible Bandowe wanted out from under the club and Nate's death was the easiest way or the new guy wanted the club bad enough to kill."

"And you're certain there was no illicit activities going on?" I asked Paul.

"Could there have been a few clients giving out sexual favors for a quick buck? Sure. Are these partyers bringing in their own drugs? You can bet your ass. What we didn't find was any sign that the owner or the employees were engaged in any illegal activities. No one seems to know who the new owner is, but maybe you'll have better luck." He nodded to Josh and said, "Let him ask the questions if you decide to interview the staff because he's less threatening looking than you are."

"Aw, thanks," Josh said to Paul.

"No problem. You two have a fun night," he said before he walked off.

The congenial smile slid off Josh's face the moment he walked away. He turned between my legs so he could look me in the eye. "You fucked him, didn't you?" It was a statement of disbelief, not an accusation.

"Not these past two days," I said. "It was a year ago."

"Did you meet here at the club?" Josh asked.

"Yes."

"Then you hooked up?" he asked.

"Once."

"You weren't going to mention it?" Josh wanted to know.

I let out a deep sigh and told him all of the things I had thought about that morning. I was with Josh and told Paul so. Paul was a one-time thing and a very distant memory. Blah. Blah. Blah. He didn't look at all impressed nor did he look angry. I couldn't get a read on his mood, which was odd because I felt like I knew him so well.

"Gabe," he said, holding up his hand. His lips tilted up on one end and he looked like he was holding back a grin. "Instead of driving back home, why don't we get a hotel and you can fuck me like a stranger tonight."

"What?" That was the last thing I thought he would say.

"I know that you love me and I trust you," he said, words that meant more to me than I could possibly express. "So why not have a little fun? Sometimes a guy just wants to be pinned to the bed and fucked hard."

I just sat there staring at him in shock for a few minutes. "If you're uncertain…" the guy beside me said, snapping me out of my daze.

"Fuck you." I got off the stool and pulled Josh behind me as I made my way to the exit. I couldn't believe Josh wanted to go to a hotel instead of his own home. I knew how fastidious he could be about certain things and beds was high on the list.

"Pick a good hotel though, babe. I don't want sheets so thin I can see through them or a lumpy mattress."

I took him to the nicest hotel in the city and didn't even grimace when the guy behind the reservation desk swiped my card. It was worth the three Benjamins to know that the pillow beneath Josh's face would be soft, the mattress would have the correct amount of firmness, and the sheets had enough thread count that they didn't tear when I fucked him into the next month.

TWENTY-EIGHT

Josh

Two weeks later, I was standing in the middle of Gabe's living room looking around with my hands on my hips. There wasn't a need to buy another TV because his big monstrosity could go into the living room at my–our–house and my current TV could go into my–our–bedroom. The rest of his furniture though…

"Don't worry about it, Sunshine," Gabe said when he entered the room behind me. "As ugly as the furniture is, it's functional, new-ish, and will fit nicely in the living room."

I slowly turned to face him. I did want Gabe to share his life with me, but what I meant was him, his clothes, and his dog move in while the rest of his things didn't. The clothes and dog we had already moved. Gabe asked me to look around to see if there was anything I wanted in the living room and kitchen before he gave it away.

"I was just kidding," he said quickly when he saw the look on my face. "I have a box of things in the hall closet upstairs that I want to grab so why don't you take a look at the movies and then there are some kind of ancient iron pots and pans that my grandmother passed down to my mom, she gave them to me when I moved and…"

I didn't wait for him to finish. I headed straight to his kitchen cabinets to see if he meant cast iron skillets. I loved cast iron skillets and finding really good ones was hard to do. It seemed like it took forever to season new cast iron cookware. I opened the cabinets closest to the stove, which was where I'd store the skillets and pots, but not my guy. I searched every cabinet in the amount of time it took him to retrieve a box of stuff from the hall closet. Don't think I wasn't searching that box before I let him put things out and about. There was a balance to my home that I needed to maintain. That was a battle for another hour, right then I just wanted to know where the fuck he was keeping the holy grail of cookware.

"Don't tease me, man. Where are the cast iron skillets and pots?"

Gabe almost looked afraid when he pointed to the oven. *He kept them stored in the oven?* I released an excited breath and opened the oven door slowly. There they were, the bastions of true Southern cooking stacked inside the oven. There had to be at least three Dutch ovens and ten skillets in various sizes.

"The lids are in the drawer below," Gabe said.

"Baby, do you have any idea what I can do with cookware like this? Have you ever had a steak seared and cooked on these bad asses?" I saw an image of me standing in my kitchen spooning butter over perfectly seared meat while a potato dish was baking in the oven and Brussel sprouts were sautéing in a garlic butter and herb sauce in a separate skillet on the stove. "We need to stop at the store on the way home."

"You already have some of those pans, don't you?" Gabe asked. I noticed his ignored my comment about going to the store. I suspected he'd rather undergo a root canal.

"God love your heart, Gabe," I said shaking my head. "They're not the same quality and these pans have already been seasoned with love for decades. There's just no comparison." I pulled a skillet out of the oven and looked at it. "It's beautiful, as will be the food I cook in it."

"I have no doubts about that, Sunshine. You're the best cook I've ever known." He pinched my ass and I turned to look at him. "Don't be telling my mother I said that."

"Oh my God! I make one little mistake with the mushrooms and suddenly I'm a blabbermouth who tries to destroy your relationship with your mother." Okay, he didn't really imply that, but it was fun to harass him all the same. "You wound me, Gabe." I gave a fake sniff.

"Sunshine, however can I make it up to you?" he asked, playing along.

"Let me think about it," I said, setting the skillet back in the oven and closing the door. "How about we have a final farewell fuck in your house. I'm sure the next tenants won't be nearly as exciting for these old walls to witness."

Gabe gave me the good hard fucking the situation called for then we packed up the rest of the things. I learned that most of the stuff was getting donated, but someone actually wanted the boring old living room furniture. My guess was they wanted it for a man cave, which was fine because only other knuckle-draggers would see it there.

We stopped by the grocery store so I could buy the items I

needed to fix the steak dinner from my imagination. I was all for being treated like an equal until it came time to lug that heavy-as-fuck cast iron cookware upstairs. I let Detective Weightlifter handle that. I even told him he could thank me later for helping him get in an extra workout. I heard him grumble about working something out in my ass, but I let his comment slide.

"What are you going to do with those apples?" Gabe wanted to know. "Going to serve them as a side dish?"

"No," I told him. "I'm going to make apple crunch in the oven with *our* cast iron skillet."

"Sunshine, you say the sexiest things," he said, pressing himself against me where I stood at the counter slicing apples. "You know all of my weaknesses."

"Hmmm, I'm sure you've hidden one or two, but I'll figure them out. And when I do," I pressed my ass into his groin, "I'll own you."

"You already do," he said gruffly in my ear.

The steak, potatoes, and Brussel sprouts turned out better than I imagined. Gabe gave his usual grunts and groans while he ate, which warmed my heart and challenged me to find new recipes to please him. The smell of the cinnamon, apple, and butter began to invade all corners of our home by the time Gabe started pulling items out of his box from his house.

In all honesty, I would've gladly put out anything Gabe wanted in his home. I wondered how important they could've been since they were in his closet and not on display though. I was expecting old football trophies or accommodations of some sort. Instead, they were family pictures. My heart ached in my chest when I saw his brother's smiling face in several pictures of the two of them together eating an ice cream cone beneath a big shade tree, riding bikes, or playing in a treehouse. My favorite by far was of them as little kids dressed up as superheroes for Halloween. I noticed that his brother had been dressed as Superman and I remember Gabe saying that Dylan had been his hero, his champion.

I bit my lip to keep from crying. Once I had a handle on my emotions, I turned to face Gabe and asked, "Why didn't you have these beautiful pictures displayed at your house?"

"It never really felt like a home," Gabe said with a small shrug. The way his voice thickened with emotion told me so much more than his words actually did. In case I didn't pick up on his unspoken meaning, he cupped my face and said, "I'm home now."

"Big Daddy's home," Savage squawked.

"Even the bird knows," Gabe said.

"I wonder if the bird knows how much I love you, Gabe?" I asked.

"I do," Gabe said, pressing his forehead to mine. "I love you more, Sunshine."

I stood in his arms and thought about where I had been just a few months prior. I had known what it was like to be with Gabe, but not what it was like to be loved by him. I had known the way his naked skin felt pressed against mine, but not the sound of his heart that beat for me. I had known that there was something between us, but I never guessed it was something to live for.

EPILOGUE

Gabe

Two weeks later, Josh and I had been invited out to eat with Adrian and Sally Ann. They'd had an ultrasound the day before and wanted to celebrate the upcoming birth of their baby girl with us. Sally Ann chose an upscale steakhouse in Northern Kentucky that overlooked the Ohio River. As far as steaks went, it honestly wasn't as good as the one Josh made for me the night I officially moved in. The smug smile on his face told me he knew it too.

Sally Ann told Josh all of the details she was planning for their unnamed daughter's birthday while Adrian and I caught up on the week's activities on our different task forces.

"The Feds came back with some surprising information about the drugs Billy had in his possession," Adrian said. He had my attention and knew it. "The drugs in his urine, the ones from the school locker, and the stash from Bianca's house all trace back to drugs that had been stolen from the evidence room in an El Paso police department. Guess who worked there at the time?"

"Billy?" I whispered, not wanting the name to ruin Josh's fun night.

"You guessed it." Adrian leaned forward and continued. "When faced with the evidence against him he confessed. He brought them with him back to Ohio and had them at a storage unit. They turned up missing and he feared that the drug cartel had tracked him back home. Billy was sure they had an inside guy on the force feeding the drug cartel information. He was afraid to be around his wife and kids so he started squatting at vacant homes around town, including Georgia Beaumont's. He kept moving around in hopes that he wouldn't be caught."

"That's how he ended up with the scissors," I said to Adrian. Unfortunately, that meant we still didn't know who ransacked the mansion. "How did the drugs end up in the school?"

Adrian shook his head as if he still couldn't believe what he was about to tell me. "It obviously wasn't the drug cartel who took his drugs, it was his mother. She thought by taking them that he would get clean. She didn't realize that she'd only found part of his stash in his storage unit. She was the one who disabled the cameras in the high school so she could hide them until she figured out what to do. She wanted to help him but couldn't bring herself to turn him in. Now, she's in hot water too and out of a job. Ironically, Mary Rogers," the former principal that Delaney has suspended and cast suspicion on in the process, "was appointed as the temporary superintendent until the board convenes after spring break."

"Holy fuck! Billy told you all of this?" I asked him.

"No, Delaney came in with her attorney and confessed to taking the drugs and stashing them in the school locker. Even if Billy hadn't confessed, she had come to terms with turning him in."

"Wow," I replied.

"So, what's been up with you this last week? Anything new on the Nate Turner case?" Adrian asked.

I started to answer him, but my attention got snagged by a tall, dark, and handsome man entering the restaurant. My mouth dropped open in shock for a few seconds and then I said, "I don't fucking believe it. Adrian, either I've lost my fucking mind or Nate Turner just walked into the restaurant."

Adrian turned and looked behind him then faced me with wide eyes. "Or we're both seeing a ghost."

ACKNOWLEDGMENTS

First, I need to thank my husband and children for their constant support and encouragement. It's not easy living with a writer who often disappears into a fictional world for long periods of time. They do so many things to help me out so that I can realize my dream. I love you guys more than words can ever express.

Many thanks go out to my three best friends, Anne, Deena, and Kerry. They've stood by me, cheered me on, picked me up, and held my hand through some really rough patches. I love you girls so very much. I wish everyone had friends like you because the world would be a much kinder place.

To my creative dream team, thanks seems hardly enough for all that you do. Pam Ebeler of Undivided Editing thank you for your tireless work, feedback, and many laughs while editing. Jay Aheer of Simply Defined art is just an incredible artist and I love how she brings my words to life. Stacey Blake of Champagne Formats is also an amazing artist who does incredible interior formatting and designing for e-books and paperbacks. New to my team is Judy Zweifel of Judys' Proofreading. She does an amazing job of finding the tiniest details that make a book shine.

I would like to thank my beta readers for all the honest feedback they give me on my storyline. I appreciate you guys so much. Aimee's ARC angels are Anne, Kerry, Jason, Jodie, Kim, and Laurel. Thank you for all that you do!

ABOUT THE AUTHOR

I am a wife and mother to three kids, three dogs, and a cat. When I'm not dreaming up stories, I like to lose myself in a good book, cook or bake. I'm a girly tomboy who paints her fingernails while watching sports and yelling at the referees. I will always choose the book over the movie. I believe in happily-ever-after. Love inspires everything that I do. Music keeps me sane.

I'd love to hear from you.

You can reach me at:

Twitter - twitter.com/AimeeNWalker

Facebook – www.facebook.com/aimeenicole.walker

Blog – AimeeNicoleWalker.blogspot.com

Made in the USA
Lexington, KY
10 June 2017